UNDER THE 82ND AIRBORNE

Deborah Eisenberg was born in Chicago,
Illinois, in 1945. She won a Whiting Writers'
Award and a Guggenheim Fellowship, both in
1987. She is the author of *Transactions in a
Foreign Currency* and a play, *Pastorale*, which
was produced by the Second Stage in New
York in 1982. She lives in New York City.

by the same author

TRANSACTIONS IN A FOREIGN CURRENCY

UNDER

THE 82ND

AIRBORNE

DEBORAH

EISENBERG

faber and faber

LONDON · BOSTON

First published in the USA in 1992
by Farrar, Straus & Giroux, Inc.
Published simultaneously in Canada
by Harper Collins Canada Ltd.
First published in Great Britain in 1992
by Faber and Faber Limited
3 Queen Square London WC1N 3AU
This UK paperback edition first published in 1993

Printed in England by Clays Ltd, St Ives plc

The stories in this collection first appeared,
in earlier form, in the following publications:
"A Cautionary Tale," "Under the 82nd Airborne,"
"Presents" and "The Custodian" in *The New Yorker*;
"The Robbery" and "In the Station" in *Bomb*; and
"Holy Week" in *Western Humanities Review*.

Wholehearted thanks to the John Simon Guggenheim
Foundation and the Mrs Giles Whiting Foundation
for the time they gave me.
D.E.

A CIP record for this book is
available from the British Library

ISBN 0-571-17089-7

2 4 6 8 10 9 7 5 3 1

For

and because of

WILLIAM SHAWN

Contents

A

CAUTIONARY

TALE

"STOP THAT, STUART," PATTY
said as Stuart struggled with the suitcases, which were way
too heavy for him, she thought. (Almost everything was way
too heavy for Stuart.) "Just put those down. Besides," Patty
said, "where will you go? You don't have anyplace to go."
But Stuart took her hand and held it for a moment against
his closed eyes, and despite the many occasions when Patty
had wanted him to go, and the several occasions when she
had tried to make him go, despite the fact that he was at his
most enragingly pathetic, for once she could think of nothing,
nothing at all that he could be trying to shame her into or
shame her out of, and so it occurred to her that this time he
really would leave—that he was simply saying goodbye. All
along, Patty had been unaware that time is as adhesive as
love, and that the more time you spend with someone the
greater the likelihood of finding yourself with a permanent
sort of thing to deal with that people casually refer to as
"friendship," as if that were the end of the matter, when the
truth is that even if "your friend" does something annoying,
or if you and "your friend" decide that you hate each other,
or if "your friend" moves away and you lose each other's
address, you still have *a friendship*, and although it can

change shape, look different in different lights, become an embarrassment or an encumbrance or a sorrow, it can't simply cease to have existed, no matter how far into the past it sinks, so attempts to disavow or destroy it will not merely constitute betrayals of friendship but, more practically, are bound to be fruitless, causing damage only to the humans involved rather than to that gummy jungle (friendship) in which those humans have entrapped themselves, so if sometime in the future you're not going to want to have been a particular person's friend, or if you're not going to want to have had the particular friendship you and that person can make with one another, then don't be friends with that person at all, don't talk to that person, don't go anywhere near that person, because as soon as you start to see something from that person's point of view (which, inevitably, will be as soon as you stand next to that person) common ground is sure to slide under your feet.

Poor Patty! It hadn't even been inclination or natural circumstances that led her to Stuart—it was Marcia. And perhaps if it hadn't been for Marcia, Patty and Stuart never would have carried their association further than their first encounter, which took place almost exactly a year before the sweltering night when Stuart packed his things and left.

Patty had been in Manhattan for several weeks, living in the ground-floor apartment that Marcia had sublet to her, but Patty had been too shy to go down the hall, as Marcia had instructed her, and knock on Stuart's door, so she didn't meet Stuart until one evening when, on her way out for an ice-cream cone, she found two men chatting above an immense body stretched out across the hall floor. Bodies! she thought. Chatting! Marcia had not prepared her for this.

"Relax," said one of the men, calling Patty's attention to the thunder that reverberated around them. "She's snoring. It's a vital sign. I'm Stuart, by the way, and this is Mr.

Martinez, our superintendent, and that's Mrs. Jorgenson down there. I bet you're Marcia's friend."

"Nice to meet you," Patty said. "Should we call an ambulance?"

"Marty and I used to," Stuart said. "But it just makes her mad."

"She get so mad," Mr. Martinez said. "The mens come, they put Mrs. Jorgenson on hammock, she bounce up like Muhammad Ali."

"Maybe we should try to get her to her apartment," Patty said.

"You can try," Stuart said. "But she lives on Three, and she's even bigger when not all of her is on the floor."

"Is nice girl!" Mr. Martinez announced happily, pointing at Patty.

In fact, Patty had been ready to abandon Mrs. Jorgenson and go about her business, but Mr. Martinez's praise revitalized her concern. "There must be something we could do," she said.

"Not really," Stuart said. "She just does this for a while, and then she goes back upstairs. But she could probably use a blanket." So Patty went back into Marcia's apartment and got her Hudson Bay blanket, which the two men gently tucked around Mrs. Jorgenson.

"Nice young girl come to make home," Mr. Martinez declaimed accusingly to the hallway, "but what she see? Is Mrs. Jorgenson and floor." He turned grieving eyes to Patty and made a tiny gallant bow. "You need something, miss, you come to Marty."

"Well," Stuart said. He moved slightly, buffering Patty against the dismal spectacle of Mrs. Jorgenson. "I was just looking for a girl to make cookies with anyhow."

———

"So Marcia was right," Stuart said as he set the cookie ingredients out on his counter. "She told me you were nice. 'Caring,' actually, is the word she used, which I have to say is a word that makes me fundamentally throw up. You know, I watched you dragging in all those cartons, and I figured you had to be you. I've been waiting for you to come say hello. I thought maybe you were avoiding me."

Patty was puzzled by Stuart's probing pause. "Of course not," she said.

"Well, here we are, anyway. Yeah, Marcia talked and talked about you. Patty this, Patty that."

"Really?" Patty said. Certainly Marcia could talk and talk, she thought, but it wasn't usually by way of praise for her female friends. "Marcia and I used to be in the same dormitory. She was a few years ahead of me."

"I know," Stuart said. "You'd be surprised the things I know about Marcia. We're very tight. In fact, there was serious consideration put into my going out to Austin with her while she set up her practice."

"Oh?" Patty said. She wasn't sure why she'd expected Stuart to be glamorous, although, now that she thought about it, Marcia's descriptions of him had been studded with words like "artistic" and "unpredictable." Well, he might be artistic and unpredictable, but he didn't seem glamorous enough even for Marcia, whose tolerance had been widely remarked upon at school. But perhaps Marcia and Stuart's relationship had professional roots. "Are you involved in therapy, too?" Patty asked.

"Therapy," Stuart said. "All right. Let's get it over with. Let's just concede that therapy's the most revolting expression of the hydra-headed pragmatism of our times." Patty picked uneasily at the chocolate chips while Stuart pressed forward with the tedious sifting. "Of course, Marcia always thinks what she wants," he said, "but, between you and me, that's actually why I let her go out West alone. Total misappropriation and subversion of the insights of a few geniuses."

"But therapy can be very helpful to people," Patty protested.

"Yeah, to would-be thieves and assassins crippled by restrictive superegos," Stuart said.

"Well, I don't really know much about it." Patty felt she'd become lost on some twisting private path. "I studied graphic design."

"Uh-huh," Stuart said unreceptively.

"Actually, that's why I've come to New York," Patty said. But Stuart maintained a bristly silence as he spooned dough onto tins, so Patty glanced around for clues. "Are you . . ." She noticed stacks of paper and a typewriter. "Are you a writer?"

"In the sense that I sometimes write things," Stuart said. "Here. Or are you too mature to lick the bowl?"

"Well, what— Thanks," Patty said, accepting the bowl. "What sorts of things do you write?"

"A little of this, a little of that. Look, I really don't want to get into this thing of 'I do this' or 'I write that.' If you develop a stake in some rickety prefab construction of yourself, you have to keep shoring it up."

"But that's an unproductive way to think, isn't it?" Patty said. "I mean, people have different things to contribute. Everybody's part of a system."

"I agree," Stuart said. "And I'm the worthless part. I'll tell you something. I think that every really good system has a significant worthless sector. The rotting leftovers on which the healing penicillin mold grows. That's me. Except that now greed is shrinking the world—you know what I mean? Desire for personal gain is collapsing the entire range of

human activity into, essentially, resale value. So at this moment in history there's no room for people like me, who don't
contribute anything that's recognizably salable."

Patty hesitated. Was she being *criticized*? "But graphic
design is something I *enjoy*," she said. "And I might be able
to succeed at it."

"Ha!" Stuart said. "Maybe what you consider failure I
consider the milieu of freedom."

"Look—" He was *smug*, Patty thought. "I understand that
you think there's something wrong with my career choice, but
I don't understand why."

"That's cute." Stuart leaned back and squinted at her.
"That's sweet. You're *earnest*, you know that? You look like
a Girl Scout, with your little face, and your little sneakers
and stuff. But the problem is, you're going for the wrong merit
badge. Yeah, Marcia warned me I was gonna have to take
you in hand. And the first thing is, it's that *word* is what I'm
saying; that word 'career'—it's a meaning substitute used to
camouflage a trench. I mean, that's exactly what I'm saying:
the more you identify yourself with a set of economic expe-
diencies, the greater your interest in rationalizing indefensible
practices. And that's why people whose jobs yield a large
income or a lot of prestige are usually incapable of thinking
through the simplest thing. In fact, in my opinion, abstract
ability decreases in direct proportion to prestige and income."

"Stuart"—Patty was held in check by the tranquilizing
aroma seeping from the oven—"that is absurd. That is absolutely ridiculous. Take me, for example. I don't have any
job at all, but I don't think more clearly than anybody else."

"True," Stuart said. "But that's because you *want* a job.
You've been corrupted by desire."

"Desire has absolutely nothing to do with me and jobs at
this point." Exasperation empowered Patty to bound with
unaccustomed agility across clumps of thorny concepts. "At

this point, the relationship between 'me' and 'job' is 'need.' I need a job!"

"See?" Stuart nodded triumphantly, as if apprehending some brilliantly crafted but specious argument. "You've already found a way to construe this degraded appetite of yours as need."

"Then how do you suggest I pay the rent, please? I've been scraping and scrimping since December so I'd be able to get here and have some time to find a job—"

"Since December?" Stuart said.

"That's right." Patty was far too annoyed to remark Stuart's sudden attentiveness. "No movies, no dinners out, no—"

"You and Marcia planned this out in December?"

"What's the matter?" Patty said. "Is something the matter?"

"Listen," Stuart said. "I apologize. I don't know why I'm such an asshole. It just sort of comes over me from time to time." He looked around restlessly and tapped his foot. "Just standard-issue archaic bohemian bullshit."

"Wait—" Patty was stricken. "You have a right to your opinion."

"By the way," Stuart said. "Just what, exactly, is Marcia charging you for her miserable sty?"

"Well, I know it's a lot more than she pays for it herself," Patty admitted, "but it's still way under the open-market rate, because it's rent-stabilized. So even if she makes a big profit from me, it's still much cheaper than anything else I'd be able to get. It's the only way I could afford to come to New York and the only way Marcia could afford to leave." ("One hand washes the other," Marcia had remarked cheerfully when she explained this to Patty.)

"Yeah," Stuart said. "Marcia. I should have guessed. It was Marcia who actually drafted the Hammurabi Code of Friendship, did you know that?"

Considering that he'd almost gone to Austin with Marcia,

he was being kind of nasty about her, Patty thought. But she had to remember how quickly it had become understood in the dorm that when Marcia appeared at the door of one's room gripping a six-pack or offering the loan of her car, she had probably just slept with one's boyfriend.

"And you know what she's going to do next," Stuart continued ominously. "The instant this building goes co-op, she'll reclaim her apartment, buy it at the insider's price, and sell the tiny squalid treasure for a king's ransom."

Why was he talking about Marcia's apartment like that, Patty wondered. It was no more tiny, no more squalid than his own! (And it was true that while Marcia's apartment was now bare except for Patty's few things and Stuart's was cozy with layers of an accreted past, and Marcia's faced the airshaft and Stuart's faced the garbage cans that lined the street, the two were virtually identical.) Besides, it was Stuart's problem if he was living like that at his age, Patty thought—he must be at least thirty-five. If Marcia could do better for herself, why should he hold it against her? "Well, it seems fair enough to me," Patty said.

"Oh, Jesus," Stuart said. "I suppose. No wonder I drive everyone nuts. No wonder everyone can't wait to get rid of me."

"Stuart—" Patty said. "Hey, you should try one of these cookies! And some of what you were saying is very interesting."

"Let's just drop it," Stuart said. "I'm an asshole."

"Oh, look"—Patty cast about—"you've got Sprouse's *Tented Desert*!" What luck to have recognized the title among all those books; as she remembered, her English Lit teacher had said it was fabulous. "Could I borrow it?"

"Sure," Stuart said listlessly. "Whatever you want."

"People say it's fabulous," Patty said.

"People who admire it," Stuart said.

Patty looked at him warily. "You don't think Sprouse is a good poet?"

"He's an O.K. poet." Stuart picked a crumb from the table and glanced around for someplace to deposit it. "A small poet."

But gradually Stuart's gloom cleared, and Patty found that she was grateful for his company: she'd been lonely. When she went back down the hall, there was no sign on the floor of Mrs. Jorgenson or her blanket, but as she passed the spot where they'd lain a psychic net seemed to be cast over Patty, and later, trying to sleep, she flopped about, struggling, unable to disengage her mind from the phantom form of supine Mrs. Jorgenson. How tender Mrs. Jorgenson's puffy ankle had looked, where it was exposed by her rolled-down stocking. From the shadowy crevasse there, demons now leapt to haunt Patty.

Patty had assumed, until this night, that she'd been drawn to New York by a lodestone buried at the core of her unexplored life. And images had seemed to shimmer out from the direction of its pull—images, for instance, of gleaming white drafting tables accoutred with complex systems of shallow drawers; a wineglass, held in a powerful, manicured (ringless) hand, which cast a bouncing patch of brightness on table linen; the balcony of a brownstone where a marvelous man lounged while he waited in the surging twilight for the woman inside to finish dressing.

But now, as Patty lay in bed, what she saw was herself—herself as Mrs. Jorgenson, distended and bleary from poverty's starchy diet; herself weeping into her gin at a darkened bar while some grimy bore expatiated incoherently into her ear; herself standing over the stove while she ate, straight from the pan, her scrambled eggs. Oh, *were* they scrambled eggs? Dear Lord, she prayed, *let* that stuff be scrambled eggs. And all around Patty's little bed circled the terror that perhaps those former shimmering lures had not been signs of some central imperative but were instead the snares of a mocking siren; that perhaps she was soon to be dashed, like Mrs. Jorgenson, against the rocks (so to speak) of the hall floor.

The weeks that followed were truly disheartening. By August, Patty had exhausted the heady sensation of exerting mastery over a new apartment, the temperature fluctuated between ninety-eight and a hundred and two degrees, and she had sat through numbers of futile interviews and sent out numbers of futile résumés. The city, in fact, appeared to be quite overstocked with women, each more ornamental and accomplished than any nineteenth-century young lady, huge quantities of whom, Patty noticed with growing terror, were waitresses.

It would be a temporary necessity, she reasoned; she would have to support her job hunt by waiting on tables. And soon her days were occupied with getting rejected for two entire lines of work, one of which she had recently despised. So in the evenings she was glad when either Stuart or Mr. Martinez would open his door to her, expanding the city that seemed to have no room for her by day.

Often Stuart was eager to share his views and his casseroles of vegetarian oddments with Patty. On other occasions, Mr. Martinez would hear her footsteps in the hall and invite her in. He would alternately extol and revile the United States while he and Patty sat together at his kitchen table eating slabs of a gelatinous confection with a plantlike undertaste and drinking a clear, stinging beverage that implied unregulated domestic production. Patty suspected it was this beverage, rather than his heavy accent, uneven grasp of English, or discursive approach to conversation, that made Mr. Martinez so difficult to understand, but after she'd had several glasses herself she could easily follow his tortuous Delphic outbursts. And she would watch, rapt, when he became agitated, either with despair or with gaiety, and swelled slightly, turning a deep translucent red, like a plastic bag filling with wine.

One evening Mr. Martinez, unsteady in his doorway, beckoned to Patty. "Miss, miss," he whispered. His apartment was dark except for the flickering of a few candles, and it was saturated with the fragrance of his arcane beverage. "Come, missy," Mr. Martinez said, drawing Patty over to a photograph that was propped up on a shelf between two candles.

She glanced at Mr. Martinez, but he only stared at the picture, breathing heavily and holding her hand in both of his. She peered back through the darkness and scaled herself down to enter the picture. Oh—there was a field, a great golden sweep of field distantly edged by tiny pointed mountains, and there were people sitting at a table in the foreground: an elderly couple, a young woman, and four or five children. They all had broad, appealing faces, like Mr. Martinez's, and black hair that gleamed in the sunlight. Sunlight poured down. The people smiled into the sunlight—dazzled, yielding smiles. Sunlight poured down on them and out from the picture into the dark room where Patty's hand, in Mr. Martinez's, was beginning to register discomfort.

"Mr. Martinez," she said, but he was transfixed, and tears ran down his face in rivulets. "What is it, Mr. Martinez? What is that picture?"

"But this is—" His eyebrows flew up, his arms dropped to his sides in helpless incredulity. "You do not know this? This is . . . *Colombia*." He sat down at the kitchen table, and, laying his head upon his folded arms, he sobbed. "This is *my wife* . . ."

The next day Patty filled out yet another job application and waited in a line of girls that snaked up several flights of stairs. Clearly her chances were poor. But she didn't really care—she was back in the dark room where she'd stood the night before next to Mr. Martinez. She had remained with him for a time, patting him on the head, but the rhythm of his sobs did not alter, and eventually she tiptoed out, closing the door behind her.

After reaching the front of the line she entered a room, where a man sitting at a wide desk took her application and put it aside without glancing at it. "What do you want," he said, looking all the way up, then all the way back down, her, "days or nights?"

"Nights," she said.

"I don't have nights," he said.

"Days," she said.

He looked up, then down, her again. "I don't have days," he said, and turned away.

Maybe she'd had enough. The thing to do was to sit down, get a bite to eat, and think rationally about her next step. It had come as a jolt that life was something to be waged, rather than relied on. And yet, Patty reminded herself, everyone on earth must have the wherewithal for it. Even Mrs. Jorgenson had the presence of mind to exist; Mrs. Jorgenson, in fact, had so developed the knack of being herself that she could fall down on the floor and lie there snoring. Whereas if she, Patty, were to fall down on the floor, Patty thought resentfully, she would only have to pick herself up again, feeling foolish.

Just who were all these people in this city? And how did they survive? The stakes were so high, the margin of comfort so slim, and yet Patty was surrounded by people who had managed to find a place for themselves here. Look at Mr.

Martinez. How incredible that he was in New York, Patty thought as she entered a restaurant that had just opened up near her apartment. Something was working in the depths of her brain, churning up disturbances that broke as they surfaced, like muddy bubbles rising from a swamp. Yes, how incredible that all of them were here: herself, Mrs. Jorgenson, Stuart, the girls waiting in the line today, Mr. Martinez, the bulky, bearded, pear-shaped man with tiny feet who stood near the jukebox now, in the otherwise unpopulated restaurant, staring at her. Here they all were, an entire—well . . . *confraternity*, sort of, of strangers, all brought together here by . . . by what? What was it they had in common? Was it something fundamental—something too profound to be grasped? Or was it something . . . *extrinsic*, manifest in, for example, er—she studied the bulky man, who was ambling toward her—frayed belt loops?

"Want something to eat?" the man asked. "Or did you just drop by to admire me?"

"Oops," Patty said, shifting her gaze to the menu he offered. "I'd like—" Right. Who cared why they were there? They were there because . . . because they were there. "O.K. A beer and a medium-rare Jarlsburger."

"I haven't got my liquor license yet," the man said. "And the meat hasn't been delivered today."

"Uh-huh," she said. "Well, how about orange juice and scrambled eggs with bacon?"

"Meat," the man said, poking his large haunch. "Have an omelette. You'll like the Chive 'n' Chèvre." He wandered off through a swinging door, from behind which awful metallic crashings began to issue, and returned to Patty's table at a rather faster rate. "He says I've wrecked his pans," the man announced cryptically just as a shockingly tall and starved-looking man burst through the swinging door.

"And what else, Arnold," the tall man raged, "is where's

my check, huh? Where's my check? You promised! Can I
have it? Are you going to give it to me? No? O.K. That's it."
He paused on his way out to kick the jukebox.

Arnold watched the door close before sitting down at Patty's
table. "Always in a hurry," he said. "I would have had it for
him tomorrow." He regarded Patty, chin in hands. "Can you
cook?"

"No," Patty said. "But I'm not really hungry."

"Too bad," Arnold said. "I need a cook."

"I can waitress," Patty said. "Do you need a waitress?"

"What don't I need?" Arnold rubbed his eyes. "Do you
have a lot of experience?"

"Actually—" It was futility that kept Patty honest. "I don't
have any experience."

"So what?" Arnold rubbed his eyes again. "I don't have
any business."

That was not an idle boast, as it turned out. Arnold kept
the restaurant open all night in hopes of compensating for
his lack of a liquor license by scooping up, while his com-
petitors slept, the restless wanderers disgorged from the bars
at closing time. Thus far, however, Arnold's business had
remained conceptual, and Patty had emerged virtually empty-
handed every morning at six o'clock after a long night of
staring toward the door. Occasionally, of course, someone
would come in, causing both Patty and Buddy, the new cook,
to panic from overexcitement and inexperience. Errors leapt
from them like sparks from struck flint, and they would soon
exhaust the self-conscious customer with nervous attentions.

Stuart reassured Patty over a celebratory sunrise supper
he prepared for her during her first week of work. "Listen,"
he said. "By the time the place gets busy, you'll be an ace."
As he reached over to pour her a glass of fancy fizzy grape
juice that had set him back substantially, Patty noticed the
tiny trucks emblazoned on his matted flannel pajamas.

"Stuart," she said fondly. "But you shouldn't be so proud of me—I can't even make enough to live on, you know."

"Well, you can't interpret that as a personal shortcoming," Stuart said. "It's just the fiscal structure of the city these days—Manhattan isn't going to just hand itself over for any little bag of beads now. All these rich bastards driving up the property values have kind of made it impossible for everyone else. I used to be able to scratch up a living with enough left over to do stuff—go to movies, eat out, spend the day observing humanity. Now you want to sit someplace for more than five minutes you got to slap down forty bucks for some kind of noodles with duck feet and grapefruit."

"I don't know." Patty was a bit irritated by Stuart's display of sourness just at the moment she was beginning to feel up to New York's idiosyncratic rigors and to adapt to the glare of its treasures. "Actually, I'm getting to like it."

"It's still New York," Stuart said. "But it's changed. You're practically a kid, so you don't know. Besides, you've just gotten here. And, believe me, you're lucky, because you're one of the last. No one except millionaires can afford to come here. Or stay, if they get here. Manhattan's just a playpen for rich people now, but it used to be paradise, Patty, I'm telling you—a haven for the dispossessed. People used to come here who couldn't go anyplace else on earth—stainless, great-souled, fucked-up fugitives, who woke up somewhere one morning and said, 'Hey, who are these people who call themselves my parents? These people are not my parents.' 'What is this place that's supposed to be my home? This is not my home.' This city was populated by a race of changelings, Patty, who kept things new, people who can't be replicated, who are really alive while they're alive—a dying race. And now it's being overrun by gangs of plundering plutocrats, the living dead, who clone themselves in bank vaults."

"Stuart—that is completely illogical. You want something

that's always new but you don't want anything to change. And I think you're being horribly unfair to all businessmen and professionals on the basis of a few overeager examples."

" 'Examples,' " Stuart said. " 'Overeager.' 'Examples of a few overeager Storm Troopers.' Listen, I'm not talking about Ben and Jerry, I'm not talking about Jonas Salk, I'm not talking about responsible 'businessmen and professionals.' I'm talking about tunnel-visioned profiteers and parasites—and they're surrounding us right now, munching mâche with walnut oil. You think it takes Alaric or a fleet of nuclear submarines to destroy a city? I'm telling you, Patty —destruction is irreversible, I don't care what its source is. You're very casual about this because you don't remember anything."

"Of course I remember things, Stuart. I'm not an infant. And I'm not as ignorant as you think, either."

"You don't remember anything," Stuart insisted. "How could you? You don't remember Jean Seberg, you don't remember Joris-Karl Huysmans. I bet you don't even remember semiotics—"

"Everything changes, Stuart. It's not a tragedy if something changes—"

"As to particulars, not as to value! We were *proud* to be wretched refuse. We had bookstores. In the fall old men sat under the gray sky on benches littered with gold leaves and played chess. Girls wearing plaid skirts carried flutes and sheet music. Back then people thought about sex—"

"People still think about sex," Patty objected involuntarily.

"You call that sex?" Stuart said with bitter, preoccupied opacity. "And you could drink O.K. cheap wine at tables with checked cloths."

"So what! Who cares what kind of tablecloths were in fashion when you were my age? All I'm saying is that after two months of crawling through the streets I'm a waitress in a restaurant with no customers!"

"And you should be unbelievably Goddamned grateful," Stuart shouted, "to have been blessed with a job that won't cheapen your mind!"

But business remained slow, Arnold was no more forthcoming with his paychecks than formerly, and the paychecks that law obliged him to dispense to a waitress were close to meaningless anyway. The restaurant had acquired one steady customer, George, but George was too poor to leave much of a tip. Still, Patty was pleased to wait on someone who endured with unsatirical equanimity the storms of cutlery that rained from her hands. And Buddy was thrilled to have a subject of refined tastes on whom to perform culinary experiments (gratis, when Arnold wasn't around).

"Oh, my, Patty," George said one night. A slightly soiled gentility permeated his soft speech, and his elegant face changed constantly under fleeting shadows of emotion. He was certainly from America, but from what part or circumstances Patty was unable to guess. Even George's age Patty couldn't pin down to the decade. "All this standing around must be very tiresome for you."

"It is, really," she admitted.

"*I* know." George brightened. "Why don't we play a game?"

"All right," she said.

"That's the spirit." George beamed expectantly. "Shall we play 'What Famous Monarch'?"

"O.K.," Patty said. "How do you play?"

"Ah," George said. "Well, for instance, I think of a certain famous monarch, and I think of something about that monarch, and then I say to you, 'What famous monarch blah-blah?,' for example, or 'what famous monarch blah-blah?' "

"Maybe you'd better go first," Patty said.

"Very well." George gathered himself into thought. "What famous monarch . . ." he said meditatively, "preferred being under a horse to being on one?"

Under a horse . . . under a horse . . . Patty ransacked her crated-up years of education. "Oh, George," she said with disgust, "Not Catherine the Great!"

"Well, that was an easy one," George said primly. "Just to show you how to play.

"Your turn," George said later, as Patty cleared his plate and wiped his table, scattering crumbs all over his trousers.

"Well . . ." Patty said. Besides, she didn't know anything *about* history. She didn't know anything *about* monarchs. Ah! (Hee-hee.) "O.K., what famous monarch is ahead of the times in a German museum?"

"Ahead of the times . . ." George looked pained. "Hmm.

"Well, I give up, Patty," he said some minutes later. "That's a toughie."

"Nefertiti!" she announced.

"What?" George said. "But Patty—that doesn't make any *sense*, dear. I mean—well, a *head*, after all. That is, naturally I could have mentioned any number of royal portraits. But 'ahead' of the *times*—I mean, *whose* times, exactly? Do you see? You see, it's a pun, dear, but it doesn't make any *sense*."

Patty slunk around cleaning tables and consolidating bottles of ketchup until George's good humor reasserted itself. "Speaking of ahead," he said, "what famous monarch became a head of a church because of a child?"

"Mary?" Patty ventured unhappily.

"Mary?" George said. "Which Mary? I'm afraid I don't understand."

"Well . . . the Virgin Mary?"

"Gracious, Patty, I really don't think you could call the

Virgin Mary a *monarch*. Or the head of a church, exactly. I was referring to Henry VIII, of course."

"O.K.," she said. "So then what famous monarch lost her head over a child?"

"Anne Boleyn," George replied, giving Patty's hand a consolatory little squeeze.

Arnold's business eventually began to pick up, and Patty felt that she could repay some of Stuart's generosity. He was beginning to look a bit mangy, in fact, so she took to inviting him over for breakfast before she left for work in the evenings. Besides (she had to be honest), she was a terrible cook, and Stuart actually enjoyed cooking.

"Guess what," Stuart announced one night as he broke eggs into one of Patty's bowls. "Rand fired me today."

"What?" Patty said. Rand published a small magazine, for which Stuart wrote about film. "I thought you and Rand were buddies. Doesn't he take you out drinking with him?"

"Yeah," Stuart said. "He's really upset about this, but apparently he and his wife had a big fight."

"So I don't get it," Patty said. "What's that got to do with it?"

"Well, I was trying to do him a favor," Stuart said. "I feel so sorry for him. His wife's absolutely nauseating, you know—and one thing is, she likes to have these parties to show off people she's met to people she's met, and she makes Rand bring someone from the staff each time. So last month I was the sacrifice. And she grabs me, and she's telling me that Devereaux is 'a genius,' 'the only American auteur,' and what do I think of him. And I try to be noncommittal, because I don't want to be forced to say, 'But lady, he's just one more crypto-fascist Hollywood cowboy.' So she tells me I've got to write about him. She's *met* him. He's 'a remarkable man.' So 'penetrating.' And then she turns that cash-register face to me and she says, 'He doesn't suffer fools gladly.' Well, that's something that gets to me, Patty. It just does. When someone looks at you like that and says, 'He doesn't suffer fools gladly,' what they mean is 'He doesn't suffer fools *like you* gladly,' or maybe only 'He doesn't, *like you*, suffer fools gladly,' but in any case it's definitely a challenge, don't you agree? Still, to be accommodating, I go to this screening of *Pulsepoint*, only it seems like Devereaux *does* suffer fools gladly. In fact, it seems like fools are Devereaux's favorite thing. So that's kind of what I wrote my piece about."

"Good going, Stuart." Patty sighed.

"And she sort of took it out on Rand, because I guess she'd planned this big party especially to invite Devereaux. Poor Rand. Here, I think this is done."

Patty was just about to start in on the plate of fragrant French toast Stuart had put in front of her when a small commotion erupted in the hallway. Stuart opened the door to inspect, and Patty, hovering behind him, saw Mrs. Jorgenson sprawled out in front of the mailboxes while a well-dressed man and woman bickered in undignified descant over her stately snores.

"Phyllis," the man was saying, "I really don't think this person ought to be lying here like this."

"We're going to be late," the woman said. "Why do you always have to be Mr. Nice Guy?"

"She wants a blanket," Patty said thickly from behind Stuart, and two sets of icy blue eyes stared up at her.

Mr. Nice Guy went upstairs to get a blanket, and Patty realized that he and the woman (who now stood next to her in uncomfortable silence) must be the art dealers who had recently moved into the apartment above Marcia's. Mr. Martinez, in whose view their arrival represented an influx of undesirables, had informed Patty that the couple had taken the apartment—small and shabby as it was—in anticipation of a move to co-op. "Now you will see," Mr. Martinez had predicted grimly, "they make takeover." And certainly the first sounds of renovation were already militating against Patty's daytime sleep.

For an instant Mrs. Jorgenson stopped snoring and opened her eyes, exposing a malevolent but impersonal irony—the expression of a tough old animal in a sprung trap. "Bugger," she said obliquely. As she resumed her snoring, Mr. Nice Guy returned, bearing a blanket, which he draped ineptly over her while his wife fidgeted with distaste.

Patty and Stuart went back to their breakfast, but the inky cold pressing in at the window had contracted the apartment; the chairs and table felt cramped and brittle.

"As you said, Patty." Stuart nodded morosely at his French toast. "Everything changes. It's not a tragedy."

Patty looked at Stuart closely. "Your apartment *is* rent-stabilized, isn't it?"

"Yeah," he said. "Of course, I'm due for an increase in November. But it is rent-stabilized."

"You're due for an increase? In November?"

"It hardly matters," he said. "I'm a couple months behind anyhow."

"You're *behind*?" Patty put down her fork.

"Well, Marty intercedes for me with Mr. Feltzer."

"But that can't go on forever, Stuart." Stuart was just *sitting* there, watching the butter and syrup congeal on his French toast. "Stuart!"

"I know. It's my own fault. You don't have to tell me, Patty. I ought to have done things differently."

"Now, just relax, Stuart. Let's think this out. There must be something—I mean, you can always—"

"See, Patty? I've made my own bed here. No one owes me a thing."

"But you could always . . ." What *could* he do, Patty thought. There would be no point in his looking for a cheaper apartment—people had to scheme and connive for apartments ten times the price of Stuart's. "Well, you could just for a while . . ."

"No, Patty," Stuart said, hollow-eyed. "You want your own life. You don't need me around."

"But actually, Stuart—" Oh, why *her*? Why *her*? "Actually, I think you'd better."

So Stuart set up his little bed in Marcia's kitchen and fitted his belongings in among Patty's. At first Patty felt as if she were in the eye of some oddly dissipating hurricane. Stuart was jumpy and he hankered after physical activity, but he was also frail and cursed with notably poor coordination. He would leave eagerly for a little run or to shoot baskets with the towering boys who hung around the lot on the corner, only to return almost immediately, fretful, winded, and streaming with sweat. It was Patty who opened stubborn jars, while Stuart, in an unbecoming agony of humiliation, shook out his cramping hand.

Still, he was clean and tidy, although one wouldn't have guessed it to look at him, and he good-naturedly performed the household chores, at which Patty was useless anyhow. The standard of Patty's meals rose, while their cost fell, and for a while Stuart had a run of luck with part-time jobs—he worked happily for a small press until it went out of business, and he received several checks when some of his writing was performed as "soundscapes" at a club, before he told the owners they were pretentious—so he was able to manage his share of the rent.

When Patty returned from work in the mornings, Stuart would wake up long enough to read her to sleep. If it had been an ordinary night at work, he would pick up whatever he himself was reading, and Patty would soon be bored into somnolence. But if it had been a busy night and Patty was wide awake, Stuart would read old, strange, majestic tales of princes turned into swans; swans believed to be second-rate ducklings; suitors who would be magically invested with insight that enabled them to choose the correct path, door, direction, or answer; nearly blameless girls imprisoned within evil trances; and soldiers or poor boys whose wits were to secure them brilliant futures. And as Stuart read, Patty would glide into sun-dappled dream forests where she encountered these creatures, known so well to her, though they were hidden temporarily, in their false conditions, from themselves.

But the independent unit created by two people is an unstable compound, a murky bog in which wayward growths flourish, and it was not long before Stuart decided that he and Patty ought to be sleeping together, a view he began to express (as Patty experienced it) with mosquito-like persistence.

"No," Patty said.

"Why not?" Stuart said.

"Because." Where were all those marvelous *men* she'd been promised by herself? Why did she have to discuss this with *Stuart*?

"So why because?"

Patty fixed him with a look intended to fracture his cheery insensitivity. "Because I'm not attracted to you, Stuart."

"You would become attracted to me if you were to sleep with me," he argued affably.

"But I'm not going to sleep with you," she said.

"Don't you see the beauty of it, Patty? It's sound in every way—politically, economically, aesthetically. You and I would be an entire ecology, generating and utilizing our own energies."

"I'm not here to . . . to provide physiological release for you," she said.

"Why not? I'm here to provide it for you. Listen, you're going to start suffering from pelvic distress one of these days. There could even be colonic or arterial consequences, you know."

It wasn't fair, Patty thought—Stuart obviously felt entitled to win every argument just because he knew more words than she did. She could only repeat herself stubbornly while he continued to whine and orate, disguising his little project in various rationales, until it seemed that one wolf, in different silly bonnets, was peeping out at her from behind a circle of trees.

"All right," she said to Stuart one night. It was miserably cold outside, but she was off work, and she just couldn't face the harangue that would flow unobstructed if she stayed in the apartment with Stuart. "All right. I've had it. This is it. Out."

"What?" Stuart said, having been halted in midsentence.

"Out." She reached for one of her own suitcases and started loading it with Stuart's neatly folded clothing.

"What are you doing?" he said, aghast.

"Out. Now. Out, out." She picked up the suitcase in one hand and shooed Stuart to the door with the other. "This is enough to get by on for a while. Let me know where you are and I'll send the rest on to you."

"You know," Stuart said as he trotted down the hall in front of her, "Marcia kept saying 'Oh, Patty is so *centered*. Patty is such a *woman*,' but actually, Patty, you're a very nervous person."

On the street Patty flagged down a taxi. "Take this guy to

Port Authority," she said, giving the driver a ten. She shoved Stuart into the back seat next to his suitcase and ran along behind the taxi as it took off, flapping her skirt.

As she walked back down the hall, whimpering, Mr. Martinez peered out from his doorway. "The mens—the mens —" he said, his voice vibrant with commiseration. "They must do this thing. Do not cry, missy. He will come back."

But, back inside the apartment, Patty did cry. She cried and cried, from exhaustion, rage, loneliness, remorse, and relief. And when she'd finished she walked slowly to the phone and dialed the number Marcia had given her.

"Hello, Marcia," she said stonily. Patty was not sure why she had called, but she knew, with a weariness that must accompany the end of a lengthy and sordid police investigation, that it was necessary. "How are you?"

"Fine," Marcia said. "I'm feeling very good about myself."

"Splendid," Patty said.

"Good Lord, you sound awful," Marcia said brightly, and instantly sobered. "There isn't some problem about the apartment, is there?"

"Marcia," Patty said, becoming fully aware of her own suspicions as she voiced them, "you promised me to Stuart."

"I did not!" Marcia said. "Heavens, Patty, what can you mean?"

"He never even knew, the poor sucker, did he! For six months you plotted to palm him off on me, and he never even knew."

"Calm down, Patty." Hah! At least Marcia sounded alarmed—undoubtedly she'd expected Patty to remain a credulous, pitiful schoolgirl forever. "I'm serious, Patty. You'd better learn how to deal with your feelings before you do something really self-destructive."

"And furthermore, Marcia"—the room swarmed with vi-

sions of pores, ducts, glands, nodes, hairs, and membranes
—"he's *disgusting*!"

"He's only as disgusting as you are to yourself," Marcia
said serenely. "Honestly, Patty—I simply thought you two
would enjoy one another."

Even in the airshaft the weather was dismal, and Patty sat
and watched a cruel sleet slide down the windowpane, until
Stuart showed up, a few hours later, looking as if he'd been
fished up from the Styx. Patty opened the door without a
word, and without a word Stuart came in. He parked himself
in front of the cold stove, his eyes fixed unseeingly on the
filthy puddles forming around him.

Patty experienced a wrenching meld of triumph and defeat.
If it had crossed Stuart's mind (and it certainly must have)
to seek refuge with Marcia in Austin, he, too, would have
had to face the grim truth that Patty had been lured to this
apartment so that Marcia could (and with a clear conscience!)
leave him behind. Well, Patty thought, she had been set up,
but in point of dreadful fact she was fiercely glad to see Stuart.

Later, as they lay in their separate beds, Patty spoke gruffly
into the dark. "Are you all right now, Stuart?"

He hesitated, but misery conquered pride. "I'm cold."

He snuffled, and when Patty climbed in with him and he
turned his back to cuddle his bony shoulders against her, he
was indeed shivering. "Want to read to me, Stuart?" she said.

"O.K.," he said, gladdening instantly and switching on his
light. "Let's see. O.K., this is *Tristes Tropiques*. And right
here Lévi-Strauss is propounding his interpretation of the face
and body paintings of the Caduveo, some of the last living
Brazilian Mbaya-Guaicuru:

> "But the remedy they failed to use on the social
> level, or which they refused to consider, could

not elude them completely; it continued to haunt them in an insidious way. And since they could not become conscious of it and live it out in reality, they began to dream about it. Not in a direct form, which would have clashed with their prejudices, but in a transposed, and seemingly innocuous, form: in their art. If my analysis is correct, in the last resort the graphic art of the Caduveo women is to be interpreted, and its mysterious appeal and seemingly gratuitous complexity to be explained, as the phantasm of a society ardently and insatiably seeking a means of expressing symbolically the institutions it might have, if its interests and superstitions did not stand in the way. In this charming civilization, the female beauties trace the outlines of the collective dream with their make-up: their patterns are hieroglyphics describing an inaccessible golden age, which they extol in their ornamentation, since they have no code in which to express it, and whose mysteries they disclose as they reveal their nudity."

How happy Stuart seemed, Patty thought despairingly, to be back from his banishment, to have the little glow of his reading lamp around him. How happy he was with this damned book—his constant companion these days.

By the time Patty woke, Stuart was out and about, but the depression beside her in the bed was still warm. She thought of her own cold bed in the next room, and without taking the time to change or make coffee she climbed up to the third floor and knocked on Mrs. Jorgenson's door. People had pushed her around, she thought—people had taken advantage of her. "Mrs. Jorgenson," she called. The peephole underwent a telling alteration as Patty stared into it, but all she could hear was a peculiar sibilance, as of Dobermans running lightly through crumpled newspaper. "Mrs. Jorgenson—listen, Mrs. Jorgenson. This is Patty, from downstairs. It's winter, and I'm cold. You have enough blankets now, Mrs. Jorgenson, and I want mine back." She put her ear to the door, but there was only that continuous rustling sound. "That's my good Hudson Bay blanket," she called into the doorframe, "that my parents gave me when I was little to take to camp. It's mine, Mrs. Jorgenson, and I want it!"

"Whore!" Mrs. Jorgenson yelled from inside. *"Prostitute!"*

In December, Arnold acquired his liquor license, and business increased radically. By that time, practice had eroded Patty's gross incompetence, but no one would have been equipped for the onslaught of customers that poured through the doors all night long. Soon it became necessary for Arnold to hire reinforcements, and with other waitresses working on her shift Patty's job, now lucrative, became more or less bearable as well.

Most of the cooks, bartenders, and waitresses with whom Patty worked took the grueling terrors of restaurant life in good part. Together they would fear, face, endure, and fear afresh the Sisyphean ordeal of customers in exchange for the flexible schedule that allowed them to continue their dancing classes, their short runs Off Broadway, their studies of Indo-European, or the pursuit of voluptuous amusements.

Patty, who had intended to strike no such bargains with life, became increasingly impatient with the easygoing attitude of her co-workers, but there was one waitress, Donna, by whom Patty was deeply impressed. Donna was a tall, good-looking woman around Patty's age, who during the week supervised a direct-mail campaign for a knitwear empire and on the weekends moonlighted as a waitress. "But not for long," she told Patty. "And you'll get out of here soon, too."

"I hope so," Patty said. "But look at Buddy and Menlo and Sheila—they've been here almost as long as I have."

"Don't be so hard on yourself, Patty," Donna said. "Those guys are lifers."

Lifers. Yes, Patty thought, compared to Donna the rest of them were children, playing. And perhaps in twenty or thirty years they would still be clustered near the waitress stand, and she with them—wrinkled children, playing.

The customers, in contrast, seemed veritable incarnations of passing time. Someone would come in every night for a month and then disappear altogether. Romances would blossom and die, people and their involvements would develop in unpredictable directions.

"Isn't that the truth, Sugar?" said Ginger, a customer to whom Patty commented one evening on this phenomenon. Ginger was the gorgeous but moody prima of a troupe of huge male dancers engaged for a long run at a nearby theatre. They danced as women, and they came in often after work, sometimes in dashing rehearsal sweats, but more frequently in full flamboyant costume and makeup. Tonight, the yellow gossamer wings attached to Ginger's gown set off his pearly black skin and imperious, fantastical beauty. "Yes, things sure do move along in Manhattan. You drop by your favorite *boîte* one time, and you say, 'Where's Hank?' And they say, 'Hank?' And you say, 'Hank, you know, sweetheart, the guy who *sits* here every night?' And they just shrug, like they never heard of him. I go home and see my momma, Sugar, she's still chasin' the same chicken around the yard." Ginger allowed his slanting lids to dip for an instant in dismissal.

Almost the only one of the pioneer customers who still

appeared with frequency was George. "Tell me, Patty," he said one night, "what famous monarch . . . gave forth a fatal dazzle?"

"I really don't know, George," Patty said testily. "I'll think about that while I wait on some of these other people."

Everything was going wrong that night. Toast was too dark, drinks were too light, customers temporized over the tiny menu while the second hand sped, but if Patty told them "Let me give you a moment," they would grab her wrist. "Don't move!" they'd say. "I know what I want. Um, Lois, you go first." Arnold cowered in the basement abusing substances and gloating over the books, even though the kitchen was running out of soup and potato skins and ribs. And it was near Christmas, so nobody was tipping and everyone was upset, and it was a long time before Patty got back to George. "I give up, George," she said.

"Spoilsport," he teased. "Just *guess*."

"I don't *know*, George. Oh, all right—Marie Antoinette."

"Marie Antoinette?" George looked stunned. "Marie Antoinette was a famous monarch, Patty, but she did not give forth a fatal dazzle. The famous monarch who did give forth a fatal dazzle was Louis Quatorze, the Sun King."

"What about the affair of the diamond necklace?" Patty demanded. This was *not* how she had imagined her adulthood. "What about that?"

George balanced his chin on a finger and thought. "Well," he said, "I suppose that counts. But do you know, Patty"— he improvised a rueful smile, and his tone was light, although vitality was draining rapidly from his face and voice—"I don't think you care about Louis Quatorze. I think you only care about female monarchs."

"Actually . . ." Patty said. All around her, people were demanding food, drink, clean spoons, napkins, the fulfillment of infantile fantasies, sweets, smiles, anything they could get away with. "Actually, I don't really care about any monarchs, to tell you the truth."

But when things calmed down, Patty returned to George's table penitent. "How're you doing here, George?" she asked.

"Fine, Patty," he said with awful self-possession. "Please tell Buddy it was delicious. Patty, do you know what George III's mother said to him?"

"No, George," she said. "What did she say?"

"She said, 'George, be a king.' " George gazed out over Patty's head at a distant empire. " 'George, be a king.' . . ."

And when Patty returned to George's table later, she found only more change than he could afford, she knew, and on his plate a pile of little bones that suggested he'd curled up there and died.

One night at work Donna announced to Patty that she was quitting. "I've met this man, Fletcher. Some corporation has hired him to develop a magazine about the media, and I explained to him that he should put me in charge of circulation."

"That's great, Donna." Patty sighed.

"And it's just about time for you to start leading a real person's life yourself. Listen, Patty, keep in touch. You never know—something just might turn up at the magazine."

At least Patty had the opportunity, while she languished at the restaurant, to scrutinize the apparently inexhaustible parade of customers for information that would lead to her missing drafting table, her brownstone, her escort. It may seem that because there is not much room for certain kinds of elaboration in the act of ordering something at a restaurant little is expressed by it. But in fact the very restriction of the situation is the precondition of deep grooves through which individual personalities are extruded with great force. "You do *that*?" is what your waiter or waitress or bartender is thinking as you place your order. "You're like *that*?" And although you may assume that you are behaving pretty much as everyone before you has behaved in a similar situation, that is a serious misconception, one not shared by those who stand and face you.

Patty had no leisure for the random yield of disinterested science, but as the months slid by she was able, through diligent observation, to harvest a crop of utilitarian specifics from the people who paused in front of her, in unwitting demonstration of the selves they had tended and grown in the extreme climates of the city. In spite of Stuart's alarmist denunciations, Patty persevered in maneuvering her appearance from undistinguished wholesomeness to the assertively stylish, with only several errors, such as the silk-wrapped nails, acquired at great expense, that felt like lobster claws extending from her fingers as they clicked against her tray.

Still, Patty was forced to note, while many of the customers were graced with beauty or wit or marvelous clothing, few seemed to have achieved a far-reaching or reliable measure of the success that she had assumed New York offered for the asking. Luck must be in scant supply these days. On the other hand, perhaps people came to this restaurant during some sort of interim stage, or limbo; certainly Patty never knew how people fared before they started coming to the restaurant or how they fared after they stopped. People seemed simply to appear and then to vanish. She hadn't seen George, for instance, since the night of the unpleasantness. Life had moved on for him. Or, as she once shamefacedly reflected, she had forced it to move on.

And then, at the beginning of summer, Ginger told Patty

that he and his company were going to California. "I just hate to leave, Sugar. But, Lord—the overhead these days! It's just too steep for an artist. Here, don't you look so sad now. Take a load off your feet for a minute."

It was a slow night, and Patty let Ginger lift her onto his lap, where she nestled contemplatively against his papier-mâché breasts and admired the steely sheen of his arm, folded so gently around her. His arm was as smooth and hard as steel, too, as Patty's finger, trailing idly along it, discovered, but its surface was as welcoming as satin. And this surface —which seemed more lovely to Patty than skin, less perishable, just as precious—raised on her own a velvety nap as she shifted, straining for some position of perfect rest.

"Oh, look," Ginger said, while Patty let the back of her hand enjoy the delicious indentation from which the curve of Ginger's shoulder flared. "Look how sweet! Look at those tiny pink nails, that little milky face. And freckles." Patty closed her eyes to better appreciate Ginger playfully favoring one freckle, then another. "Long, long lashes." Ginger brushed his cheek against Patty's lashes, and when she opened her eyes again the eyes that gleamed back were feral and slanting. "Little flower mouth," he said, and Patty's mouth opened, too, as he arched, letting her glide it from his jeweled earlobe down his polished neck and along the sweep of his collarbone, but there was a quick explosion in her brain as "Waitress! Waitress!" someone called, and Patty scrambled trembling to her feet, scraping her shoulder against papier-mâché.

Patty had developed the habit of routinely clambering in with Stuart when she got home, for warmth and company, but that morning she prowled back and forth across the apartment. Stuart didn't wake up, so eventually Patty poured herself a glass of cranberry juice and drew up a chair across from his bed, where he lay in a little humid wad, wheezing, appearing to become more and more exhausted as he slept, like a ship-wreck victim unconscious on a seaborne plank. How painful a sight it was! How painful it was to be reminded that Stuart's helplessness was something beyond a manipulative ruse! Patty and Stuart had laid to rest the question of sex (sex between the two of them, that is), and although Stuart raised it from time to time, he did so clearly in the spirit of commemorative iteration. It almost made Patty sad that he had come to be as uninterested, actually, in the prospect as she was herself. She sipped at her cranberry juice, watching him, thinking.

Her presence must have made itself felt, because Stuart wheezed mightily, thrashed, and flung himself into a sitting position. "Patty," he said.

"Stuart," she said, "what famous monarch gave forth a fatal dazzle?"

"Come here and give me a hug, Patty-Cake," he said. He moved over to make room and politely turned his back to her.

"Come on," she said. "Please guess what famous monarch gave forth a fatal dazzle."

"Well . . ." He sighed. "O.K. Jupiter, then."

"*Jupiter*," she said. "That's a stupid guess. Jupiter isn't even a monarch."

"Oh, yeah?" Stuart cleared his throat. "Well, listen to this, Miss Smarty:

> "*Oh, thou art fairer than the evening's air,*
> *Clad in the beauty of a thousand stars.*
> *Brighter art thou than flaming Jupiter.*
> *When he appeared to hapless Semele:*
> *More lovely than the monarch of the sky.*
> *In wanton Arethusa's azure arms,*
> *And none but thou shalt be my paramour.*"

When Stuart stopped, a spectral resonance hung in the room as if a cello had been playing.

"So?" Patty demanded, forcing back tears.

"So Jupiter's the *monarch* of the sky," Stuart said. "Get it? And he also fries Semele, which, in my opinion, is, like, an irrefutably fatal dazzle. Anyhow, what do you care?"

"It's just a game," Patty said miserably. "What Famous Monarch."

"Oh," Stuart said. "Trivial Pursuit for right-wing extremists. Anyhow, all monarchs give forth a fatal dazzle. Fatal dazzle is the sort of sine qua non of monarchy. The steady effulgence of enlightened self-government, for example—"

"Stuart," Patty interrupted, "I don't want to talk about this." Morning had arrived in the airshaft; a thousand stars had dimmed. Mr. Nice Guy and his wife would be waking just above Marcia's ceiling, and, above theirs, Mrs. Jorgenson. "I'm tired, Stuart. I'm lonely. I want a real boyfriend."

"Well, Patty," Stuart said softly. She could feel his laborious breathing behind the fragile arc of his rib cage. "I just can't help you there."

Customers generated themselves from air; where there had been one, now there were twenty. Patty rushed back and forth in terror, first for menus, then, thinking better of it, for knives and forks.

"Don't fret, Sugar," said a man, putting a calming arm around her. From the prodigality and exquisite subtlety of the painted designs that covered his body, Patty realized that this man was a chief.

"Take a load off your feet. We Brazilians tend to be hunting-and-gathering peoples." And the band was indeed now plucking burgers and drinks and platters of ribs from under the tables, from out of the waitress stands and light fixtures.

"I never thought of looking there!" Patty said, astonished, but the chief was moving off with his band as they continued their hunt into the forests of the ever-expanding restaurant. "Wait," she wheedled. "Please—I'll get your bread and butter . . ." But the wonderful painted people who had paused so briefly in her sleep on their way off the face of the earth were disappearing through the trees. "Please don't leave!" she cried loudly, waking herself up.

"I'm here for you, baby," Stuart murmured from out of his own dream.

Baby! Patty propped herself up on her elbow and stared at Stuart's pale, knotted face. Who in God's name could *Stuart* be calling *baby*?

"Stuart," she said that afternoon over coffee. "I think I've let myself get sidetracked somehow."

"Hey, are you wearing some different kind of eye makeup these days?" Stuart asked.

"No," Patty said. "Listen, Stuart. It's time for me to start doing something interesting."

"You are doing something interesting," he said.

"That's not what I mean, Stuart, as you know."

"If you're not careful," he said, shaking a finger, "your wish will come true and you'll wake up one morning shackled to some corporate cutthroat who cracks jokes about his interior designer."

"Slurp slurp," she said.

"Look, you're too poorly informed to be familiar with the behavioral and attitudinal alternatives that are history's legacy, but trust me, Patty. You're at a crossroads here. We're all soldiers in the battles between historical forces and you'd better look down at your uniform to see what side you're fighting for before you do something you'll be sorry about."

"Stuart, are you telling me that I ought to be a waitress for the rest of my life?"

"It's honest work," he said.

"Honest!" Patty said. "It's *funny*. TV and books and movies are full of *waitress* jokes. But it's extremely *hard work*!"

"What do you think work is?" Stuart said. "What do you think people have been doing all these millennia? What do you think less privileged people do? Not less intelligent, not less attractive, not less deserving—less *privileged*. Just because history has tossed a bouquet to your weensy little culture, you think actual work is an ignominy, a degradation—"

"You know"—Patty was *not* going to let Stuart outtalk her—"considering how . . . how *entranced* you are by the sanctity of toil, it's a wonder you never indulge in any yourself."

"I've tried," said Stuart, instantly in the right.

"I know." Patty held up her hand. "I take it back."

"I've tried waiting on tables, I've tried moving furniture . . ."

"I know," she said. "I know I know I know I know, never *mind*. Yaargh." He had tried. It was indisputable. He had tried waiting on tables, but, being Stuart, was confined to low-income jobs in dingy coffee shops or delis, where he was fired before his first shift was out, having kindled, to his own perplexity and the manager's fury, little feuds that sprang up like brushfires at the tables and in the kitchen. He had tried moving furniture—for three days he'd gone off in the mornings with fear in his eyes and returned in the evenings looking shocked and broken. On the fourth day his body had refused to raise him from bed and reproached him with racking pains. He would have tried, gladly, to drive a taxi, except that he couldn't drive and no instructor would let him learn, and when occasionally Patty had insisted that they travel by taxi, Stuart wedged himself back in his seat, peeking through his fingers and gasping in such a way as to provoke the driver into a murderous bumper-car rage. "But you know what, Stuart?" Patty bore down on her powers of expression. "It seems to me that if it's a foregone conclusion you're going to fail at a given undertaking you might examine your own motives to see whether there's something hypocritical about them."

"Hypocritical!" Stuart said furiously. "And you used to be *nice*."

"*Caring*—a word that makes you throw up! I used to be caring."

"Nice. You used to be pretty nice. Nice. A little, pretty nice glob of unformed humanity who couldn't put two words together. Now, barely one year later, slimy sophistries drop from your lips like vipers and toads."

"Wait!" Patty said, standing. Because the most incredible thing had just occurred to her. If she was going to get on with her life, it was not only she who had to get a job—Stuart would have to be gotten a job as well! As things stood, he couldn't possibly afford an apartment of his own, and she couldn't just put him out on the street to starve. Even Marcia, after all, had left him provided for, and now it was Patty who had to help him, whether he wanted help or not. "That's not what I meant, Stuart," she said ingratiatingly. "I expressed myself poorly. I only meant why should you wait on tables or move furniture when there are so many other, better, things you're suited for?"

" 'Better.' " Stuart sniffed.

"Better paid, then, if you prefer."

"Patty," he said, "just what are all these things I'm so well suited for?"

"Well, I don't know, Stuart. How should I know? Why couldn't you . . . write copy, for example?"

"What is copy, actually?" Stuart said. "Is it anything like prose?"

"Or be a reviewer again, for some publication. Or get something done with some of your poems? After all, you're an artist, really."

"Yeah, and why don't I rack up a bunch of grants while I'm at it, and have my picture taken for magazines? '*Artist*' —you know what you think an artist is, Patty? You think an artist is some great-looking big guy in a T-shirt, with a bottle in one hand and a paintbrush in the other, who has five hundred thousand dollars zooming around the stock market, and a car like a big shiny penis."

"Stuart," Patty said patiently as she tried to inhibit a telltale blush, "please don't be revolting. The point is that I have complete respect for your convictions, no matter what they might be. It's just that I worry."

"Don't worry," he said.

"Well, I do worry. And I'll tell you one thing I'm especially worried about right now. The Nice Guys. Yesterday Mr. Martinez told me they want a duplex. And you know what that means. That means they're going to have to get someone out—either us or Mrs. Jorgenson. And Mrs. Jorgenson isn't going to go without making trouble. We're an illegal sublet, Stuart. We're not supposed to be here. Especially you. We could get Marcia evicted!"

Stuart sighed. "I'm sorry, Patty. I know you want me to leave."

"Oh, Stuart," she said guiltily. "I just want you to find something that will make you *happy*."

"But Patty." He looked at her. "I *am* happy."

———

Patty, however, had stumbled upon a decision lying in her path, and during the next few days she treated Stuart with the solicitude due to the condemned.

But when she called Donna, there was a bad moment. A minuscule silence preceded Donna's first words. "Oh. Patty," Donna said then. "Right."

So Patty judged it best to come straight to the point: she wanted to talk to Fletcher at the magazine. She was aching for an outlet for her talents. She had developed a feverish interest even in layout, which he could surely exploit. If there was nothing open in that line at the moment, perhaps she could meet him, in case something were to open up in the future. Or in case there was anything. Anything at all.

"Unfortunately, it's not the greatest timing," Donna said. "Everything's all sort of set up now."

"But if we could just meet," Patty said.

"I could give Fletcher your number," Donna said.

"And you know what?" Patty said. "My roommate's a writer. And he's had a lot of journalistic experience."

"Well," Donna said, "the problem is, Fletcher already has a lot of writers."

"I understand," Patty said. She took a deep breath to clarify her mind. "Anyhow, it might not work out with Stuart. He's like a lot of artists—very unpredictable, if you know what I mean. Kind of dangerous."

"Mmm . . ." Donna said. "Dangerous . . ."

And when Patty finished talking (talking and talking) Donna said, "Well, we might as well all have dinner one night when you're not working. At least we'd—at least we'd get a chance to, you know . . . meet."

"Patty," Stuart said. "Why do I have to do this?"

"You just have to, Stuart, you have to." Oh, God, Patty

thought. If she weren't careful, Stuart's suspicious nature might lead him to the conclusion that she was trying to market them both. "Donna's asked me to do this, and I can't go alone, because she's just . . . finding her way around with this guy, who also happens to be her employer, and who, I understand, is a very serious and profound person, incidentally, so she wants to be with some people who are . . . pleasant. And . . . pleasant to be with. And, by the way," Patty said, to change the subject, "you're not planning to wear that shirt, are you?"

"What's the matter with my shirt?" he said. "I thought nerds were considered fashionable these days."

"Not actual nerds, Stuart. Just people who look like nerds."

"Patty," he said. "I really don't want to do this."

"Forget about the shirt, Stuart. However you're comfortable. I just don't want to walk in looking pathetic and desperate."

"Desperate about what?" Stuart asked shrewdly.

To pacify him, Patty agreed to forgo a taxi. They picked their way uncompanionably in the steaming evening through a cluster of shapeless creatures who sat at the subway entrance, surrounded by bags that appeared to be stuffed with filthy, discarded gifts, muttering to themselves in garbled fragments of some lost language. Mrs. Jorgenson would undoubtedly be joining them—assuming Patty could protect herself and Stuart—when the Nice Guys got their duplex. Well, Patty thought, good riddance.

Patty grew increasingly ill-tempered as she and Stuart sweltered underground, waiting for the shrieking train. And by the time they reached the restaurant her mascara was creeping downward and she was cross through and through. So this is it, she thought, looking around at the mirrors and linen, at the graceful sprays of freesia. So this was where everyone had been while she'd been eating Stuart's barley-and-zucchini casseroles.

Donna was already at a table with Fletcher—a man, as it turned out, of unparalleled presentability. "He*llo*," Patty said.

"Well, well," said Donna, across whose face was written "I thought you said this guy was an *artist*." But Donna was not one to let the failings of others cloud her mood, Patty knew, and by the time drinks had been brought she was mollified.

Donna had buffed herself up to a high gloss in the months since Patty had seen her (nothing wrong with *her* mascara), and she was talking with Fletcher of matters entirely foreign to Patty. But strangely, Patty realized, Stuart could manage this conversational obstacle course strewn with technical matters peculiar to periodicals and the private lives of various people involved with them; Stuart knew how to join in.

Obviously, however, Stuart participated entirely without pleasure. It was for her sake, Patty thought, because of her injunctions, and therefore the situation was— Heavens! The situation was dangerous!

Just as Stuart began to fidget noticeably, a new waiter appeared, to deal out menus.

"Oh—" said Fletcher, evidently startled to have been faced with someone as handsome as himself. "The pasta's excellent, incidentally, but I'd avoid the fish."

Patty looked at him bleakly. Why were they all here? This wasn't an interview; it wasn't—it wasn't— She couldn't even think of what it was that this wasn't. She looked at the prices on the menu, and she looked at Donna and at Stuart and back at Fletcher. *Fletcher* didn't care what this was or wasn't; he was just having dinner!

Nerves had dismantled Patty's appetite, and the menu

seemed to be written in Esperanto, so when the waiter returned Patty simply tagged along with Donna and Fletcher.
"Fine," she said. "I'll also have the salade panachée and
then the perciatelli all'amatriciana."

The waiter turned and stared at Stuart. "O.K.," Stuart said
hopelessly. "What the hell."

"*Certainly*," said the waiter with deferential contempt.

"Who does that kid think he is?" Donna said as the waiter
left. "He's a *waiter*."

Fletcher continued the line of thought he'd been pursuing
with Donna as the waiter returned with their salads. "So my
point is that Jay Resnick is doing a feature series on Saffi
Sheinheld for *Dallas by Daylight*. And Saffi happens to be
the senior vice-president of SunBelt, *Dallas*'s biggest account.
Now, I would consider that ethically questionable."

Ethically questionable— That *fool*, Patty thought. There'd
be no holding Stuart now. "Hey, Stuart"—she foraged wildly
in her salad—"this purple thing is a *pepper*."

For a while Patty struggled to match the fun bits of her
salad with his, and although Stuart suffered quietly, he looked
like a rag doll that had been thrown over a cliff, and soon
Patty felt that she, too, was teetering on the brink.

"Donna tells me you're in graphics," Fletcher said, flinging
Patty a rope.

"Terrific field." Patty swung to safety. "So incredible, for
example, how design, or even layout, can send these tiny,
subtle signals. 'Buy me,' for example, or—"

"Visual appeal," Fletcher agreed, glancing up as the waiter
arrived with their pasta. "Crucial." The waiter smirked.

"Is that *bacon*?" Stuart demanded, pointing at his plate.

"It's *only* a little pan*cett*a," the waiter said.

"I understand you're into film," Fletcher said obliviously
to Stuart.

" 'Into'?" Stuart said. " 'Film'?"

"Look," Patty said, plunging into her salad and unearthing a greenish disk rimmed with hair. "I bet no one else has one of these!"

"Or have I misunderstood?" Fletcher said to Stuart as if Patty hadn't spoken.

"Kind of," Stuart said with an equability that made Patty's heart plunge. "What I really 'am,' see, is mentally ill."

"Yes?" Fletcher was guarded but ready to be amused.

"Yeah," Stuart said. "Mental illness. An exacting mistress. It doesn't leave me a lot of time for other things to be . . . 'into.' Like racquetball. Or parenting. Or leveraged buyouts."

Patty looked down at the table, struggling against an untimely smile, and then looked meekly back up at Fletcher. But Fletcher had been enveloped, during the silence, by a glacier. His disapproval gleamed faintly out from behind centuries of ice, which Donna's voice splintered like a hatchet. "I don't think that's very funny," Donna said. "A lot of people actually *are* mentally ill, you know."

"Patty—" Stuart yelped.

"All *right*, Stuart," Patty said, getting to her feet. "Stuart, you didn't eat any of that pancetta, did you? Stuart has a . . . a sensitivity to various additives used in pork products." She was sick of this; she didn't care how ridiculous she sounded; these people had never intended to help them. "And you can just never tell when it might— Listen, Stuart, we'd better get you home before you— Here, this should cover our share." Stuart in tow, she made her way clumsily to the door.

On the way back to Marcia's in a taxi, Stuart was oddly tranquil. And it was he who, after minutes of silence, spoke first. "I'm sorry if I put a crimp in whatever the hell you were trying to accomplish," he said quietly.

Contradictory responses raced through Patty's brain for expression, and clogged. "Give me a break, Stuart," she managed to say.

"I understand," Stuart said. "Your better judgment's been under a lot of pressure."

"Stuart—" Patty was gratified to find that indignation was the attitude forceful enough to distinguish itself from the mute tangle choking her. "Please don't talk to me as if I were a criminal. Don't talk to me as if I were a psychopath. I know the difference between right and wrong. It was wrong of me not to be more forthcoming with you. It was wrong of me to wreck a good opportunity through carelessness. It was wrong of me to waste all that money. I know that what I did was wrong, and I'm trying to apologize." But Stuart just hunched over and looked out the window, where the lights were streaming by. "Stuart—"

"Take it easy, Patty," he said. "I'm not angry."

"Then don't act like this," she said. "Just criticize me, please. Give me a lecture."

But Stuart only patted her hand as if she were an overtired child, and it was when they got back inside the apartment that he himself took his things from the closet and packed them up. "Where will you go?" Patty said. "You don't have anyplace to go." And when Stuart took her hand and held it for a moment against his closed eyes, she might have been touching a fallen leaf or petal, or the wing of a chloroformed butterfly.

After Stuart closed the door behind him it was very quiet. And then it kept on being very quiet. Patty had to force herself to stand up and go to the door.

Outside, the evening trembled with threats of a summer storm, and the air was alive with residues of color. In the growing dark the sky was beginning to twinkle with a thousand little windows.

Mr. Martinez smiled up at Patty from the stoop, where he sat watching a bunch of spindly, raucous, big-eyed children as they danced in some sort of circle game, playing with a violent urgency, competing against the approaching storm for what was left of the evening. "Hello, miss!" Mr. Martinez said.

Patty smiled at him absently. How beautiful that restaurant tonight had been! And now, of all things, she was hungry. If Stuart hadn't left, they could at least have gone someplace, for a cheap bite. Well, it hadn't been *her* fault that he'd left—it hadn't been her *fault*.

As Patty stood, lost in thought, she saw George walk by. "George!" she cried, clattering down the steps. "George!" She tapped him on the shoulder, but the creature that turned around was not George—oh, surely not George—but some awful ghoul with sunken cheeks and stained, broken teeth and eyes that burned as she shrank back. "Sorry," she breathed. "A mistake."

"Mistake!" he shrieked. "Sorry! Always sorry, sorry, sorry. Well, I do life, and I do death. Pass this block, blah-blah, blah-blah. Pass this block, we never see *you* again." A flash of lightning illuminated the awful creature as a contraption of bones in retreating white silhouette, and her own eye sockets flashed white, too, around her, before she blinked and looked back over her shoulder.

In an island of street light Mr. Martinez still sat blissfully watching the ring of dancing children. Everything was just as it had been a moment before: the little scene, the street, the building where Patty had lived for a year; everything was just the same, of course, yet it all looked slightly uncanny —looming and mutable—as if it were something she'd known only from photographs.

"Mr. Martinez," she tried to call, though Mr. Martinez himself seemed newly a stranger, and her voice, hoarse and ghostly, hardly carried back to her own ears. The smallest of the dancing children spun, and leapt into the center of the circle. Street light glanced off the child's tiny gold earring, and Mr. Martinez, with narrowed eyes, rocked back in delight, flinging his arms wide in a tap dancer's gesture of embrace. But for what? Just what was the guy so pleased about, anyway, Patty thought irately, but his arms stretched wider and wider, and he smiled as if he were smiling at the sun.

UNDER

THE 82ND

AIRBORNE

TWO PALLID EGGS, POSSIBLY the final effort of some local chicken, quivered on the plate as the waitress set it in front of Caitlin. The waitress raised her canted black eyes, and behind her Caitlin saw Holly entering at the far end of the room, flanked by two men. Holly's hair was blond now, a terrible kitchenette color, but her face was Todd's exactly, or what Todd's had been at that age. Incredible: Caitlin and Todd had been as young as Holly was now; Holly was now so old—as old as Caitlin and Todd had been! And in the moment before Holly and the men reached her table Caitlin had all too much time to contemplate this stunt, a stunt that had taken twenty years to prepare.

Perhaps she'd been rash to make this trip; certainly she'd had something in mind other than this dingy place and Holly and her friends trooping in like judges. A restful gathering on the beach, something of *that* sort—coconuts filled with rum. A respite from New York, where life had begun to feel chaotic and shapeless, during which she could reconnoiter with all that now seemed to be left of her past—Holly.

For some time, things in New York had been going along just well enough to ignore. Then recently Neil had begun to complain—to formulate an exhaustive catalogue of complaints, each item of which Caitlin considered no more than a shabby justification for seeing other women. Which he was more than welcome to do, as it happened, although, in point of sheer fact, there was also the rent to be considered.

Caitlin temporized, spending more and more time at the bar where she worked, waiting for life with Neil to take an upward turn, or for something else to come along, but in the silence that followed Neil's noisy departure Caitlin's surroundings became audible—the daily din of the customers reliving, as she poured their drinks, the talismanic episodes of their pasts; the ghoulish whispering of her own future. And when she understood that there was no one waiting to replace Neil—no one at all—her life roared in her ear like an empty shell.

The problem was, she thought, she'd let herself lapse; she had not been on a stage for some time after Holly was born. When she took up work again she'd had a brief spate of good luck but then job offers became more and more infrequent. She grew out of the roles to which she'd been suited; she grew into no others. And the truth was, she realized, astonished, she hadn't performed for years now—it was probably years since she'd even auditioned.

In the course of one week she forced herself to attend two open casting calls where scores of people had waited in a large room, some of them women her own age, who were quite clearly too old for the part for which they, and she, were trying out. These women had dressed carefully, as she herself had, to appear nonchalant and young, and, sitting there, had looked at her with something like hatred. At the second audition the script rattled in Caitlin's hands, and the director, a boy in a fashionably floppy suit, stopped her after she'd read no more than half a page. Later someone told her that the calls were a union requirement—that both shows, in fact, had been cast before the calls took place.

When she returned to the apartment after the second audition she examined herself in the mirror. Her gray-blue eyes were still clear and wide, her pale-brown hair still gave off light. From a distance she could have been a girl, but tonight her face was disfigured by the meaningless history of a stranger. Surely her intended self was locked away somewhere, embryonic and protected. She searched the mirror, but the impostor on duty there stared bafflingly back.

She had a drink, and then another, straining through the tumult of her panic to understand what she was to do, and then it came to her that she must see Holly.

"What's the matter, Mama?" Holly said guardedly when Caitlin reached her on the phone.

"I'm glad to talk to you, too," Caitlin said, thrown as always upon hearing Holly's light, high, rapid voice, her slight Southern accent.

"It's after midnight," Holly said.

"It took me long enough to find you, you know," Caitlin said, although, strictly speaking, she happened to have Holly's new number, which Todd's sister Martha had included in one of her infrequent but vigorous letters of ill-concealed denunciation. "You didn't even tell me you'd moved."

"Did someone just dump you, Mama?" Holly said. "Is that it?"

Caitlin shrank inward. When Holly was a child she'd arrive every summer, a distrustful little stranger from Todd's world, with Todd's accent. More recently she and Caitlin had spent several weeks a year together. Not enough time, of course. But still, had it been Caitlin's fault? "You've got my number," she said. "Call when you have time."

"No, wait, Mama, don't," Holly said. "Don't. I'm sorry."

Holly was taking a break from school, she said; she'd been planning to let Caitlin know. She'd moved in with her boyfriend, who was in business. He traveled a lot, south, to other countries. Daddy liked him—he was alert. He spoke some Spanish. Sometimes she went with him on his trips. She was fine, she said; happy.

"Are you happy?" Caitlin said. "You sound tense."

"I'm happy, Mama," Holly said. "I told you."

Caitlin let a moment elapse.

"Sorry," Holly said.

"Listen," Caitlin said. "How about this? Come visit—why not? We'll have a great time. We'll go around New York like tourists. And then you'll tell me all about your friend. I've been auditioning like a madwoman, and I need to relax, too."

"I don't need to relax," Holly said. "I'm relaxed. Besides, Mama— Listen, I'm sorry. But this is just not a good time —Brandon and I are going on a trip."

But she'd been *counting* on seeing Holly . . . "Well, then," she said. She held the phone in dazed confusion for a minute or so, trying to think of a way to disengage herself from the conversation before she cried, or said something she would regret. But then she heard herself asking, to her own surprise, "How's Todd?"

"Daddy?" Holly said. "Oh, Daddy's O.K. Business has been bad, though, lately," she added. "He seems sort of worn out."

Todd's busty secretaries, his little pocket Christmas calendars, his showroom of clownish plumbing fixtures—could Caitlin have despised them so much if they were not indestructible? How terrible if they should turn out not to be. "I'm sure Linda's taking good care of him, though," she said.

"Yes . . ." Holly admitted uncertainly.

"Everyone gets older," Caitlin said. "You wouldn't believe it if you saw me."

"Mama—" Holly said. "Are you O.K., Mama?"

"Fine," Caitlin said. "Anyhow."

"Wait, Mama—" Holly said. "Please."

Caitlin waited while Holly readjusted the phone.

"Listen," Holly said. "Well, anyhow. So Brandon and I have to take this little trip now. Anyhow, otherwise—" Holly stopped. "I mean it would be really nice to see you. But I mean, we're not going to have any time on this trip. This is a business trip."

"Well, if that's the only problem," Caitlin said. "I'm a terrific traveler." Before Holly was born she'd spent quite a bit of time on the road, back and forth between California and New York. "No one has to take care of me—I love to go off on my own and explore."

After a minute Holly sighed. Then she spoke. "All right, Mama," she said. "O.K."

Within three days Caitlin had made all her New York arrangements, bought a plane ticket to the town whose name Holly had spelled out for her, and acquired, under Holly's instructions, a visa. But when she changed planes in Miami early one morning, she wondered if there was something she'd failed to take into account. "What does your friend do in that place?" Caitlin had asked Holly on the phone. "It's *business*, Mama," Holly had said. "Anyhow, what do you care? It'll be a vacation. It'll be warm." And Caitlin packed a suitcase full of festive, warm-weather clothing, new and borrowed. But the few other women waiting at the gate were prim and sour; aside from them, and some miserable-looking boys whose heads were practically shaved, and several thickset athletic types incongruously bad-tempered in their colorful, open Hawaiian shirts and cutoffs, the passengers were pale men with briefcases, who sat forward in their chairs, looking neither to the right nor to the left.

The silence at the gate grew more and more concentrated

until a few minutes before the plane was to be boarded, when a portly woman in Bermuda shorts strode in. A little blue sailor cap bobbed on top of her iron-gray hair, and she gripped a small boy by the arm. "Guess what he's got in there!" the woman said. She released the child's arm to thump the knapsack he was wearing. "He's got a Big Mac! Every time we come up, we stop at McDonald's last thing, so he can bring a burger or two down to his brother." The boy rubbed his arm and blinked resentfully. His face was small and peeled-looking, and there were bluish shadows beneath his eyes. "I hope you got yourself one," the woman said to Caitlin. "Because you're not going to be having one for a while, I guess, are you?"

Caitlin offered the minimum smile and extracted a fashion magazine from her bag.

"Who are *you* with?" the woman said, settling heavily into one of the tiny seats near Caitlin.

"Excuse me?" Caitlin said.

"Excuse *me*, excuse *me*," the woman said, raising her hands as if to ward Caitlin off. "Well, I don't mind talking about my people then. Because we stick strictly to religious instruction. Of course, we're required to distribute a certain amount of aid as well, but out there in the countryside religious instruction is the thing that really counts, isn't it?"

"Really," Caitlin said, casting a glance at her magazine.

"You bet your boots it is," the woman said. "Arms them against temptation. Of course"—she chuckled—"I suppose arms arm them, too. But seriously, you've got to reach them first, don't you? Their hearts are good, you can take that from me—they're honest, and they're hardworking, despite what you hear. But they're gullible, you see; they're still Indians, when you get right down to it. And the Cubans and the Catholics come sidling along, telling them that God loves the poor. And we know where *that* leads, don't we? So we do what we can with shoes and rice—these people don't eat potatoes, you know. And leadership's planning a home for the widows and orphans, so they see that we intend the best for them. Not that there aren't risks." She raised a stern eyebrow and looked piercingly at Caitlin. "I hope you don't mind my asking," she said, "but is this your first time down?"

Caitlin looked up from her magazine, but the woman's features were like a pile of root vegetables screening her expression. "It is, actually," Caitlin said.

"Well," the woman said, relaxing her scrutiny, "you're all right in the city, aren't you? Fewer mosquitoes. You can get quite a decent hunk of meat, too, you know. And there are several clean English-language cinemas—I mean, if you can stand the blood."

On the plane Caitlin watched with relief as the woman in the sailor cap proceeded past her up the aisle, pulling the boy, from whose knapsack trailed a suggestion of grease. "Chin up!" the woman called, and the man in the next seat glanced at Caitlin.

"Completely insane," Caitlin explained, to put the man at his ease.

"Yes?" he said. He seemed doubtful.

"I couldn't believe my ears," Caitlin said. "Hamburgers. Indians. Subversives . . ."

"Tend to be a problem, I suppose," the man said. "They say not, of course, but one expects them to put a good face on it. Still, one never knows—in Guatemala things really are under control." He raised his eyebrows and nodded at Caitlin. "To tell you the truth, though," he confided anxiously, "this is my first time down here."

"Footloose little crowd," Caitlin said. "Aren't we?"

"Ha-ha," the man agreed. "You see, we've been doing

quite a decent business in Guatemala and Salvador the last few years, and the office thought, Well, why not give it a whirl? All these places are so darn hungry for trade—terms are favorable, and there aren't so many silly restrictions as in some places I could mention."

Caitlin glanced across the aisle, but the situation there didn't look much more promising—there were only the ill-tempered men in cutoffs, who were already drinking from cans of beer they must have carried on with them.

"And things being what they are at the moment," the man continued, "there's a lot of disposable income clanking around down there, believe it or not. Not per-capita speaking, of course—per-capita speaking, still just about the poorest damn place in the hemisphere. Well, I mean except for Haiti."

Haiti—Caitlin had been in a play once, with wonderful costumes, about voodoo. "I always think Haiti's so fascinating," she said.

"Really?" The man looked somewhat alarmed. "Incidentally, what is it that brings you here?"

"My daughter." Caitlin smiled at him. "Isn't that amazing?"

"I'll say," the man said.

"Well, I was practically a child bride, of course," Caitlin said.

"Yes?" the man said. He appeared to be puzzled. "And is she at the Embassy, your daughter?"

"Embassy?" Caitlin looked at him. "What on earth for?"

"Oh, sorry," he said. "I just—no, I guess not." He glanced at her, inventorying her in a category she couldn't identify, and then receded into a private melancholy. Caitlin returned in irritation to her magazine, and the man bent over his open briefcase, shadowy preoccupations playing across the pale screen of his face. But when the stewardess came around he grew morosely cordial again. "Can I get you a drink?" he said.

"Thanks," Caitlin said. "Just a vodka tonic, please."

"Bourbon for me, dear," the man said to the stewardess. "Terrif."

"That's better," he said, turning to Caitlin a few minutes later. "You know, if you and your daughter would care to stop by for a drink, I'm at the—well, here." He took a business card from his wallet. "I'll write down the name of my hotel."

"Thank you," Caitlin said. Underneath the scrawled name of the hotel was printed "TechNil, Cleaning Products for the Home, Harvey Gumbiner, Vice-President in Charge of Distribution."

"And if the two of you are planning to be down here through the summer," Harvey said, "they'll probably be having their party at the Embassy on the Fourth. They do in most places, anyhow. Wonderful custom, in my opinion—usually the event of the year. Any U.S. citizen, of whatever stripe or persuasion, is welcome to attend. People come from every sector of the business community. Hot dogs, hamburgers—just like your own back yard. Corn flown in fresh . . ."

Caitlin adjusted her seat backward. No, it had been a good idea, this trip; there would be new people, parties, interesting men . . .

"But don't misunderstand me," Harvey said hurriedly. "You do hear of the occasional embarrassment in these sensitive areas. Episodes, poor taste, so on. Seems odd, but that's human psychology, isn't it?" He frowned at his empty plastic cup. "*Our* money, *our* protection, but people seem to feel funny about that sort of thing. More blessed to give than to receive, I suppose. Well, another drink?"

"I shouldn't," Caitlin said, looking around for the stewardess.

The airport was a stark little affair outside of which a sad mob waited under the bloated sky. Inside, in the lines where papers were to be checked and stamped, luggage was to be inspected, and unconvincingly ornate money was to be issued, Caitlin's fellow passengers once again looked away from one another, tense and silent. Harvey disappeared quickly into the maw of the baggage-claim area, the disheveled beer drinkers were nowhere to be seen, and even the woman in the sailor cap seemed to have been seized with a seriousness of purpose. She went through her tasks quickly, with a cold efficiency, and when she passed by, her mouth set, neither she nor the boy with her seemed to recognize Caitlin. An official of some sort appeared, to speak to the cluster of furtive-looking boys from the plane, who were now standing right behind Caitlin. Their pale scalps glimmered like mushrooms through their short hair, and a damp fear came off them as they responded to the official's question, nodding soberly, their faces a shifting balance of expressions—resignation, eagerness, rage, and obedience—that canceled each other into an unstable blankness.

A mournful taxi-driver brought Caitlin, without commentary or questions, to the hotel where Holly had directed her. There Caitlin registered with a woman whose listlessness was almost overpowering. At least the woman spoke English, Caitlin thought—in fact, it seemed that almost everyone did.

Caitlin's room was an undeceiving simulation of luxury. Streaks of disinfectant testified to its cleanliness, and the faint stench of synthetics recalled best-forgotten mornings in motels. Caitlin followed a thunderous choking into the bathroom, where the toilet was paralyzed in a permanent flush.

She washed her face with the fibrous soap that had been provided and inspected the other complimentary toiletries—tiny plastic packets, bonded shut, of shampoo and bath foam in violent, improbable colors.

She sat on the bed and looked out the window. The hills around the town were covered with vegetation, fecund but dying; the town appeared to be constructed of pale, decomposing, organic concrete. There were fingerprints on the bleary clouds. No sense unpacking—she'd move to a happier hotel later. She left her suitcase in the closet and went downstairs to the restaurant, where she was to meet Holly.

The restaurant was the color of dying vegetation. Most of the customers and all of the waitresses had heavy black hair and black, slightly slanting eyes that made their ordinary suits and dresses look to Caitlin like disguises. She ordered breakfast. Where was Holly?

It was twenty years ago that Caitlin had found herself pregnant. She'd been on tour, in a small revue that had become unexpectedly popular, and she'd met Todd in the bar of the hotel where she was staying with the other members of her company. His childish respectability, his crafty innocence were comical, but he was very good-looking, and Caitlin was slightly drunk, and the whole thing was irresistibly ridiculous, not only to her but also to the boys from her cast, who were with her in the bar, waiting. In the morning, Caitlin let herself be persuaded to spend the night with Todd again, and by the end of the week he took her breath away.

She swung back and forth across the gulf between her attraction to him and the stunning tedium of his conversation. At first the sensation was like a toy. The boys in the company came down with a group fever; Todd was, they agreed, delicious. The boys made up stories—uproarious, hyperbolic romances—in which Todd starred opposite Caitlin, the surrogate. All the boys, and Caitlin, too, would be weak with laughter by the time Todd appeared after the show to take her home, and then the boys would become pouty and sultry, throwing Todd into good-natured confusion. It didn't matter, Caitlin thought; the show would be moving soon.

But then she was pregnant. She would wake up in the morning and the fact would be waiting to claim her. During the day she would be blanketed by a dullness that was impossible to fight off—she couldn't grasp anything for more than a moment.

Of course, she could get rid of the baby—not much problem there—but then what was it she'd been planning for the whole rest of her life? The truth was, she thought alone in her hotel room, she couldn't count on having this sort of job forever. And each time she brought herself to consider her course of action, what presented itself in place of an answer was a question once again.

For whole minutes the world would be suspended, and she would feel emptily cheerful, even happy; then she would remember what was happening inside her and a heavy fear would press her down. Days and days passed in this way, and then one day, among the shreds of feelings that rose and fell around her on harsh little gusts, a sort of hope appeared. Gradually, it grew in substance and weight, and one night she had a dream.

She dreamed that she was lying in her bed, exhausted and despairing, but then she noticed a wonderful piece of furniture against the wall, all covered with rosettes and cherubs. She got up from bed and opened it, and there, sparkling in the darkness, was the solution to her problems.

It was a ridiculous dream, but when she woke up it struck her with the force of an actual possibility that the means for her happiness was right inside her. When she told Todd she was pregnant, his face registered a self-satisfaction that made her sick with rage, and then immediately he began to plan.

For some time after they were married, Todd would plead with Caitlin to tell him what he'd done, but eventually he stopped, since it was clear that he'd done nothing. Later, he would beg Caitlin to stay, in a mounting voice and a mawkish, lofty, and fraudulent tone that drove her into venomous frenzies of threats. During several of these outbursts Holly had been in the room; she'd pushed at Caitlin's knees and shrieked as though Caitlin really were going to leave that very second. "Don't! Don't!" Holly would cry. "Mama, don't *leeaave*—" and then, for days afterward, the three of them would be shaken and fearful, shadowed by the horror of things that had almost been done.

When Holly was three and a half, Caitlin really did leave. Todd was courteous and formal—he had become a great deal more self-possessed since his days at the hotel bar—but his efficiency in the matter of Holly revealed a long-entrenched and fully assimilated hatred, of which Caitlin had been entirely unaware. He had little trouble insuring that Caitlin's access to Holly was legally limited; evidently he had been ready for some time.

Now, as the waitress moved away, Holly appeared—different in immeasurable tiny details from the person who existed in the custody of Caitlin's imagination—and gestured to one of the two men with her. "Mama, this is Brandon," she said in her rapid little uninflected voice. "My fiancé."

Although he looked hardly older than Holly, Brandon had a finished, knife-edged glint. His eyes were shockingly blue and expressionless, and his hair was a lucent, pure flax color, to which Holly had attempted, apparently, to match her own.

Fiancé? Later, when they could really talk, she must tell Holly not to do this.

The other man, Lewis, must have been practically twice Holly's age. He was large and a bit soft-looking. His curly hair was greasy, and coarsened from the sun; a pitted nose stuck out between his mustache and his aviator sunglasses. He wore jeans, and a short-sleeved shirt under which Caitlin could see a faded, rose-colored T-shirt clinging sensually to his broad torso.

They sat down with Caitlin, and Lewis ordered breakfast for himself, Holly, and Brandon in Spanish. Holly's natural expression, Caitlin noticed, was still stubborn and slightly worried—even as a toddler she had been literal-minded and deliberate. But she had lost some of Todd's starchy look, and the tank top and shorts she was wearing suited her better than the ruffled things she'd favored as a child.

Brandon stretched out his long legs and looked appraisingly at Caitlin. But Holly blinked rapidly, then glared at her plate and rubbed at a splotch on it with her thumb.

"Well," Caitlin said.

"Glad you could take the time to come down here and join us all, ma'am," Brandon said to her quietly. He turned the blue beacon of his stare on Holly. "Aren't we, sweetheart?" he said, and she looked up at him, her mouth open.

Brandon looked oddly clean, as though he'd just showered off some identifying characteristics, and his brilliant, empty eyes could have belonged to an animal—some creature attuned only to the most minute signals of scent and sound. His accent was identical with Holly's, but his speech was alarmingly controlled. Fiancé! Well, of course it was all back in fashion now—table settings, shame, property agreements—but it seemed such a short time ago that no one had gotten married. No one, of course, except Todd.

Holly cleared her throat. "So, what about those auditions you've been doing, Mama? You find anything good?"

Caitlin pushed her hair back. "Nothing," she said. "Everything around is shit."

"An entertainer, huh?" Lewis said, poking his fork toward Caitlin. "You know, I admire entertainers. I always had a bit of a secret letch to be an entertainer myself. I played the drums when I was a kid, drove the whole neighborhood nuts. Then when I got back from Vietnam my buddies and I had a band. Gross National Product—" Caitlin could see him look at her behind his aviator glasses. "Maybe you remember it?"

"Not really," she said politely.

" 'Not really,' " he mimicked. "Surprise, surprise—no one fucking remembers. What do you want? We played exclusively scummy neighborhoods."

Holly and Brandon attended to their food with fastidious absorption, but there was a disturbance occurring in another part of the room. "*Buenas*," someone was declaring loudly. Caitlin turned around to see a young man going from table to table, greeting the customers.

"*Buenas*," he announced, stopping at their table. "How are you fine people today?" His accent was so slight as to seem just a crisping around the edges of words. "I'm Ricky." He extended to Caitlin a hand in a little black backless glove that snapped at the wrist. "Just down from Miami?"

"Miami?" she said. His clothing looked like a scout uniform from a pornographic movie; his bare, heavily muscled thigh was level with her face.

"I like Miami," he said. His hands settled lightly, one on Holly's shoulder, one on Brandon's. "People there are friendly, not like here. *This* place—bunch of crazy refugees trying to stab you in the ass all the time." He kneaded Holly's shoulder absently under the strap of her tank top. "You got a plane?" he said to Brandon. "Maybe I'll go up with you this weekend."

Holly had turned a bit pink, but Brandon was looking thoughtfully into the distance.

In the silence, Ricky seemed to notice his hand on Holly's shoulder. He lifted it and waved. "O.K., good people—see you at the club."

Brandon resumed eating and Holly continued to poke at her eggs as Caitlin looked from one to the other. "Friend of yours?" she said.

Brandon's look of extreme neutrality intensified. Neither he nor Holly looked up. "Because if you ask me," Caitlin said, "there's such a thing as just too stoned."

"Oh, we all know each other down here," Lewis said. "Not like Guatemala. Here, everything's under control. A place for everyone, everyone in his place. Small operation, enough pie to go around; smoothly functioning system of checks and balances."

"Remember when we used to play that game, Mama?" Holly said suddenly. She turned to look at Caitlin. "Remember that? We played 'We're in Holly's room, in our house, in Durham, in North Carolina, in the United States of America, in the Western Hemisphere, on the planet Earth, in the solar system, in the universe . . .' "

Holly's room, with its new furniture and the glut of horrible bears from Todd's family. How could Holly remember that? She wouldn't even have been four. She had played soberly with her bears and teacups while Caitlin, in a reverie of scene-study classes and rehearsals, had brushed the light, sweet hair back from her face and the two of them had pursued, in the stale, fruity afternoon sunlight, the protean task of being mother and daughter. "I remember," Caitlin said.

"Well," Holly said. "Now we're in the restaurant, in our hotel, in Tegucigalpa, in Honduras, in whatever it is, in the Western Hemisphere, on the planet Earth, in the solar system, in the universe . . ."

" 'Honduras' . . ." But where were the white sand and palm trees, vacationers spotting one another amid crowds of perspiring natives and trading private, approving glances? Well, of course, Caitlin knew, there were all kinds of other things going on now in this part of the world. "Just what exactly is this stuff we keep hearing about down here now?" she said, trying to construct something solid from fragments she'd heard on television.

"You might be thinking of the war, ma'am," Brandon said.

"Yes . . ." Caitlin tried to remember. "Well, there's a war here, of course."

"No, ma'am," he said.

Caitlin looked at him sharply. If only she'd been able to have Holly with her in New York more often! "Do you think you could find something else to call me?" she said.

"Mama—" Holly began, but Brandon touched her wrist, and she looked down at the table.

"Well," Lewis said, standing. "I'll just be off to freshen up a bit."

Brandon nodded to him, but Holly just stared at her plate, eyebrows furrowed. How helpless she looked! Caitlin reached over to her. "My baby," she said. "Your hair used to be such a lovely ash brown."

"Hash brown, Mama," Holly said. "Like yours."

"Honey?" Brandon said. He turned to Caitlin. "It's a hard thing—here she hasn't seen you in so long, and then you have to be going off again so soon."

"No I don't," Caitlin said.

"Yes you do," Holly said.

"You know what?" Caitlin said, rage distending the words. "Why don't we go to the beach right now, before some of us start to get mean?"

"What beach?" Holly said. "Besides, Brandon has to work this afternoon, and I have to help him."

"Now, sweetheart," Brandon said. "I've got to go out to Palmerola, load up all that stuff for Salvador. You don't want to hang around for that, do you?"

"Yes I do," Holly said to her plate in a particularly little voice.

"Well, I can go with you," Caitlin said.

"No you can't," Holly said.

Caitlin turned to her. "Enough," she said. "First you drag me to this terrible place, then you say I can't even come with you this afternoon."

"You can't," Holly said. "They won't let you. Besides, I didn't drag you anywhere. You invited yourself."

"I beg your pardon," Caitlin said.

"I'm sorry," Holly said. "I'm sorry."

"Well," Caitlin said. "I certainly did not invite myself."

"Well, you did," Holly said, "you certainly did. And now you're already complaining again, just like you always do. Just like you're some princess and I'm something that washed up one day on your—"

"Do we have to—" Caitlin said.

"You act like I come from a *pig*sty. You act like Daddy and I are I don't know whats. You're ashamed of me. Look —you can hardly even look at me."

"How can you say that! Do you think I would have stayed with your father for fifteen minutes if it hadn't been for you? If it weren't for you I wouldn't be able to recognize your father in a police lineup."

"That's *exactly* what I—"

"All *right*," Caitlin said. "If you don't want me here, I'll leave."

"So, good!" Holly said. "Leave! You think you can just show up somewhere and be all *charm*ing and—and *love*ly, and then whatever you've done won't matter, and someone will bail you out of whatever stupid slimehole you've fallen into. You think you can just walk away from anything and then by the time you turn around again everything will be just the way you want it to be. It makes me just want to throw *up*!"

"Honey?" Brandon said softly. "Sweetheart? We're in a *res*taurant." He turned to Caitlin. "She's overexcited."

"I can see that, Brandon," Caitlin said. "I'm her mother."

Brandon stood. "I'm just going to take her away now, and we'll give you a call later when we're feeling better."

"That's what *you* think," Holly said furiously. She stormed out of the room while Brandon held out his hand to Caitlin.

"Pleasure to meet you, ma'am," he said with opaque calm.

Jesus, Caitlin thought. How idiotic. Holly would be sorry later—she always was. But in the meantime . . . Oh, well. Out for adventures. She sighed and looked at the swamp on her plate; how on earth had the others managed to eat these miserable, depressing eggs?

The hilly streets were crowded. Puffs of dust and low, slowly roiling clouds veiled the chalky buildings and churches, and groups of black-haired schoolchildren in blue uniforms flowed around Caitlin, as yielding as a haze of gnats. Men and women passed with soft, despondent expressions; at first, Caitlin smiled cheerfully at them, but the smiles they returned were conciliatory and apologetic, as though hers were something to be evaded, or endured.

Those shorn boys on the plane had been soldiers, of course,

Caitlin thought. But who were all these other Americans? Like the burly, red-faced boy who was drinking a beer as he walked. His bright red T-shirt came toward her. "FEED THE HOMELESS TO THE HUNGRY" it said. "Gramma's looking good," the boy himself said and belched into her ear as he lurched lightly against her.

She steadied herself at a low wall and rubbed her ankle, fuming. When she looked up she saw that she was in a stone plaza, where a knot of ragged people was forming around something. She joined the grimy crowd and saw at its center a man sitting on a blanket, surrounded by small heaps of dried plants, a large trunk, and jars of smoky liquid, inside of which indistinct shapes floated. Of course, Caitlin couldn't understand what he was saying, but his voice rose and fell, full of crescendos and exquisitely disturbing pauses, and his eyes glittered with irony as he gathered up all the vitality that had dissipated from his dusty audience and their torpor burned off in the air crackling around him.

The women in the crowd giggled and tilted their heads against one another's shoulders; the men squirmed and smiled sheepishly. Suddenly the man on the blanket went still. He stared, then lifted his arms high and plunged them into the trunk, from which he raised, as the women screamed and scattered, a great snake that seethed luxuriantly in his hands. Caitlin found herself clinging to a barefoot woman, who smiled to excuse herself, and then, as the crowd drew together again, the man on the blanket placed the twisting snake around his shoulders and reached into the trunk for a second time.

This time what he drew forth was a small white waxy-looking block. The crowd peered and craned. The man looked sternly back and silence fell. He passed his hand across the block, and as the crowd sighed like a flock of doves rising from a tree, the block began to foam.

In an instant the onlookers were rushing forward, drawing
from their pockets bills as worn and dried out as they themselves were, which the man on the blanket collected, passing
out bars of soap in a blur of speed.

And then it was over. The man had packed up his herbs
and his snake and his trunk—the bottles and blanket, everything gone, leaving only a few dazzled lingerers and Caitlin,
who was penetrated by a rich sorrow.

She took her compact out of her bag and looked in the
mirror. *Oh*. Time to redo her makeup and sit down for a
refreshing snack. She looked around. Hopeless. But up on
the rim of town she saw a towering structure. Perhaps that
was where all the cafés and nice shops were. To cheer herself
up, she bought a clump of sticky candy from a little stand
on the street to eat while she walked.

The steeply inclined streets curved up across little ravines
choked with garbage, and, with every dip or turn as Caitlin
drew nearer, the massive tower disappeared and then loomed
again in the tinted, fumy air.

Up high the town was more prosperous. Houses were set
back from the street behind dry gardens. Spectral cars slid
by, their occupants invisible behind black glass, and muscular dogs strained at their tethers, baying as Caitlin passed,
or snapping their teeth. She paused for a moment, breathless
from the heat, and the garden beside her heaved—heavens,
there was a man in camouflage clothing!—and she turned
away quickly, to find herself right in front of the towering
building. It was Harvey Gumbiner's hotel.

Beige light draped the vast lobby, masking clusters of
people. "Praise the Lord," someone seemed to be saying,
and something stirred in a deep chair. Pale men, like those
on Caitlin's flight, spoke quietly, disclosing the contents of
their briefcases to dark men in sunglasses. A group of back-

packers with Bibles whispered in a corner. A breathtaking girl walked by dreamily with a blond man of about fifty, who looked permanently soaked in alcohol. He wound her long black hair around his hand. She whispered something to him, and he smiled, closing his eyes, her hair still coiled around his hand like a leash.

Caitlin found Harvey in the bar with a man named Boyce—from the Embassy, Harvey explained. Boyce's eyes were inflamed, and he scratched at himself. "Allergies," he said unhappily and waved to a group of waitresses, who leaned against the bar, gazing out the window like convicts, or children. One disengaged herself, walking slowly, and shifting her weight from haunch to haunch. She stopped, swaying slightly, at their table, still looking out the window as though she were asleep.

"Is the rum here sensational?" Caitlin asked. The waitress smiled helplessly, then shrugged. "O.K.," Caitlin said. "What's to lose? Cuba libre, please. *Bless* you," she said to Boyce, who had choked.

When her drink arrived, she told Harvey and Boyce about the man with the amazing soap.

"That's impossible," Harvey said. "Soap that lathers without water?" He squinted at Caitlin. "How much did this 'soap' cost?"

"Two of those things," she said. "The red ones."

"Two lempiras!" Harvey said. "It cost two lempiras? That's damned expensive, you know—that's about a dollar."

"Seems reasonable." Boyce rubbed at his eyes. "If it doesn't require water. After all, they don't have water."

"Of course it requires water," Harvey said. "Soap requires water—I *know* soap. Obviously, it's some sort of trick. Two lempiras! You know, this is a very expensive country. I mean considering how damn poor it is. I stopped to buy some batteries this morning for my radio? And two batteries cost me thirteen lempiras! Now, I call that damned expensive."

"Well," Boyce said, waving his hand slightly, "what you see here in Tegucigalpa is a dual economy. The international community that's arrived with all the expansion confuses the picture; the wealthy Nicaraguan émigrés, the new-rich military—" He cleared his throat furiously. "Excuse me. No, what I mean is that the prices you're seeing confuse the picture, because those prices are for foreigners, not for Hondurans. Out in the smaller cities—Choluteca, for example —you don't see those prices."

Harvey frowned. "Still," he said. "I mean, look: two batteries for my radio cost me thirteen lempiras. Now, that simply has to affect the people in—what did you say? Choluteca."

"Well, *no*," Boyce said. "Because my point is, the people in Choluteca *don't have radios*."

"Ah. How do you do?" A well-dressed man had stopped at their table to address Boyce. "Excuse me, I shan't interrupt."

"Well," Boyce said. "Mr. Best." He looked away, but Harvey was already introducing himself and Caitlin. "O.K." Boyce sighed. "Might as well sit down."

"My, my," Mr. Best said. "I see that all our friends are arriving."

"*Oh* boy," Boyce said. "*That's* right—entire international press corps. Another couple of hours they'll be clogging the pool like lemmings."

Caitlin looked around and saw that men and women with large bags slung over their shoulders were filtering into the bar. "Why so many reporters?" she said.

Mr. Best smiled and motioned for drinks from a waitress who was idly stacking glasses in a pyramid at the bar.

"It seems, my dear," Harvey said, as the pyramid of glasses

tumbled to the floor, causing convulsions of giggles among the waitresses, "that you and I have arrived on a rather tense day. The White House has announced that Nicaragua invaded Honduras last night."

"Oh, that's what it is," Caitlin said, trying to remember. "Honduras and Nicaragua are at war—"

"Well," Boyce said. The three men looked at Caitlin. "Not exactly."

Harvey glanced at Boyce, then turned to Caitlin and smiled. "You see, *we're* in Honduras. And Honduras is a democracy—everything is fine here. But next door in Nicaragua? Well, about nine years ago the dictator there—an extremely unattractive man—was overthrown—"

"By Communists," Boyce and Mr. Best said simultaneously.

"Yes," Harvey said. "And, of course, that's no good. So we give money to Nicaraguans who liked it better the other way—the Contras, they're called—to fight the new government. And we let the Contras encamp here in Honduras, where we can—"

"Excuse me," Mr. Best said. "One slight correction." He twinkled charmingly at Caitlin. "Honduras is a neutral country—the Contras are *not* here."

"No, the *point*," Boyce said loudly to Caitlin, "the point *is* that Honduras is a highly sensitive strategic area. Of course we have financial interests in the region—we've never attempted to deny that—but the point is that, *strategically* speaking, Honduras is money in the bank. And that's why the Soviets and the Cubans are stirring up these indigenous movements all over the place. Otherwise, *Jesus.* I mean, these people are pacific; they don't know what's going on—they're *farmers*, for heaven's sake. And that's the point, you see— that we're not just here because we go all gooey inside when we think about the relationship between free enterprise and democracy!"

Caitlin looked at him. She liked to travel. But this was not traveling.

"I can see that I haven't convinced you," Boyce said gloomily. "I can see you think I'm overestimating the danger in order to justify intervention, or God knows what kind of things you've been reading. But that's not true, it's not *true*. Think of the proximity to the United States, think of Cuba, think of the Canal. When's the last time you really thought about the map? I want you to close your eyes and picture the map."

Caitlin took a sip of her drink, and in the reddish mist behind her eyelids tired, dusty figures—like the people in the stone plaza—scrambled across a confused surface. But then flat colors began to mass: the blue of North Carolina, sweet pink of New York, orange of California; little mountain ranges and lakes, little capitol buildings jogged up and down, waiting to be superimposed. They fanned out over the map, the map swung into the night, a light shone in North Carolina from Holly's room, where Holly sat alone, in her tiny rocker, cradling a bear, waiting. The rum came up Caitlin's straw again, washing it all away in a flood of gold as she opened her eyes to see Mr. Best watching her with a faint smile.

" 'Mr. Best,' " she said slowly. He was dark, and very attractive. "Are you from Honduras?"

"I live much of the time in Tegucigalpa, but the import-export business requires an unfortunate amount of travel. It becomes a chore."

"Yes." She looked at him. "I'm an actress, so I know."

"Ah." Mr. Best raised his eyebrows. "An actress . . ."

"But just what brings you here?" Boyce said suddenly.

Really, Caitlin thought—from the moment she'd gotten to her plane people had behaved as though they'd never seen a tourist before. But she only glanced at Mr. Best and laughed. "My daughter's fiancé is in business here, and the two of them invited me down. So, of course, I drop everything I'm doing, I hop on a plane, and as soon as I get here they have to dash off to some other town. Pomarola, I think they said."

"Palmerola—" Boyce said.

"Palmerola," Harvey said, glancing at Boyce. "That's no town—that's the U.S. base, isn't it? Where the U.S. Army is?"

"*Honduran* base," Boyce said. "Where the *Honduran* Army is."

"Quite right." Mr. Best twinkled at Caitlin again. "The U.S. Army is not here."

"And just what," Boyce said, reddening, "does your daughter's fiancé do?"

The force of his interest confused Caitlin for a moment, but she composed herself in the calm emanating from Mr. Best and remembered the conversation at breakfast. "Oh, Brandon's quite the entrepreneur. He has his own plane and he flies around from country to country."

"Really," Mr. Best said thoughtfully. "A young man I ought to know. Let me give you my card; perhaps we could all meet for dinner one evening." Boyce stared in astonishment as Mr. Best extracted a card from his wallet, but when Caitlin reached over to take it Mr. Best frowned and replaced it. "Sorry," he said, selecting another, "that one was . . . incidentally—" He stood and turned to Boyce. "I believe I'm expecting something from you today?"

"Yes, yes, yes," Boyce said. He raked his hands through his hair. "Stop by the Embassy. See my secretary. . . . Oh, God," he said as Mr. Best left, "I'm so *tired*. Oh," he said sourly, as Lewis came through the entrance. "Hello, Lewis. Long time no see."

" 'Long time no see,' " Lewis said. "Kinda catchy. Well, well, well, this appears to be a most congenial company."

Boyce picked petulantly at the label on his beer bottle, but Harvey held out his hand. "Harvey Gumbiner," he said.

"You're putting me on," Lewis said, drawing up a chair. "Hello, pretty lady." He patted Caitlin on the shoulder. Whatever "freshening up" meant to Lewis, it did not include changing his clothes.

"You two know one another," Boyce announced accusingly.

"So the joint's already jumpin', huh?" Lewis said.

Caitlin looked around. By now most of the chairs were occupied by journalists, and a small, good-looking dark girl with a camera over her shoulder pirouetted lazily by the window. "Attractive young people," Harvey said, looking at the girl. He picked up a handful of peanuts from a dish on the table and shoved them into his mouth.

"All waiting to watch the 82nd Airborne Division fall out of the sky," Lewis said.

"*What?*" Harvey said.

"Well, naturally," Boyce said sheepishly. "We could hardly not respond, could we? I mean '*Reds*,' get it? '*Invading a democratic ally*.' "

"The *82nd Airborne!*" Harvey said, turning to Caitlin as though this were supposed to mean something to her. "Well, you and I certainly picked one hell of a day to show up."

"Relax," Lewis said. "There's no one here for them to fight with—this is a photo op."

"In fact," Boyce admonished, "this is a very important moment. Which requires documentation. Because when everyone back home sees this footage, of all these courageous paratroopers diving into the jungle, they're going to understand the danger; they'll see what an invasion means, and maybe then they'll get it through their heads why we're here. Why I'm here, why I've been posted in this Goddamned cow town for the last year and a half. Year and a *half*, mind you. No restaurants, no night life, white-trash hoodlums out at Palmerola *terror*izing the women. My *God*," he said to Caitlin. "I mean, have you seen Guatemala *City*?"

"Cheer up," Lewis said. "A job's a job."

"What the hell is *this*—" Harvey interrupted. Caitlin followed his horrified gaze to where Ricky was goose-stepping through the lobby in his khaki shorts and black gloves.

"Just Ricky," Lewis said. "On his way from the casino, looks like."

"He's not *American*, I hope," Harvey said.

"We don't strictly have jurisdiction over him," Boyce said stiffly to Harvey. "We don't strictly have jurisdiction over the casino—"

"No, but if it *offends* you so painfully," Lewis said, "why don't you just—"

"This is a free country," Boyce said shortly. "We intend to keep it that way. Now, if you'll excuse us, Mr. Gumbiner and I have a—"

Lewis picked up Boyce's beer bottle and waved it. "Be our guests," he said. "Goodbye."

"That Boyce," he said as Boyce and Harvey disappeared through the lobby. "You don't blame the laundromat 'cause you've got dirty laundry, right? I mean, if you want clean hands, stay out of the kitchen. Because people ought to stand behind what they do. You should say, 'Well, look, these things are what we do. Because we believe in certain things. So we have to do certain things.' " There was something odd, Caitlin thought, about his distant look, as though he were peeking out from behind it to check her reaction. "Anyhow," Lewis said, abandoning whatever he'd been driving at, "I've got to admit he's pretty cute. *Rotten* liar, isn't he? Poor guy, he's never going to get out of Tegucigalpa."

"He sure got out of here in a hurry," Caitlin said. *And* with Harvey, her fallback position for dinner.

"Hope it wasn't something I said." Lewis held up the beer bottle and nodded to a waitress.

"Hello, Lewis." One of the journalists sat down. "Sorry to interrupt."

"How sorry?" Lewis said pleasantly. " 'Cause I'm just curious."

The journalist closed his eyes and smiled briefly, turning his back to Caitlin. "Bingo," he said. "All kidding aside, though, I want to know something about this invasion."

"What's to know?" Lewis said, and winked at the waitress who was setting down his beer.

"I'd like to know, for example," the journalist said, "if there *was* one; I'd like to know, for example, if any Nicaraguans actually crossed the border."

"Got me," Lewis said. "No one knows where the border is. Yuk yuk. Of course there was an invasion, honey bunch—didn't you hear that on the news?"

"You know what, Lewis?" the journalist said. "Don't you ever worry that someone might mistake you for garbage and throw you to the sharks?"

"Look at me, pal," Lewis said, putting down his bottle. "What do I look like to you? Joint fucking Chiefs of Staff? If you want the story, why not go out and get it? Or better yet, why not just sit tight in Washington and listen while they tell it?"

"Thanks anyway, man." The journalist tipped his beer slightly and sauntered off, nodding self-consciously to the good-looking dark girl, who didn't see him.

"Rude little cliché-bound bastard," Lewis said. A muscle

jumped in his arm. "I give the guy enough information to jam a memory bank, and look at the way he acts."

"So he's an asshole," Caitlin said. "That's his problem, not yours." She hadn't followed the conversation, but that much was clear. "And you were very open with him." She nodded. Then nodded again.

"Yeah." Lewis closed his eyes. "Well. Mutual respect, in a manner of speaking."

After a moment he opened his eyes again. "Look. Look at this spectacle; look at this mass of human waste. In a few hours, not forty kilometers away, the sky's going to be black with specks—the 82nd Airborne floating down, all the cameras in this room pointing up. Photographs of vines, photographs of specks, give the folks back home a look at what it means to live near Communism. What do you bet three-quarters of these jerk-offs were in Vietnam, photographing specks and vines? After a hard day's work, they're going to come back here, sit around the pool, talk about the old days. Sit around the pool here, Panama City, San Salvador, Managua, get all weepy about how they sat around the pool in Saigon, Vientiane, Phnom Penh, Bangkok. Hey, now they get to do it all again. Specks, vines, flames, buddies fallen in the line of duty yada yada, brings tears to the eyes." He paused and darkened. "You're thinking who am I to talk, right? Vines and specks, we all got a taste for it back then."

So . . . yes. So why *was* Holly here, exactly? "I hate this place," Caitlin said.

"So what are we waiting for?" Lewis said. "Fresh air! Countryside!" He motioned to the dreaming waitress for a check. "Come on, we're out of here."

Lewis's jeep clung like an animal to the road as it undulated away from town. Clay-colored earth covered with acres of shacks, made from what looked to Caitlin like garbage—cardboard, plastic, scraps of wood—gave way to sunlit valleys and grand, pine-covered hills. Caitlin gazed out the window, until Lewis switched on a tape and driving rock and roll obliterated the landscape. "Our sound," Lewis said. "But kids are still growing up on it. Isn't that wild? We were rebels, but we created this enduring institution. Now it's just one more thing that's always been there. But for me it always sounds like that time when it was just invented. Remember what it was like? Remember how loose and new everything was?"

Caitlin remembered. There was always something happening, and something good just about to happen—no end of things ahead. Someone always had money, night horrors were gone by morning, the nasty and boring bits melted away in rainbows. "We had fun," she said.

"Yeah," Lewis said. "We had fun. But you know what?" He frowned and switched off the tape. "For me, there was a certain parting of the ways from you guys. During the war they used to ship us over to Bangkok to chill out. And a lot of times, in the bars, we'd hear the new songs, we didn't know what was going on. The lyrics, I mean. What was everybody talking about? It was *our* home, right? I mean we were *representing* this place, we were fighting for its stuff, this was our generation. But evidently back at 'our home' there was this whole other life going on. So, I mean, who were *we* supposed to be?

"Now look," Lewis said a few minutes later as they pulled off the highway onto a dirt road. "What do you see?"

"I give up," Caitlin said.

"That's right," Lewis said. "Nothing. You can zip up and down all day long and never know these villages are here."

And as he spoke, in fact, a little village was unfolding like paper flowers in a glass of water. First there was only the dusty road, and then there were oxen, with flowing horns and long Egyptian faces, and ribs that stood out, stretching their hides, yoked to a cart with great wooden wheels. A small boy sat astride one of the oxen, his ribs protruding, too, above his swollen belly. He sat and stared as the jeep passed, though Caitlin waved, and then the road was lined with painted walls, velvety in the sun, with openings that led into what must have been tiny homes or shops.

Lewis parked where the road stopped and the walls opened out onto a little village square waving with lilies, in the center of which sat a few wooden benches in the shade of an enormous tree, whose bluish bole shot up and up to a dense and massive dome of leaves floating, very green, against the deep, even sky. Tiny birds darted and chattered. In the heat, little yellow butterflies danced above the high grass, making the air around them flicker, but a chilly darkness was pouring down stone steps out of a church that faced the square. Doves, resting among the cracked angels on its immense wooden doors, ruffled up as Caitlin and Lewis passed through.

Phantom colors dropped from the high windows. A barefoot woman knelt, her hair streaming down her back, and far away, in the shaft of light that pierced the altar, Christ hung bleeding and serene in his perpetual agony. "Let's go," Caitlin whispered. "I want to go."

The heat was intense, but it didn't seem to bother Lewis. He guided Caitlin out behind the church to a lane where, inside tiny painted rooms, she could see some rough pieces of furniture, or a case or two of soft drinks and shelves that held a few cans or sacks of food. On one dirt floor huge and glossy avocados lay mounded like a heap of slumbering animals, and through another doorway Caitlin saw a circle of old men in coarse clothing playing oddly shaped stringed instruments. They sang in a fragile harmony, and a pale marine light came from their dark eyes as they listened intently to the notes their fingers released, their faces skeletal and papery. People disappeared inside as Caitlin and Lewis passed, and children hung back.

The lane branched off into mud paths. A stream glittered; beyond it low dwellings were nearly hidden by blossoms and vines that festooned them like hair ribbons. Caitlin looked around and saw no one. "Let's go," she said. "These people are strange."

"They're just paranoid," Lewis said. "Probably think we're looking for Communists."

"Why would they think that?" Caitlin restrained a childish giggle of apprehension.

"Why not?" Lewis said. "It's a good place, come to think of it. Look at these people—they're starving. Didn't you see their faces?"

As Caitlin looked again, a child burst from the wide silence and flashed across a field, all brown legs and bright tatters. Tiny points of fear sparkled across Caitlin's skin—she turned and ran herself.

Lewis caught up with her easily at the church. "Hey," he said, holding her by the wrist, "take it easy. I want to take your picture."

"Come on," Caitlin said. "Let's get out of here."

"I said I want to take your picture," Lewis said. "What's the matter with you?" He turned her wrist until she fell back onto the stone steps. "Smile," he said, lifting a little camera she hadn't noticed him carrying.

She stood up, staring at Lewis in fury, and teetered for a second.

"Sorry," he said. "I get all excited to have English-speaking company.

"Look," he said, opening the car door for her. "Not bad, huh?" He handed Caitlin a little snapshot, newly extruded from his camera, in which she sat, an awkward smudge on stone steps, one hand grasping the other wrist.

She grasped her wrist as the road buckled and writhed beneath the jeep. She looked terrified in the picture, she looked ill. These people were starving—she wanted to talk to Holly. Could Holly have meant those awful things she'd said at breakfast? Where *was* Holly? Caitlin had come to see her. She wanted to see *Holly*. "I feel terrible," she told her.

"I didn't really hurt you"—but it was Lewis, answering lightly—"did I, sweetheart?"

"Lewis—" The heat was *phenomenal*; Caitlin wanted to reach under Lewis's shirt and dry her forehead on his soft, rosy T-shirt, but it was covered with dark, wet patches. "I don't feel good."

"You don't feel good?" Lewis glanced at her. "Listen, you didn't eat anything funny today, did you?"

"I didn't eat anything today," Caitlin said. "Just a bite of those shitty eggs at breakfast. And a piece of candy on the street."

"On the *street*?" Lewis said. "You *ate* something on the street?" And then Caitlin was sick all over his car.

"What, are you ignorant?" Lewis said later as he put her to bed in her hotel room. "You should never eat stuff on the street." The toilet, still flushing violently, crashed and thundered behind his voice. "Anyhow"—he poured a glass of water from a jug on the bureau—"take two of these little jobbies, and you'll be fine in a couple of hours."

"Lewis," she said. "Lewis . . ."

"I'll be checking on you later," he said from the doorway.

"And I plan to see you as good as new. Now, you want me to send someone up about the toilet? 'Cause that thing is fucking barbaric."

Caitlin's eyes felt grainy and far too large. The room was grainy. It broke up into sizzling whorls of black and white dots; zigzags were breaking from her head. The sound of running water was supposed to be refreshing! Boyce said they didn't have water; so why didn't they take some of hers, whoever they were? Flowers and butterflies throbbed through the torrent—eyes glittered behind them. In the stone plaza, ragged throngs clamored for magic soap, its secret existence undetected by the imperial magnates who swarmed through the Miami airport, dangerously close. They weren't true, those things that Holly had said at breakfast, and the proof was that she was *here*. Why had she come, if not to see Holly, if not to see what had happened to all that time she'd had! And Holly was too harsh; things *could* be undone, with a little imagination—repositioned, seen in a different light. Except—except that she was so sick; because if she were sick and *dying*, then everything that had ever happened would stay forever, just the way it was right now.

Beyond the screen of Caitlin's illness Holly was sitting, dipped in some phosphorescent substance, happy, light. Caitlin struggled and thrashed, trying to call out to Holly, but it was Lewis once again who answered her. "Ready to get up?" he said.

"Did Holly leave?" Caitlin said.

"Holly?" Lewis said. "You've been asleep for hours."

"I have to talk to Holly," Caitlin said.

"They're not back yet," Lewis said. How had he gotten into her room again? He must have taken her key. "How about something to eat? We'll go down to the strip—check out *le tout* Tegoose."

"I'm not hungry," Caitlin said. "When is Holly going to be back? I want to wait for her."

"Forget it," Lewis said. "They won't be back. Not tonight. It's almost midnight now, and *no* one does these roads after dark. Anyhow, you should get out of here for a bit; get some air."

It was true. Caitlin felt weak and strange. The toilet still thundered, and this room that Holly had put her in was hot and sour and stinking.

In the floating pools of darkness by the elevator, two men in uniform lounged. "Relax, princess." Lewis guided her into the elevator, and the door shut her into safety. "Those guys weren't waiting for you." But they'd been carrying what must have been automatic rifles. Just like that man, Caitlin realized, she'd seen earlier in the garden near Harvey's hotel, though she hadn't taken it in at the time. Now he, and others she'd hardly noticed, began to march toward her, in their various uniforms, through her memory. They'd been by the side of the road, in shadow, now that she thought of it, yes they had, and in town, perched high above the thronging people, watching. On the way out Caitlin and Lewis passed by the restaurant, where waiters who looked like champions now circulated instead of the waitresses, sleek and unsmiling.

The streets were so steep and curving that now, in the dark, the little lights—the lights of street lamps and houses—appeared to be strung all up and down the air. "Yeah, it's pretty at night," Lewis said. "And pretty in the day when the sun's out—brightens it up like a little smile. Funny place to use as a control panel, though, isn't it? Wouldn't think to look at it that it's one of the premier cities in the U.S. Just like Chicago—except for this thing of location, I mean."

Lewis opened the door with a flourish onto his apartment

—a single room one flight above a small, shuttered store. There was hardly any furniture—just a bed, a television, and a night table next to the bed which held a lamp, a carved box, an ashtray, and a fishbowl containing a little goldfish and an ugly ceramic castle. One of the walls, though, was layered like a child's bulletin board with clippings and photographs and insignia, including a Confederate flag and an Iron Cross. "Little TV?" Lewis said. He lifted his shirt to unstrap a holster and pistol, which he put down on the night table, and reached over to switch on the set.

It grew bright, and tiny men drifted across it in parachutes. Groups of them bloomed and bloomed, darkening the screen again, and then the scene was gone, replaced by the street where Caitlin had been walking earlier in the day. She saw the stone plaza in the background, and streaming by in the foreground children in school uniforms and crowds of men and women with their soft, defeated expressions. "But in downtown Tegucigalpa today," an announcer intoned sonorously, "it was business as usual for—"

"Enough?" Lewis said. He turned off the volume and sat down on the bed.

"Lewis—" Caitlin said. True, they hadn't been waiting for her, those guys by the elevator. But they had been waiting for someone. "Let me ask you something."

"Sure," he said. "Here, you pick." He handed her the carved box, which was filled with thick joints. "All export quality."

As she bent over him to accept a light, her glance fell on a snapshot pinned up among the things on the wall behind him. Although the figure in the snapshot seemed to be a man, the body was so mutilated that Caitlin could not be sure. Patches were torn from it, and the arms and legs were twisted, but the young face was shockingly intact.

"That was a union guy," Lewis said. "He stirred up a lot of big trouble in a lot of little towns. Hey, why the long look? Don't you understand what's going on? Don't you know what kind of world those people want us to live in?"

Caitlin handed him the joint and watched his eyes narrow with pleasure as he inhaled. They smoked for a while quietly, passing the joint back and forth, and Caitlin thought of her hotel room—the little room that had harbored her in her sickness. "Lewis—" she said.

"This is that guy's chain, in fact," he said, pulling at the neck of his T-shirt to reveal a silver chain. "You know, I never talked about this to anyone before, but I have this fantasy that the guy's got a wife somewhere—a widow. Very beautiful, very innocent, and she has this matching chain. And someday I'm going to see this beautiful Honduran girl somewhere with a bunch of little kids, wearing that chain, and wham—just like that I'll be married, have a family life of my own."

"What does Brandon do for a living?" she said.

"That what's been on your mind?" he said. "That what's been bothering you?"

She shrugged, watching him.

"Good," he said. " 'Cause I was afraid you were getting bored with me."

"No," she said. Out the window the little lights burned merrily.

"Good," he said. "I'm glad to hear it. Well, you can relax. Brandon's strictly in transport. Well-regulated, high-paying, protected work. Mostly doesn't even know what his cargo is. Kids these days, very sensible—no romance in them at all. Butch—hey, Butch," he said, tapping the fishbowl. "Come say hello to my new friend. Isn't she pretty? Isn't my new friend Caitlin pretty? Ach," he said, turning away from the circling fish, "fuck you. To tell you the truth, Butch isn't particularly gregarious. You know, some people say that a fish is not a good pet because it's not an affectionate companion. But I say, hey—who are you to evaluate the affection of a fish? You look in the bowl, and you see what you see. Furthermore, that is one ridiculous way to approach the question of a pet. Because, for instance, what is a pet? A pet is another little consciousness to balance out the fact of your own, which can otherwise sometimes feel like—how can I put this?—like the whole bowl. So there a fish qualifies, right off the bat. Then you have to think, well, what are the specific features of a fish? And they are (a) a fish floats, which is a good quality in and of itself; (b) a fish does not have to be walked, which the same; and (c) a fish has a very wise, eternal type of nature. Whew." He took the little camera from his back pocket and stretched out on the bed with an arm over his eyes. "No high like a reefer high."

"No," Caitlin said. She accepted a fresh joint from him and sat down in the corner, leaning against the wall.

"Of course," Lewis said, "each fish as an individual is not eternal, which is the down side of fish. To give you an example: I was recently living in the Philippines. Got myself all set up with a fancy tank and a fish to match—a particularly beautiful and pleasing specimen, a sort of blue-and-yellow-banded disk with a flirty tail. Well, that fish swam up and down, around and around its little castle there, thinking its own private thoughts from one end of the day to the other. You could watch that thing for weeks on end and never move—no matter what you'd seen during the day, no matter what, that fish would put it all in perspective. It was a very beautiful being. But one evening I was having a little drink with some buddies, and one thing led to another and so on and so forth, and, what with this and that, by the time I got home, which was not for a couple of days, as it happened, when I walked in the door, there was that fish, lying on the surface, belly up."

"Maybe you should feed this one now," Caitlin said. The fish looked agitated; it was darting back and forth, bumping against the glass. "I think it's hungry." Or maybe it was suffocating—the bowl was filthy, with trailing bits of pale debris floating around in it.

For a moment Lewis seemed not to have heard, but then he lifted the ashtray from the night table and flung it against the wall. "Fucking fish," Caitlin heard him say through the noise of the impact, which was reverberating around and around her like a lasso about to snap tight.

Ten steps to the door, not more than ten. But the door itself was on the other side of the bed. Lewis lay back down, looking at Caitlin past the fish. "Hey," he said. "What are you doing down there on the floor?"

Those boys from the plane had looked so easily damaged, with their shorn heads, and dangerous, like a litter of newborn animals, squirming blindly, and clumsily exposing their tiny teeth and claws. "Do you have your orders?" the official at the airport had asked them softly, and they had nodded, pale and helpless.

"Come here," Lewis said. He reached over and unscrewed the bulb in the night-table lamp. The room flickered nervously in the greenish light from the TV, and the mounds of Lewis's reclining shape—his big legs, his broad torso and shoulders, the hair curling up from his forehead—looked to Caitlin like a landscape; perhaps little figures in parachutes were already beginning to choke the air beyond it, spreading out like spores all over the villages in the distance, the breathing hills and living valleys.

The day Caitlin had left, really left, Todd (by which time

she was no longer welcome to stay) the sky had been as silken and pure as a banner. Holly had not cried at all that morning, or even seemed to understand.

When the taxi arrived to take her to the airport, though, Caitlin had cried. She'd knelt down beside Holly, holding Holly's little face in her hands, but Holly had hardly seemed to see her. "Can I go play with Patricia today, Daddy?" Holly had said, turning away as though Caitlin were invisible, as though Caitlin had simply ceased to exist. "Can I go play with Patricia?"

"Hey," Lewis said.

Caitlin started. She saw the fish darting and circling in the flickering light, bumping against the glass as though at any moment its cloudy little bowl could be a great fresh pond, strewn with leaves and flowers.

"Look," Lewis said, "I thought I told you to come here."

THE

ROBBERY

FROM THE BED WHERE SHE LAY
with her feet propped up on a pillow, Jill could see out into
her garden, now in its most lavish aspect, and beyond, over
the hedge to the Binghams' lawn, on which their white house
floated. It looked as pristine and enigmatic as a freshly ironed
dress, but only two days before, someone had forced the lock
on the door while the Binghams were out, and had raged
through, appropriating some of their possessions and leaving
others in ruins.

"We should have invited them tonight," Jill said.

"The Binghams?" Nicholas said. "We never invite the
Binghams."

Nicholas, just out of the shower, was wrapped in the most
beautiful, soft robe. As he walked by the window the last
shining strokes of sunlight fractured around him as though
he were an emissary from some wholly harmonious universe,
and Jill was newly abashed by his perfection. But right behind
him, across the lawn, the Binghams, previously so hale and
confident, were falling at this very moment—turning and
turning in bottomless space. Jill steadied herself, rubbing her
cheek against Nick's robe as he sat down next to her. "It's
just that I dropped over to see them after work today. They

seemed so shaken. Really, we should make a gesture . . ."

"But we couldn't exactly invite them now, could we?" Nick pinched a lock of Jill's yellow hair into a little switch and brushed at her face with it. "If you want, you can . . . *bring them a casserole.*"

Nick said it to amuse her, Jill knew, but occasionally she would be overcome by an actual little terror that he really did yearn for something beyond their enveloping domesticity, that he might simply disappear one day back into the city, the palace of steel and glass that rose above the lake, bright blowy evening and nights dense with reflections and murmurs.

The city. As a child, Jill had driven in with her mother, to go to one of the stately old department stores, or to a matinee when the ballet came to town. She always wore one of her nicest dresses then, and Mary Janes with white knee socks. "Lock your door, Jill," her mother would say, and at that moment the earth seemed to become transparent, and they would drive toward its center, penetrating worlds and then worlds. When they reemerged on the surface, which was settled on a human scale with houses and shrubs and newly covered driveways, her mother would draw in her breath deeply, and the road would heal up behind them and become opaque. But later the hidden day would emit around Jill the troubling light of a dream, and she could see herself and her mother sitting across from one another in the wood-paneled restaurant that smelled deliciously of rolls; she could see how they'd watched from the red plush seats as tiny figures spun and trembled on the distant stage, how they'd driven without stopping past sidewalks that glittered with glass and heat where congregations of thin black people sat on stoops fanning themselves and staring with inturned concentration and then along lakeside boulevards where the very rich strolled in the breeze and mild sun.

"Don't go away," Jill said, reaching as Nick stood.

He smiled and disengaged himself. "So, who are we to-night?" he said, disappearing into the dressing room.

"No one exciting, I'm afraid," she said. "Bud and Amanda. Kitsy and Owen."

"No one exciting!" he said. "Had you not realized that Kitsy has ensnared Bud?"

"Nick, no." Jill frowned. "What makes you think such a thing?"

"A deep source," Nick said. "No, but after all—subtlety is hardly Kitsy's strong suit."

"What is it about me?" Jill said. "I never see these things."

"You," Nick said, "are not meant to see such things."

Jill surveyed her distant toes for a moment. "Poor old Owen. Poor Amanda. Anyhow," she said, "I don't believe it." Jill never believed the intermittent tales about Kitsy. She suspected that people made them up simply because Kitsy was so irresistibly unlikely a subject of the stormy infatuations and disappointments to which she was rumored to be susceptible. And Kitsy and *Bud*! No, impossible.

" 'Poor Amanda'?" Nick said. "Is that what I heard you say? 'Poor *Amanda*'? Poor Owen, yes. And poor Bud—obviously he's only obliged Kitsy in order to get some response from 'Poor Amanda.' But you watch—Poor Amanda won't even do Bud the courtesy of being jealous."

"Oh, dear. Well, in any case—" Jill sat up slowly, appearing in the mirror behind Nick. "I suppose I should go downstairs and see how things are going." Was it the light, or were there circles under her eyes?

Nick concentrated on the mirror, toweling his wet hair. "Amanda's problem is that she considers herself to be irresistible."

"Well, she is very beautiful," Jill said, letting herself lie back again into the square of sunlight that spilled over the pillow, "as even you must admit. And I think you're hard on her. She loves Bud, in her own way."

"I wouldn't absolutely count on that if I were you," Nick said, but he turned from the mirror to smile directly at her.

Jill really did like Amanda, and so, she was sure, did Nick. Nonetheless, it was partly for the pleasure of Nick's protests that she would praise Amanda, whom she had known ever since Amanda had arrived, the new girl in Jill's sixth-grade class, from California, the golden place where people's fathers went when they got divorced. Amanda, equipped with bright loops of hair and an amazing charm bracelet, had been immediately and steadily the center of attention, and even then, her calm, puzzled stare of displeasure had been a terrible thing.

"Oh, and Susan and Lyle are coming," Jill said. "Is that better, or worse?"

"That's good," Nick said, returning his attention to his hair. "I like them. And it's fun to be charming to Susan."

"Nick, that's wicked. You know it makes her uncomfortable."

"It doesn't," Nick said. "Why?"

"Because," Jill said, and stopped. It amused Nick, she knew, that she considered her Jewish friend exotic.

"Because why?" Nick said.

"Because she's—oh, you know Susan. I mean she's so . . . *intelligent*," Jill said, and was rewarded as Nick exploded in laughter and gathered her up.

"You're wonderful," he said. "Do you know that? You're perfect." And Jill tingled with a sheepish pride, like a child who has fortuitously performed some clever act. "By the way," Nick said, stepping back to study her, "how are you feeling?"

"Fine," she said. Although actually, she noticed, she was feeling rather queasy. "Much better."

There had been no need, after all, for Jill to check on anything in the kitchen, where Roo had everything completely in hand.

"Dressing—" Jill said. "Should I make some?"

"All done," Roo said.

"And the silver?" Jill said.

"Everything's done, Mrs. Douglas," Roo said.

Four years earlier, when Roo had come to work, Jill had asked to be called by her first name, but Roo had simply, magically, caused the suggestion to vanish. Although the small formality had come to appear to Jill an implicit and constant antagonism, at the time she had hardly noticed—she had been far too grateful to have someone in the house who could take care of things so marvelously well.

It was Amanda who had arranged it. Jill had been about to have Joshua, but she hadn't wanted to leave work, and she had interviewed, she told Amanda, full scores of half-wits and psychopaths. Then, one week before Joshua was due, Amanda called. "Lucky Jill," she said. "I've got something for you."

Subsequently, Amanda had not only become further involved with Roo but had involved herself with Roo's family as well. Amanda had helped out financially when Roo had her own baby, James, two years ago, and Amanda had helped Roo's sister May get into a nurse's training program. Moreover, Amanda successfully waged an ongoing campaign to shame the entire neighborhood into providing odd jobs for Roo's older brother, Dwayne, though he was too passive and defeated, Jill thought, to do a decent job of anything, even were he not taking drugs. And so, suppose she were to go completely insane and fire Roo because she couldn't stand the tension, Jill had several times reminded herself, the fact was she would have to answer to Amanda.

Happy shouts floated into the kitchen from the yard. Jill went to the window and saw Joshua and James working away with paper and crayons in the back yard, under the casual supervision of Katrina, who lay next to them, sunbathing. "It sounds like the boys are having fun," Jill said.

Roo relented and smiled.

"I think I'll go out and inspect," Jill said. She hoped Roo didn't think her own little smile was cowardly.

"Joshua is making a portrait," Katrina said, shading her eyes from the late glare and smiling up at Jill. She pulled up the straps of her inadequate bathing suit and sat up. Jill looked away for an instant. If she were that girl's mother, she thought, and then remembered that Katrina's mother was someone far away. "What is your picture, Joshua?" Katrina said.

"Mommy," Joshua said, without looking up. He was absorbed, or so it seemed, in his drawing, and Jill obligingly bent over to admire it: yellow crayon hair, round blue crayon eyes, pink crayon cheeks—it could have been a drawing of Nick's idea of her. "How pretty, darling." And what a dazzling little boy Joshua was; how exactly like Nick. "Thank you."

"This is a picture of you, Mommy," Joshua insisted with academic clarity.

"And what about James?" Jill bent down over James's squiggle-covered paper, and James looked up at her wide-eyed. He was so dark—much darker than Roo. "What is that, James?" she said.

"Mommy . . . ?" James said. He looked at Joshua, who did not respond.

Jill resisted a potent impulse to pick James up. Her new baby would be—she was sure of it—much more approachable than Joshua, sweetly dependent, and cozy.

"That's mine—" Joshua yelled, grabbing for a crayon that

James had casually reached for, and James started to wail as the crayon split in two.

"Joshua," Jill said. "You've frightened James."

"He broke it." Joshua's face was bare with outrage. "It was mine. I was using it, and he took it."

"It will work just as well like that," Jill said. "Look—poor James. He's frightened."

Joshua stared at her. "This is really not fair," he announced.

"Look, Joshua—" Katrina said. "Look at that little animal in the tree! What is that called? Look, look, look—" And Joshua did look while Katrina picked up James, who was now bellowing with sorrow.

It was too complex, Jill thought as she returned inside, it was too difficult. How could Joshua be expected to know how to behave or to feel? And James—surely it couldn't be good for James. Of course Jill wanted the boys to be together on an entirely equal basis, but there could be no pretending that their situation was identical—how could there be? With Roo *working* in the house? It would be transparently false of her to pretend such a thing, and therefore unsettling to both the boys.

Yet, even as it was, she felt that she seemed to be in the wrong about something, and that no matter what she did— since things would necessarily remain unsatisfactory in one way or another—it would still seem to be she who was in the wrong. But what more could she do? Every action, every thought, was fastidious. Yet it was as if they were engaged in some secret war, the terms of which were known only to Roo. Well, she was just going to have to speak frankly, she decided, as she stepped into the kitchen. "Roo—" she said.

"Yes, Mrs. Douglas," Roo said, but the blood that was crashing in Jill's ears drowned out her thought.

"I don't know what I was about to say," she said. "Isn't that silly? Oh—in any case, I tried to think of anything I might need Dwayne for, but I'm afraid I don't have anything right now."

Roo didn't glance at Jill, though she must have known, Jill thought, that she was desperate to have something done about the garage. "Yes, Mrs. Douglas," Roo said.

"At least there isn't anything at the moment," Jill said.

Still, perhaps it was best that Roo understand that Jill did not intend to have Dwayne around her house again. After the last time, when he'd done the floors, Jill had been so concerned that she actually checked the silver, as absurd as that was, she realized when she calmed down. But he had been so high—"I'm sorry," Jill said.

"Dwayne's out in St. Louis now, anyhow," Roo said. "He's got something steady."

"Well, that's wonderful," Jill said. Wonderful, though if Roo had only bothered to mention it earlier, they could have avoided this dangerous exchange.

"Mother," Joshua said from right next to Jill.

"Hey, now," Roo said. "Where did you come from?"

"Mother, do I get to help you?" Joshua said.

"Aren't you going to say hello to Roo?" Jill reminded him.

"I want to help you," Joshua said.

"Don't whine, please," Jill said. "We're all finished. Look, Roo's even finished with the fruit salad."

"Roo?" Joshua said.

"Yes, baby." Roo ruffled his hair, and he smoothed it out automatically.

A year or so earlier Jill had been bringing a stained tablecloth down to the basement to be laundered, and there was Joshua, sobbing in Roo's arms, absolutely shrieking, really, with an extravagance that was unfamiliar to Jill, as

Roo rocked him. When they saw Jill, Joshua stopped crying immediately, and Roo set him down. Joshua walked out then, right past Jill, and Roo turned back to her work as Jill stood, holding the tablecloth. The truth was that Jill had been riven by jealousy at the time. Of course she was ashamed of her jealousy later, and she had regretted that, after the episode, Joshua had become so formal, really rather distant with Roo. Still, even that formality was better than the actual rudeness Joshua was displaying this afternoon. Where could he be picking that up?

"Roo," Joshua said, "is James coming back again Tuesday?"

"Depends on whether May's working Tuesday," Roo said. "If May can't mind him for me, I'll have to bring him."

Joshua sighed theatrically and scuffed his feet.

"Joshua," Jill warned.

But Joshua overrode her. "He doesn't play right. He breaks things. He's too little."

"I know, baby," Roo said. "That's why you've got to be patient with him." But Joshua shook her hand from his shoulder, sighed again, and scuffed his way loudly to the screen door, which he allowed to slam behind him.

"I don't know what *that's* all about," Jill said, burning. "He adores James. He's always asking for James."

Altogether it was a relief when the doorbell rang. Owen and Kitsy were the first to arrive, and when Jill opened the door, Owen was already in the middle of a bow. "Goodness me—" he said. His voice was a graphitelike emollient, a granular medium in which the words spread out soothingly.

Jill laughed and kissed him. How innocent he made the world seem; he was so completely himself, rueful and mysterious, precariously balanced, like an underwater explorer.

Behind thick, gogglelike glasses, his eyes swam in unstable magnification.

"Mosquito," Kitsy said, slapping.

"Uh-oh," Nick said. He put an arm around Kitsy and gave Owen a pleased, telegraphic nod. "Let's run for cover."

"Let us," Owen said, wandering inside. "Possibly the shelter of the bar . . ."

"What to drink?" Jill asked.

"They've got me on Scotch tonight," Owen said vaguely.

"Gin-tonic, please, darlin'," Kitsy said. "A healthy one. I've been doing battle with the tomatoes all day." Kitsy smoothed back her oat-colored hair as her attention traveled across the room, randomly encountering and dismissing objects. "I don't know how you do it all," she said. "And with a job. Jobs, tomatoes, Joshua . . ." Could it be true, Jill wondered, about Kitsy and Bud? Kitsy was so . . . like a parakeet on a perch—blinking and rounded over her prim little feet. But when the doorbell rang, Kitsy didn't move, though her eyes brightened and narrowed.

Bud and Amanda and Susan and Lyle arrived in a clump and were reabsorbed, after some initial milling, into configurations that left Jill with Bud and Susan. Bud looked controlled, Jill saw—possibly furious, and when, in another part of the room, Amanda laughed, he closed his eyes almost blissfully for an instant, before turning his attention, with surplus force, to Susan. "So where do you get all these wonderful garments, Susan?" he said, tugging at a tassel on the large shawl she wore.

"Oh—" Susan waved her hand and laughed, but Bud waited unyieldingly with a half-smile and lifted eyebrows. "All right," Susan said. She cleared her throat. "Well, this particular one's from Mexico. And it is lovely, thank you, Bud, isn't it?" She turned to Jill, and her large eyes looked lost, and metallic. "You know, when Lyle and I were back in March, we didn't see anything of this caliber. Hardly any cotton at all, in fact. Isn't that odd? It was my understanding that they grew it."

"Cash crop," Bud said. "Grow it for export."

"Oh, yes," Susan said dubiously. "Well, that doesn't sound so good, does it?"

Clearly Bud was beginning to enjoy himself now, Jill saw, that Susan was flustered. Really, he was rather attractive with that little space between his teeth and his raffish, dark halo of receding hair. "Hear you've been having the worst kind of trouble with that painter you and Lyle have in your beach house," he said.

"Gracious, this *drink*," Susan said. "Naughty Jill." But Bud only looked down at his glass and swirled the ice patiently, so Susan, patting at a fan-shaped ornament that was struggling upward from her heavy hair, sighed and continued. "I'm afraid it did turn into a bit of a melee," she said.

"What a shame," Bud said. "But very generous of you and Lyle."

"Well, the man's an enormous talent," Susan said. To her astonishment, Jill saw Kitsy direct a damp, shining glance in their direction, but Bud shifted slightly, so that his back was squarely to her. "And the dreadful truth is that Lyle and I hardly ever use the place. So we thought, now isn't it criminal to waste it like this when there must be—oh, well . . ." She laughed self-deprecatingly.

"Not a bad way to pick up a bargain," Bud said. He laughed along with her, then made an elaborate display of sobering. "Oh, Bud, how vulgar," he said in falsetto.

"Not that Lyle and I minded for ourselves," Susan said, reddening. "But the Foleys found trash all over their beach. And they actually had to call the police about the noise . . ." Bud clucked sympathetically.

Susan, having gained momentum, was now irrepressibly

confidential. "We did manage to get him out finally," she said. "But there was quite a scene. He *pointed* his finger, and accused Lyle of 'artistic imperialism' if you can believe it."

"Artistic imperialism—" Jill laughed. "My!"

"Yes—" Lyle said, joining them. Towering over Bud, Lyle rocked mournfully back and forth on his toes, and pushed his floppy hair behind his ear in discomfiture. "It really was funny." Jill smiled at his baffled sorrow and put an affectionate hand on his arm. He was like a gigantic boy, with those glasses and that pink, open mouth.

"Mrs. Douglas—" Roo said. She stood just behind the entrance to the living room, holding James.

"Yes, Roo," Jill said. Roo had changed into very high heels and a white dress that Jill had kept in the closet for two years after Joshua was born, before coming to terms with the probability that she would never fit into it again. "Come in."

"I'm just saying the taxi's come," Roo said.

"Oh. Well, thank you, Roo." But she'd never—she'd never seen Roo actually wearing the dress. "Good night, then."

"Oh, Roo," Kitsy called. "Don't you look stunning." And there was a silence as Roo turned slightly to readjust James, exposing the fine articulation of her arms, and her narrow bare back. Where could she be going like that, Jill wondered. And with James—

"Hello, James," Amanda said, raising her glass slightly.

"And will I see you on Tuesday, then, Roo?" Jill asked senselessly.

"Yes, Mrs. Douglas," Roo said, her face scrupulously expressionless.

Jill sighed. If only there were still people in the world like the people who had worked for her parents—people made flexible and melodious by their hard lives; special, quiet people with gentle hands and outlandish, old-fashioned names. Jill remembered one woman in particular, Evaline, and her husband, Vernon, who had helped occasionally in the yard. Jill hadn't thought about them in years, she realized with surprise. How she had adored them! But then once—sometime, she did not remember when, sometime when she was a child—her mother had told her something: a story about a past that Vernon and Evaline had in common, things that had happened before they'd met, even before they'd been born.

And the story was (Jill's mother had been doing her nails, Jill remembered, when Jill had gotten her to tell it) that Vernon and Evaline each had a grandparent, or grandparents, who had been slaves, whose own parents had been taken to America—kidnapped away from their families, bound up in chains, and put on boats with other prisoners whose language they could not understand. And then they had been brought to America and sold.

Jill stood very still. She felt as though she knew what her mother was telling her, but did not know, at the same time, and she wanted her mother to tell her again, but for some reason she did not dare to say so. " 'Sold'?" she repeated very, very quietly.

"That's what I said, Jill." Her mother spread out her fingers and stared at her nails with a sorrowful, absent irony.

So, they'd been sold. And bought—just like the little lizard Jill's father had bought at the circus for her. "But you must never, never mention this to them," her mother said. "They would be terribly hurt."

Jill's throat was dry, and her skin prickled oddly. "Why, Mother?" she said.

"Because," her mother said. Then she looked at Jill, as

though Jill had just come into the room, and stood up. "Because, Jill, it was their own people who did that to them." And after that, Jill had felt very shy with Vernon and Evaline.

"How she does it," Kitsy said, when the door closed behind Roo. "And that adorable little boy."

"You send her home in a taxi?" Bud said.

Jill laughed, and the memory of Evaline and Vernon and her mother dispersed. "Do you think we're rich like you? Just to the station."

"I was going to *say*," Bud said.

"I suppose she has to go all the way to the far side of the city," Kitsy said. "What a saint that girl is—but, oh, that dreadful brother!"

"The Utterly Worthless Dwayne," Nick said.

"Not utterly," Amanda said, and sat down. "Roo adores him." She crossed her legs and surveyed the little gold sandal dangling from her high-arched foot. "He practically brought her up, you know."

"Be that as it may"—Kitsy addressed Amanda's shoe—"things are otherwise now."

"Mmm," Amanda said. And in the pause Kitsy's comment flopped about like a stranded fish. "Incidentally," Amanda added, "he's doing something creative about his problem, finally."

"You don't mean to say he's hocked his needles?" Nick said, and Bud laughed shortly.

"How ashamed you'll be, Nicholas," Amanda said, "when I tell you that he's joined a drug-rehabilitation program in St. Louis."

"A drug-rehabilitation program—" Jill frowned. "Are you sure? That's not what Roo—"

"Of course I'm sure." Amanda raised her eyebrows slightly. "I helped him get into it."

"Quite a triumph, Amanda," Nick said. "But it could be short-lived."

Amanda smiled faintly, but Jill was distressed: It was part of Nick's charm that he was contrary, absolutely intolerant of hypocrisy. But therefore—because he considered Amanda's activities to be merely adornments that issued from vanity rather than conviction—Amanda could provoke him into assuming and defending truly unattractive postures.

"After all," Nick said, "this is your little project, not his, isn't it, Amanda. A man like Dwayne is almost certain to drop out. Just look at the statistics."

"Nick," Jill said.

"He'll tear through a wad of state money," Nick said. "Or Bud's money, if that's what it is, and then he'll drop out, and we'll all be back where we started, except that his self-esteem, and Roo's hopes, will be shattered."

"I'm sorry to admit," Kitsy said, "that I think Nicholas has a point."

"Oh, my—" Owen's voice spread into the room. "Look at this tray, all undefended and just littered with shrimp."

"These *are* delicious, Jill," Lyle said. "Anyone else? Kitsy? Amanda? Bud?"

"No, thanks," Bud said. "So how's life in the futures, Lyle?"

"What?" Lyle said. He looked up, his mouth open. "Oh, picking up, Bud, thanks."

"The thing is, Amanda"—Nick leaned back in his chair—"you're not doing anybody a favor. Dwayne is just pulling your strings."

Amanda made a little face at Nick and pushed her gleaming bracelets up her arms. "You do have to agree," she said, "that Dwayne would have had a very different life if it hadn't been for the war."

"Isn't it strange, Amanda," Nick said, "how everyone

would have had a different life if it hadn't been for everything? Certainly I agree that men like Dwayne had a very hard time. Yes, it was easier for white kids to avoid the draft; yes, the men who did end up fighting were treated pretty badly—and by people who never had to confront the issue of what they themselves would have done if they'd been drafted. But you've got to remember, Amanda, that it's possible to have any number of responses to a problem, and I think that *you'll* agree with *me*: no one *has* to take drugs, and no one *has* to become a criminal. Now, I was as opposed to that war as anybody in this room. But in hindsight, we see—whether we like it or not—that, once there, we should have stayed there. Look what happened the minute we left. But here are Dwayne and his friends, behaving as if they're the only people in the world who ever had a difficult time. 'Oh, us poor black veterans— sacrificed to do the dirty work of the U.S. government . . .' Well, of course I'm sympathetic to their situation—it's unfortunate; no one would deny it, but the truth is that this position of theirs is untenable. And it's disingenuous. Because, in point of fact, it was those very men who stood to *gain* from being in the army. They picked up some valuable skills, they picked up a free education—"

For a moment Amanda's face was white, but then she laughed and shook back her hair. "You're really quite a Nazi, you know, Nick," she said.

"And don't you forget it, Fräulein," Nick said, smiling at her slowly.

"Frau, to you." Amanda smiled slowly back.

"Jill—" Owen glided in front of her, severing her attention from—from what? Jill felt a gust of irritation. "Now I have a serious question for you," he said.

Nick got out of his chair and walked to the window. He stared out, in the direction of the Binghams'.

"And that question," Owen said, "is this. Does Joshua plan to put in an appearance before dinner, or must I hunt him down?"

"I'm afraid I told him he had to stay upstairs," Jill said. "He was a horror this afternoon."

"Not Joshua," Kitsy said. "It's not possible."

"Alas, it is." Jill stopped for a moment, overcome. "In fact—well, as a matter of fact he was gruesome to poor little James. And absolutely rude to Roo."

"Roo-too-roo," Lyle said. "Roo-too-roo—"

"What are you saying, Jill?" Nick said, turning from the window as Lyle tossed a shrimp in the air and caught it in his very pink mouth.

"The truth is," Jill said, "I think Joshua sometimes resents sharing Roo." She didn't dare look at Nick. "And Katrina."

"He knows how to share," Nick said. "I've seen him share very generously with his friends."

"It must be hard for him in his own house, though," Kitsy said.

"Certainly," Bud said. "I know I wouldn't share Katrina with anyone."

"No one imagines you would, Bud," Amanda said, as Kitsy erupted in a volley of tiny coughs.

"Excuse me," she gasped. "Swallowed."

"This is something I don't enjoy hearing, Jill," Nick said.

"He was just tired today, honey," Jill said. "I don't think Katrina gave him his nap."

"Nick," Amanda said quietly, "you're making a scene over nothing."

Nick looked at her, then took a large swallow of his drink.

"In any case," Owen said, taking Jill's arm gently, "I'd quite like to see the little viper."

"He'll be thrilled, Owen," Jill said. "He was asking for

you all afternoon." And at that moment, she felt so grateful
to Owen that she might have been telling the truth.

Upstairs, Joshua welcomed Owen with a bonhomie and
poise that caused Jill's eyes to brim. He presented Owen with
a select offering of toys and stood back as Owen, sprawled
out on the floor, affected to be defeated by the workings of
first one, then another. "Don't be discouraged, Mr. Plesko,"
Joshua said. "These things take time."

Owen put down a little plastic hammer and sighed. He
really did look sad, Jill thought.

"Does Mrs. Plesko like toys?" Joshua asked.

"Mrs. Plesko has a way with a toy," Owen said. "She's
younger than I am, you know. By virtually hundreds of years."

"Do you think she'd like to come play, too?" Joshua asked
hopefully.

"No more come-play tonight, Mr. Joshua," Katrina announced from the doorway.

"Katrina—" A bolt of candor cleared Owen's face as he
struggled to his feet, and his eyes loomed up behind his
glasses like fish.

Katrina lifted her light, springy hair from the back of her
neck for a moment and smiled at Owen. "Joshua," she said.
"It's time for our bath."

Owen's expression had resumed its unclear underwater
shiftings, but Jill had seen enough. "Well, Katrina," Owen
was saying, "it looks like you've been in the sun." He looked
down at his shoes.

"This sun—" Katrina closed her eyes and leaned her head
back. At the opening of her shirt, Jill saw, was a little triangle
of skin that glistened as white as her teeth. "I could spend
my whole life under this sun . . ."

Owen started to speak but looked down at his shoes again
instead.

"So, Joshua." Katrina smiled. "Are we ready?"

But Joshua had gone oddly sullen. "I have to see my dad first," he said. "Tell my dad to come upstairs."

"He can't," Jill said sharply. But then she knelt and hugged Joshua so hard he squeaked. "I'm sorry, darling. Not right now." As they went downstairs together, neither Jill nor Owen spoke.

Everyone else had gone out into the garden, and Jill and Owen, drawn out behind them through the French doors, were able to disengage from their distressed intimacy. Jill paused on the terrace and watched as the others fanned out across the sloping lawn. They drifted alone or in twos among the spires of delphinium, and the peonies, whose huge blossoms shed a waxy glow and a lovely, tormenting fragrance. The colors of the lawn and the flowers intensified with the dark; the night was saturated with the concentrated colors of summer. Beyond the hedge, lights showed in the top story of the Binghams' house. Little clusters of sound sparkled in the air like fireflies—the chiming of glass, leaves clicking against one another, Amanda's tiny, shimmering laugh. Jill closed her eyes, and the sounds intermingled, into a distant surf. For a moment, Nick was behind her. His hand moved up her neck, then down. He let her hair glide through his fingers. When she opened her eyes, he was gone.

By the time they all sat down to dinner, they had become an ensemble; the night and the garden had uncoiled the skein of associations and habits, memories and dependencies that ran between them, dropping it over them in a loose net. Jill lifted her glass, and the amber sea in it moved—these were her friends.

Bud was asking Owen's advice about a lawsuit he was considering bringing against an account, Lyle was counseling Kitsy about London hotels, Nick was unusually animated—

Susan *was*, in fact, enjoying the focus of his charm, Jill saw, as he embarked on a lengthy and involved anecdote; her large eyes misted with effort as she nodded, listening intently. "But how true!" she said earnestly when Nick completed his story and burst out laughing. Amanda twirled between her fingers a little flower she had broken off in the garden, smiling at it quizzically.

"Isn't that the Bingham house?" Lyle asked. "Right next door?"

A silence fell. "Yes . . ." Jill said.

"So terrible," Kitsy said.

"Just what exactly was it that happened?" Lyle asked.

"Well, it might not seem like much to you," Kitsy said. "But it was devastating for them."

"No," Lyle said, "all I meant was—"

"Of course they're insured," Kitsy said. "But it's their privacy, isn't it? And to have one's own home *invaded* like that! Those poor old people—they never did anyone any harm."

"I don't know," Bud said. "Spencer's a hard man on the golf course."

Kitsy cast a reproving glance at her fork. "You know what I mean, Bud," she said.

"Doesn't he make pesticides?" Susan said, and looked brightly around the table. "I mean, didn't Mr. Bingham manufacture pesticides?" she said.

"Well—" Nick stopped smiling. "Actually, there are new studies indicating that if pesticides aren't used, a plant will produce its own, much more toxic, sub—"

"That's so strange," Susan said. "Or really, there's nothing really strange about it, is there? And that's—I mean, Mr. Bingham manufactured pesticides and there's nothing strange about that, and someone broke into his house, and there's nothing strange about *that*, either. But don't you sometimes have the terribly vivid sensation that under this thing we refer to as 'life' is something that—how do I say this?—that there is this thing going on, and we *make* it, or it makes itself, possibly, and then there is this other thing that it looks like, or seems like, which is only sort of a top view of the first thing. A reflection, if you see what I mean. And usually those two things are exactly alike, or at least, reasonably alike. Or—well, I suppose you might say, they coincide, the bottom and the top. So, in any case, it's as though we decide what our lives are going to be like—we deal in futures, or we manufacture pesticides, or we take a trip to Europe, or whatever it *is*, and everything seems to be just the way we've planned it, because, in the vast majority of instances, it *is*. Exactly the way we've planned it. And so the thing that we think is going on is just like the thing that *is* going on, and everything is just the way we've decided it ought to be. But sometimes the . . . the thing on the top and the thing on the bottom are completely different—they've *diverged*, some-how, and we wouldn't even know that they'd diverged, except sometimes the thing on the bottom just pops *out*, it pops out! *Into* the top thing. Because, suppose, for instance, that one of us—oh, goes to Venice, for example, and just falls into a canal. Well, I don't suppose any of us would do that, but I mean people still *die*, for example. Not that that's exactly—but, you see, things are going on in some continuous way, somehow, and, in a sense— Well, look. If you have a party, then people talk to other people. Things happen be-tween people. Or even just happen, like somebody's baby has Down's syndrome, just to mention a—well, happen. When there isn't anything to do about it, nothing, nothing, nothing at all to do about it, because things only happen in one direction—"

Susan stopped, and a laugh bounced slowly out of Owen, like a rubber ball falling down steps.

"It's strange," Susan said, turning to him. "I don't know what I mean . . ."

Susan was never much of a drinker, Jill thought. But in fact she herself was expanding outward, and the few sips of wine she'd had with dinner were causing everything to pass over the convex surface of the evening in long, slow, luminous flashes. Nick, at the other end of the table, seemed to be at the other end of a tunnel; the gentle sounds of conversation rode at the margins of a darkness enclosing her.

There had been things—there was something about Owen . . . She had been angry, if she wasn't mistaken, but the anger had consumed itself, leaving an ashy void. And something had happened—oh, Nick and Amanda had had . . . was it a quarrel? about Roo and her brother; and something had happened with Roo—yes, Roo had been wearing Jill's *dress*, of all things. And before that was when Joshua had been so bad. And before that—oh, yes. Before that, she had visited the Binghams. Of course; she had visited the Binghams, and that must be why she felt so sad. And so ill, really—like an apple with a hidden soft spot spreading under the skin. It must be because of her visit to the Binghams that everything seemed so flat and bad—so stained.

Although Hattie and Spence Bingham lived right next door, they and their house seemed to belong to an earlier era, distant in space as well as in time. They were near eighty, Jill thought, though they'd never looked anything like it until today, when they had looked much, much older. Even their vitality, issuing, as it did, from an untroubled and unreflecting pleasure in success, seemed to sequester them in a more vigorous and brightly colored period.

Jill and Nick had attended several enormous parties or receptions held on the Binghams' lawn, which was glorious in the spring and summer with flowers and blossoming fruit

trees. The Binghams were marvelous hosts. And once or twice
a year Jill would stop over to have tea with Hattie. The heavy
drapes in the living room were always open, allowing the light
to fall in rich panels across the polished floor and the deep
silence of the old furniture, and Hattie would serve Jill tea
and slices of a dense buttery cake, as well as cookies so
fragile they almost disappeared by themselves.

But this afternoon it had been Spencer who opened the
door. "Well, Jill," he said. Without letting go of the doorknob,
he glanced back into the dim hall.

"I've interrupted, haven't I?" Jill said. "I'll come back
tomorrow."

"No, no," Spencer said, and displayed his cordial smile.
"Come in, Jill. Hattie," he called, "we have a visitor." He
dropped his voice. "She'll be glad."

"Well, invite Jill in, Spence," Hattie said, and then Jill
saw that Hattie was having difficulty with the stairs, so there
was nothing to do except wait through the painful descent.
"A visitor is supposed to come in and visit. Come in, Jill,
and sit down."

But when Jill did sit, in a generous upholstered chair near
the fireplace, there was a silence.

"I can't stay long," Jill said. "I just dropped in to say how
sorry I was to hear about—about the other night."

"Oh, yes," Spencer said, as if he were picking up a story
in the middle. "Wednesday night. Well, we'd been over at
the DeForests' for cocktails. They had a little do for that
young man—the new head of cardiology over at Lakeview.
And then we went into town for dinner. We usually do on
Wednesdays, party or no party, so you see what a bad thing
a habit is. Because this Wednesday, when we got back and
opened our door—well, it was just like being somewhere
else—it was like something that hadn't happened. I mean,

if you were to go back outside and come in again, it wouldn't have happened."

"What Spence means," Hattie said, "is that we opened the door of our own house, and we didn't even know where we were—everything torn apart—drawers dumped out, furniture every which way, papers all over the place—private papers!"

"And the dolls, of course," Spencer said.

"*We* want some tea, don't we," Hattie said.

"Hattie," Spencer said. "Sit down, Hattie—don't bother with that—"

"Not for you, you tyrant, for our guest—"

"No, no," Jill said. "I really can't stay."

"Well, Spence has to have his tea," Hattie said. "Unless he's going out. Are you going out, Spence?" She turned to Jill. "He's just been sitting around like an old man. Why don't you call Bob Niederland, dear, and play some golf? Get outside and do something."

"Why should I do anything?" Spencer chuckled unhappily. "I'm an old man, and I like it right here."

"Well, we have to have *something*," Hattie said. "Otherwise, it isn't a party."

Spencer and Jill sat quietly as Hattie made her way toward the kitchen. "Her leg is bothering her, I think," Spencer said, frowning hopefully over at Jill. "Have you noticed?"

"Not at all," Jill said, embarrassed.

The Binghams had never seemed absorbed in their own problems before. In fact, they'd never seemed to have problems, or to think of themselves at all, beyond whatever satisfaction they took from being themselves. Certainly they had never referred to their bodies, to infirmities. "And as you can imagine," Spencer said after a time, "she's heartbroken about the dolls."

"I couldn't even find the tea," Hattie said, returning with

juice and a plate of cookies that seemed to have come from a package. "Ruby and I worked all day to restore a modicum of order around this place, but I still can't find a thing. That darned thief—"

"Don't suppose he took the tea," Spencer said. He smiled at Jill. "Didn't have the style of a tea drinker."

"He got our Lacy, did you hear?" Hattie said. "He broke most of the others, or spoiled them, but he took the four or five really valuable ones, including Lacy."

"She was the first one we owned," Spencer explained to Jill. "We found her in Smoky Mountain country. The first time we went down there, the year we were married."

"Oh, the Smoky Mountains in those days . . ." Hattie said. "Well, we went back after the war once, and of course everything had changed. But in those days—well, you can't imagine—it was so remote, just those cloudy green hills and silent roads, dirt roads, with leafy little hidden enclaves here and there of those peculiar mountain people. You could hear the train whistle sometimes, from way up over the mountains, but that was as close as the world came. And they still spoke their own kind of English then, practically some sort of Elizabethan English—they were almost like an odd little race of animals. Anyhow, Spence and I were driving around up there, and we stopped in Asheville, to poke around some big barn of a place full of antiques. Junk, really—and I spotted Lacy. Can you imagine? She had a handmade lace dress and a lovely white wax face—so elegant and perfect it was almost eerie. Some poor mountain woman's dream of a lady, I suppose. And that's what started us. Afterward, we liked to look wherever we went, and eventually we found ourselves with a whole world, all sorts of nationalities, all sorts of periods. But we never looked for value. Who would have dreamed that dolls would become an item of value? Of course, everything does sooner or later, now. Isn't it funny? Old toasters and everything—all that ugly kitchen trash we hated so. But we never even thought of that. It was the feeling. You couldn't believe what people put into some of those little things—all the beauty and personality that anyone could imagine, that anyone could want in a human being . . ." Hattie sighed and looked past Jill out the window.

"And do you think that's what they broke in for?" Jill asked. "The dolls?"

"What?" Hattie said.

"Oh, there's no question about it," Spencer said. "We've been over it a hundred times, with each other and with the police. There's no question that there was someone involved who'd learned the value of the individual dolls."

"Oh—" Jill said. She put down her cookie, which was slightly stale, she noticed.

"They got Spence's Confederate rifle, too," Hattie said, suddenly indignant. "He was very fond of it."

"Picked up some loose cash, and a bit of silver," Spencer said. "But nothing much. Just enough to make it look like any old break-in. At least until we could collect our wits."

"There was stuff all over the place," Hattie said. "There was even—oh, lord . . ."

"Oh, now, it doesn't matter," Spencer said.

"He had even taken a drawer of my underthings and scattered them around," Hattie said. "You see, there was simply no need for all that violence."

"We know," Spencer said. "That's what we're saying."

"But the worst was the ones he *didn't* take," Hattie said to Jill. "Oh, you could hardly believe your eyes—little arms and legs all over the place—their bodies all twisted; sawdust, stuffing pulled out of them, porcelain faces smashed up, eyes just staring at the ceiling, or the floor, or wherever they'd been thrown. Hurled, really," Hattie said. "They were ours. We found them, we loved them, but now they're ruined, and I feel sorry that I ever brought them here. It's as though this was never our house, we just thought it was. All you could think was blood."

Through the Binghams' window Jill had looked at the hedge that hid her own house from view. Long shadows fell across the lawn, and a late, ciderlike light sliced through the room, charging a panel of tiny suspended dust particles between herself and the Binghams. Beyond it, Hattie and Spencer were insubstantial, wavering, as though they had just acquired a contagious susceptibility to old age. "I'm sorry about the tea, Jill dear," Hattie said.

"I notice that Jill keeps her own counsel," Owen was saying. "I'd give a penny, or more, for Jill's thoughts on this matter."

"I'm afraid I—" Jill ransacked the previous few moments for any words she might be able to retrieve. "Well, I'm afraid I really haven't any thoughts on the matter at all." She laughed.

That serene lawn. The china, and all that glowing old wood. What a flimsy fortress the Binghams' house had proved to be. This was what their lives had come down to—the husks of their bodies. The Binghams had valued themselves highly. They had accepted as their due many beautiful things. But the instant the robbery tore away the fragile illusion of their invulnerability, their merit no longer seemed secure, either. And what the world had rendered up to them, it was now clear that the Binghams kept on sufferance. What they had, Jill thought, what they were, could be tossed aside at any moment, just like the oldest of their possessions, their bodies.

"Susan tells me you have some night bloomers," Lyle was saying. "May I have a tour?"

"Heavens—" Jill said. Only she and Lyle were left at the table. "Thank you, Lyle—no, I'd better make coffee."

As Jill went through the swinging door into the kitchen, a shadow swelled on the wall, twisted, and broke in two.

"Jill." Nick spoke at her side. "Are you feeling all right?"

"—All right?" Jill said.

"Poor baby," Amanda said. "You were looking all green out there."

Jill looked at Amanda, and at Nick. "I'm fine," she said.

"You'll be fine," Nick said, and patted her rear end. "You know," he said to Amanda, "she wasn't sick for one minute with Joshua."

A hard presence stepped forth within Jill and faced her. Nick was selfish, this presence announced. He was arrogant; he was domineering and reckless; he overestimated his skill in all things, and underestimated the abilities of others; he drove too fast, he thought too little, he expected too much; he was careless, deceitful, and calculating. Jill had not told Amanda, she had not told anyone except Nick, that she was pregnant. "Did you make coffee?" she said.

"We were just going to," Nick said. "You didn't look up to it."

"I'm fine," she said. "I'll do it."

Jill waited until the swinging door had come to rest behind Nick and Amanda, and then she turned out the lights and sat down at the counter. Was she going to be sick, she wondered.

Out in the garden Owen was wandering among the high, pale blossoms. Shapes and lines were etched shockingly against the brilliant night, and even from where she sat, Jill could see the tense flare of petals, blades of grass arching with the weight of gathering condensation, and the creases of Owen's face, arranged, as always, into folds that might prefigure either bliss or grief. Owen bent down over a flower, his large padded backside catching the moonlight, and straightened up again as Amanda appeared on the terrace. Her arms were crossed against her chest, although the air was warm and still. She closed her eyes and tilted her face back. Her nails, her hair, and her thin gold bracelets shone. "Hello," Owen said, and the small sound was right next to Jill's ear.

Amanda opened her eyes. "Hello," she said. She and Owen smiled at one another tentatively, sadly, and then Amanda returned inside.

Alone again, Owen made a circuit of the garden. Really, Jill thought, she ought to feel pity for him. In all the time she had known him—except for that one instant upstairs tonight—even in the face of Kitsy's corrosive deficiencies, her inept, gnawing flirtations, his demeanor had never altered.

Owen stopped in the far corner of the yard, at Joshua's swing set. He pulled the swing back and released it, pausing to watch as it rocked back and forth, before he moved on. Jill turned on the light and made coffee.

When she returned to the living room, it seemed to Jill that something must have happened in her absence. Nick was again stationed at the window, gazing darkly out in the direction of the Binghams', Lyle was perched, none too steadily, on the piano bench, and Owen leaned against the open French doors, but attention seemed to be directed toward the center of the room, where Bud, speaking loudly, strode back and forth between the armchairs in which Susan and Amanda were seated, while Kitsy hovered at the periphery, as though she were unable to approach more closely. Bud's voice was poisonously reasonable, and although he addressed himself ostensibly to Susan, who watched him like a browbeaten jury, he looked steadily at Amanda, who sat, eyes closed and head back, swinging her foot.

"I'm just trying," Bud said, "to clarify what you were saying earlier, Susan, about product-liability law. That is—correct me if I'm wrong—but wasn't your point that we need those laws if we're to have any *viable* protection of the consumer, and yet, at the same time, you say, those laws are vulnerable to abuse and exploitation by unscrupulous people. Wasn't that your point?"

"I really—" Susan said.

"And all I'm saying," Bud said, "is that I'm in total agreement with you: it is no longer possible to rely on laws or institutions, because we now have a certain sort of individual who twists laws or institutions, and undermines them by using them for his or her own purposes. The rest of us can hardly be blamed if we're suspicious. Or are forced to behave cynically ourselves."

Amanda sighed.

"You laugh, my darling," Bud said. "But I'm serious."

"But are we saying—are we talking about something?" Susan said.

"Yes," Bud said, as Amanda said, "No."

"I'm a bit lost here, myself, Bud," Lyle said, turning around at the piano. "Could you define your terms?"

"You're a *deliberate* son of a bitch, aren't you, Lyle," Bud said pleasantly. "I'm simply speaking generally. About the misapplication of principles."

"But, Bud," Susan said. "It's hardly a *principle's* fault if someone—"

"How true," Owen said. "Now let us—"

"No, Lyle," Kitsy said, claiming a central position on the

arm of Susan's chair. "I think that what Bud is talking about is a climate, a climate in which people invoke principles in order to pursue their own selfish—"

"Why not let Bud persecute his own wife, Kitsy?" Nick said.

"That's right," Bud said. "Why not let me persecute my own wife. I think I was doing a damned good job of it."

Amanda smiled, but Kitsy flinched as though she'd been slapped. "Do whatever you want to your own wife. I really don't give a shit."

"Would anybody like to tell me what this is about?" Jill said.

"Nothing," Nick and Amanda said in unison.

"We're talking about a climate, Jill"—Kitsy's face was clenched with anger—"of selfishness, of turning things to our own advantage. Of taking things that belong to other people or pretending not to notice if someone else does. These are things—"

" 'Things,' " Susan said. "Does anything feel dizzy?"

"—and these are things we're all involved in," Kitsy said. "All of us. Collusion. Because take the thing we've all been thinking about all evening—the Binghams. My point is, for instance, that we're all involved with the Binghams."

"The Binghams!" Nick turned from the window with a laugh of surprise. "We're all involved with the *Binghams*?"

"Heaven knows what you're involved with," Kitsy said. "I wouldn't know." She looked at Amanda. "But one thing I do know, Nicholas, is that every one of us understands exactly who broke into the Binghams' house, and not one of us is willing to say or to do anything about it because of what some people call—"

"The plot thickens—" Lyle pounded on the piano. "*We know who broke into the Binghams'.*"

"And just who is it," Amanda said, "that we all know to have broken into the Binghams', Kitsy?"

" 'Who'?" Kitsy said. "Dwayne, obviously."

"Who's Dwayne?" Lyle said, lifting his palms comically.

"Dwayne!" Susan said gaily to Lyle, as everyone else looked at Amanda. "The brother of that girl who works here, isn't that right?"

"What on earth gives you the idea that it was Dwayne?" Amanda said, recovering. But Jill had to sit down. Of course it was Dwayne, she thought. Kitsy was right. She'd only pretended to herself because of Amanda that she didn't know. But now— "Would you mind telling me *how* we all know it was Dwayne?" Amanda said.

" '*How*,' " Kitsy said. "What do you mean, 'how'? Who else could it be? He knows the house, he's worked there. He always needs money—everyone knows what a drug addict will do for money. It had to be Dwayne. But we're trying to protect a whole group of people, even though we know perfectly well—"

" '*Group* of people'—" Amanda said. She stopped and stared at Kitsy.

"I am now going to play chopsticks," Lyle announced.

"Shut up, Lyle," Susan said gently and with unexpected lucidity.

"—Listen to yourself, Kitsy," Amanda said. "Just listen to what you're saying—"

"And you," Kitsy said. "Listen to what *you're* saying. You're saying that such people shouldn't even have the dignity of being held accountable for their own failure to adjust to society. But that's pa—"

"Do you think it was Dwayne who stole Bunny Wheeler's Majolica vases?" Amanda said. "Do you think it was Dwayne who stole that Soutine from the Art Institute?"

"—that's *patronizing*. It's not fair to *them*. Other immigrant groups have made something of themselves. Other immigrant groups haven't depended on us for help. Even if they've come from tragic situations, even if they've lost everything—" Kitsy gestured toward Susan. "Like the Jews—"

"Well, now," Lyle said. "Let's not—"

"Look at the Jews," Kitsy said. "Look at the Asians—*they've* suffered, *they've* been persecuted, *they've* been slaughtered. But *their* children play the violin. They get into Harvard. They carry out the garbage. Other immigrant groups—"

"Just one small point," Owen said, "is, immigrants are people who *decide* to go somewhere. People who pack a suitcase, buy a ticket—"

"Oh, I know it sounds ridiculous when I put it like that," Kitsy said.

"It certainly does, Kitsy," Bud said. "Amanda—"

"I know how it sounds, *thank* you, Bud," Kitsy said furiously, but as she turned to Owen, Jill saw, her expression was shockingly piteous. "And that's what I used to think, too. You know, that they'd been slaves and so on, so they couldn't be expected et cetera, et cetera—"

"But that's not even my—" Owen said.

"And, Owen, darling"—Kitsy sprang toward him, gesticulating with her glass—"the terrible thing is that you're so good and kind yourself that you don't see the terrible things that happen to people, the terrible things that people do to one another—" As she leaned against him, tears spilled from her closed eyes.

"There, there," Owen said, but his arms hung at his sides.

"I'm sorry that you're unhappy, Kitsy," Amanda said. "I'm sorry if I've said anything or done anything to cause you unhappiness. But I'm afraid I have to clear the record, because the fact is that it was not Dwayne who robbed the Binghams."

"I'd be the last to doubt your word, sweetheart," Bud said. He was breathing shallowly, Jill saw, just as she was, herself. "But just how are we to believe you?"

"Yes," Jill said, or didn't say. She saw Amanda's fluctuating color, her shining gold bracelets, as though through a fever. "How?"

"Since you must know," Amanda said. "Since it's been decided that it's absolutely everybody's business, the fact is, I checked. At Dwayne's program. Dwayne was there—in St. Louis. He was at a meeting that night—"

Jill's hand tingled, and for a moment all she heard was a breeze outside, riffling the leaves, but then there was an uproar. Kitsy was speaking loudly, and Owen turned away toward the garden. Lyle pounded on the piano, Susan, for some reason, was crying, and Bud and Nick were laughing. Nick whooped with laughter. "Amanda," he said, flinging his arms around Amanda while she stood, furiously still, "you're perfect, do you hear me? Perfect," he was saying, as the room waved around Jill, gelatinous with Nick's laughter. But Bud had stopped laughing, Jill saw. He was staring at Nick and Amanda, and it was only Nick who was laughing.

No, Susan was laughing, too, Jill realized. Susan was not crying—she was laughing. She was splayed out over her chair, laughing without pleasure or comprehension. "What's going on?" she managed to say, through fresh inundations of laughter. "Why is everybody laughing?"

"Well, that really was the worst, wasn't it," Nick said later, with satisfaction. There had been kisses, and tears, and poorly balanced hugs, and everyone had gotten out the door, though whether anybody had gotten home or not, Jill didn't care. She turned away as Nick unbuttoned his shirt—she had already changed in the dressing room.

"Tomorrow will be spectacular," Nick said. "Everyone on the phone all day apologizing. If anyone even remembers what happened—"

Jill waited until the words came of their own accord. "What did happen?"

"Nothing." He laughed. "You sound like Susan. Nothing happened. Just one of those tectonic upheavals between old friends."

"Nothing matters," she said. "Does it, Nick?"

"Well, this doesn't matter," he said. Her stare seemed simply not to reach him. She turned to the mirror and slowly combed her hair.

"You know—" He climbed into bed. "We're not going to need this blanket tonight. The thing is, though, I really do feel sorry for Owen. Not a day goes by that Kitsy doesn't make a spectacle of herself in one way or another."

"You mean that she deserves to be humiliated because she's not attractive. You think that only women like Amanda ought to be able to have affairs."

"Darling—" Nick turned to her and held out his hand. "What's the matter? You're not feeling well, are you."

"The truth is," Jill said, "that Kitsy's in a miserable position."

"She's damned fortunate," Nick said. "Owen puts up with her completely."

"Yes," Jill said. "It's like a sentence of penal servitude."

"I really don't know what you're talking about, Jill." Nick dropped his hand. "At any rate, it's over."

"Besides," Jill said. "You should have seen him with Katrina tonight. It was disgusting."

"Oh, for God's sake." Nick sighed. "Well, I suppose we're going to have to be more careful of you from now on."

In the mirror, Jill watched him close his eyes and turn.

"Would you get the lights?" he said. "Or do you want to read?"

"No." She switched off the lights. "Go to sleep."

She sat down in the chair with her feet up and her arms around her knees, watching as the night settled into the room. She saw Nick's eyes gleam for a moment in the darkness. "Look at the moon," he said, his voice thickening with sleep. "What a moon . . ."

"Nick—" Jill said.

"What, sweetheart?"

"When the baby comes, I want to stop working."

"Stop working? I thought you liked your job, Jill."

"It's only a part-time job, honey. We spend more on help than I make."

"That doesn't matter. I can afford it. If you want to work, you should work."

"But it isn't really *for* anything, Nick. It's just an office job. It isn't really very interesting. I'm not particularly good at it, I don't do anybody any good—"

"Do you want to be one of those women who just sit around the house all day?"

"Why are we married if you're so disappointed in me?" Jill said. "Did you marry me just so you could be disappointed in me?"

"This is ridiculous," Nick said. "You're exhausted. As far as I'm concerned, if you want to work, that's fine, and if you want to stay home, that's fine, too. But I don't want to discuss this any more tonight. I'm going to sleep, and I think you should, too."

"I want to stay home," Jill said. "I want to take care of my home and my children. I don't want all these strangers in my house anymore."

But Nick lay still. He looked like marble, the sheet looked

like carved marble in the pearly indigo of the room. "Nick—" Jill said. His lashes fluttered, his eyes gleamed again for an instant. He spoke indistinctly and turned.

Jill settled back in her chair, her face tilted toward the window. Cool waves of darkness slid in from outside; there was a brief, plangent rush of leaves. Below, in the garden, flowers were tossing about, sighing and giving off their tender light from generous blossoms, thick, pale stems. The grass was wet and tangled, and through it a little path led out from the far corner of the yard, past the swings, and out behind the Binghams' house. It went along behind all the houses on the block—the tidy, sleeping houses—and picked up on the next block, and then the block after that, and then the block where the new houses were being built, and the smell of wood and wet concrete wound through the air. When the path faded out, Jill found herself in a meadow, where she had never been before. Or perhaps she had—yes, she had been there, but now it looked strange, with sticky shafts of milkweed and patches of rough, sour grass pushing up from the mud. Next to her, a layer of chemical suds floated on a ditch. Though it was only twilight, Jill could see the red glare from where the city curved out in the distance, the fierce glare from the steel mills. Jill picked her way among huge spools of wire and pieces of track that lay about the burned-looking ground, and sooner or later she found a little house where she'd seen Evaline once, a long, long time ago, in a Sunday dress and a hat with wooden cherries on it. There were a few chicks in the yard, and some tires, and a half-buried old washing machine; and she must have skirted the city, because now she could even see the metal lozenges of the mills at its far side. I'd better hurry and go inside, she thought; because the greenish wedge of twilight was pressing down quickly upon her and the little house.

In the bare wooden room that was the house, many people were waiting. Jill wandered around and around among them, but they paid no attention to her whatsoever, which was odd, Jill thought, because, of all those people—old people sitting and fanning themselves anxiously, and babies who sat, distracted and silent, on the floor—she herself was the only white one. But evidently the people there were concentrating on something, waiting for something that was going to happen, and they had no time for Jill, none at all. And just as she was growing beside herself with impatience, she saw a woman stirring something on the stove from which came rich, dark tendrils of aromas, streaked with traces of something that was familiar, although Jill couldn't place it.

"Don't be rude," said a voice in Jill's ear. "You know what this is."

That's disgustingly unfair, Jill thought, and I'm going to leave; I never wanted to be here in the first place. But she could not make her way through the crowded vigil—even though morning was soaking into her sleep, and she could feel Nick pick her up and carry her to the bed, she could not fight her way through.

She was just starting to struggle in earnest when she saw the two boys—Roo's James and her Joshua. They had gotten hold of some marvelous toy, a translucent sphere inside which tiny figures whirled and orbited, and Jill watched as the thing spun, lofting into the air. She caught her breath as James tensed, his tiny face pointed with effort, but before James could catch it, Joshua reached out. "It's mine—" Joshua called, and, as the fragile thing bounced from the tips of Joshua's fingers, Jill, too, reached and cried out, just managing to wake, her hair damp and clinging to her forehead, before James was able to open his mouth.

P R E S E N T S

THE WAVES GO ON AND ON—
there is no farther shore; a boat here and there in the dark
water, a cluster of fronds, an occasional sunset. Cheryl closes
her eyes, and the warm night-blue water rushes out around
her. "Think it's really like that?" she asks. Cheryl's voice is
arresting—low, and with a city accent that gives each word
the finality of a bead dropping into place along a string;
sometimes strangers to whom she speaks pause before re-
sponding, and look, if they haven't looked before. "Think it's
really that blue?"

"Blue?" Carter glances down at his shirt. "Nothing's this
blue. Not even this. It's the lights in here—make everything
vibrate." He tips the little glass bottle in his hand and spills
a neat white line from it onto his forearm, which he extends
to Cheryl with balletic solemnity.

"You know what?" Cheryl says when her attention returns
to Carter's shirt. "It's sort of . . . not beautiful, isn't it? Sort
of—"

"Don't insult my shirt," Carter says. "Are you insulting
my shirt? That's not nice; it was a gift. I wonder why people
wear these things, come to think of it. They're ugly, they're
stale, they're not even funny, but you can't get rid of them.

They disappear for a few years, then, wham, they're back again, worse than before. Fact, I'm going to make a stand. I'll never accept another one from anybody, I don't care who tries to give me one." He taps another line neatly out from the bottle onto his forearm and inhales it, all in one fluid sequence. "Don't let anyone tell you I've lost my talent," he says.

Cheryl, leaning against the sink, smiles. "So what is it like?" she asks. "You been there?"

"Huh?" Carter says. "Ah." He presses his fingers against the corners of his eyes. "Yeah. I did a film there. It was like a film set. It was like a hotel room."

When Cheryl and Carter return from the men's room, Danny is waiting at the table, with a fresh round of drinks, in exactly the same position they'd left him. His soft dark hair, his soft white skin, his muscular roundness, his stillness—he is dark and still enough to absorb all the clatter around him.

When did Danny and Carter last see each other? Cheryl tries to figure it out. It must have been five or six years ago that Carter moved out to the Coast—long before Cheryl started going out with Danny—when she was just a child and would stop in here with her mother, Judith, for a hamburger and a soda before going back up the block to do her homework or go to sleep while Judith stayed on at the bar. Cheryl might well have seen Carter here in those days, but he would have been just one among many people who hung out at Danny's table.

Danny, of course, is delighted by Carter's unexpected appearance tonight. He has often spoken of Carter to Cheryl—their friendship, to him, is a living thing. But Carter, who seemed comfortable enough downstairs in the men's room with Cheryl, is formal here at the table, and querulously passive, as if he were being forced to wait for some event that would reveal to him exactly why, after all these years, he has taken the trouble to look Danny up.

"Put quite a dent in this," Carter says, handing the little bottle back to Danny.

"That's what it's for," Danny says. "You don't even need to ask—it's always here."

" 'Here'!" Cheryl says as Danny pats his pocket, surprising herself with her own disloyalty, but Carter only glances over at her as if taken unawares by some unidentified disturbance.

"In fact"—Danny frowns slightly—"let me lay a little of this on you."

"No," Carter says. "Thanks. This is—this is just old times' sake."

"Well, that's good, right?" Danny says. "I took a break recently myself."

"I work much better now," Carter says. "Nothing to distort my concentration."

Danny nods, smoothing things over. Or, Cheryl wonders, has he really not noticed the cruelty of Carter's remark. "They keep you pretty busy out there, I guess," he says.

"It's not too bad," Carter says. "Nothing too much for a while, though. Everything's shit this year."

"Well," Danny says, "we're always glad to see your work here. Cheryl and me. Everyone."

Carter's look, as it sweeps across the room possibly assessing conditions for departure, provokes a rustle of self-conscious laughter from girls at nearby tables.

"Carter made a movie in Hawaii," Cheryl interposes.

"Hawaii," Danny says. "Interesting. That's interesting. I wasn't aware of that."

"It was a while back," Carter says.

"You were doing a series just now, right?" Danny asks.

"Right," Carter says.

"I haven't seen that for a while," Danny says.

Carter smiles as if yielding to a barbed witticism. "The network said it was too specialized for the viewing public. Meaning the sponsors couldn't follow the plot, so they took it off the air."

"That's what I thought," Danny agrees. "That's what I thought. You know, I never saw that movie—I thought I'd seen all your movies."

"What movie?" Carter says. "Oh. Well, you might not have known. It was supposed to be—well, actually, it was supposed to be Hawaii, in fact, through some error of efficiency. Course they had to chop down the palm trees so there'd be room for the fake palm trees. But otherwise it was a good idea for a location. An exciting concept."

Danny laughs obligingly, but Carter's irritability threatens to overflow and swamp the conversation.

"At least you've got the shirt," Cheryl says.

Carter looks at her blankly, then down at his shirt. "Right," he says. "Girl on the crew gave it to me," he explains to Danny. "So I wear it from time to time, out of respect for her memory."

"Holy shit," Danny says. "She died?"

"Out of respect for her memory," Carter insists. "Because I can't remember her. Hair, I think. Or makeup. Except maybe I got it for myself, come to think of it, to remember myself by, because the thing about that movie was, my performance had the exact level of distinction and authenticity illustrated by this shirt."

Danny looks perturbed. "I don't like to miss any of your work," he says.

"You would have liked to have missed this."

"It was probably a lot better than you think," Danny says. "You probably just think that because of some personal situation or whatever. Anyhow, I'll try to rent it."

A silence falls between the two men, in which Cheryl feels ensnared, implicated.

"Anybody need to make a trip to the powder room?" Danny asks finally.

"Thanks." Carter pushes his glass away. "But I've got to sleep. I'm seeing those guys tomorrow."

"Look at that," Danny says, turning to watch as Cheryl takes a sip of her drink, a frozen Margarita. "The things girls drink—green things, pink things. The things they do. I love it. Paint, curls, things that shine . . ."

Carter looks at Cheryl. It is the first time, she thinks, that he has really looked at her. "Yes, indeed," he says.

"If it's sleeping, don't worry," Danny says. "I've got something for later that'll help with that."

Carter withdraws his look from Cheryl, erasing her. "Right," he says, accepting the little bottle from Danny. "Anybody care to join me?"

"I'm O.K. for the moment," Danny says. Cheryl looks down at her drink.

"I hate to see the guy so unhappy," Danny says, watching solicitously as Carter disappears toward the men's room. "He's seeing those guys tomorrow, I guess. Well, he's a good man."

"Excuse me a minute," Cheryl says. The tentative, probing note in Danny's voice is making her uneasy. "I want to say hi to Roy."

Although the tables are nearly full, the population at the bar is sparse, and Roy is killing time polishing glasses. "Would you look at this shit, please?" he says, holding a smudged glass up for Cheryl's inspection. "Day-shift assholes."

Roy takes a personal pride in the ruin that is the world, and there are times when each of its details provides him with a welcome occasion for disgust. But Cheryl is perfectly at home with these moods of his; he has been more or less living with Judith for nearly seven years. "Could I have a soda, please, Roy?" she asks.

"Knock it back, Princess," Roy says, handing her a Coke.

Cheryl simply doesn't like the taste of alcohol, although on nights like this when she's getting high she has to drink it to take the edge off. But it suits Roy to theorize, with infuriating magnanimity, that Cheryl's reluctance to drink inevitably stems from some of the scenes Cheryl witnessed between Judith and his predecessors—real drinkers, problem drinkers, "walking slime" Roy has called them, and Judith and Cheryl agree—who beat Judith in unassuageable furies, as if she were losing her looks to spite them. Which she would have, she's told Cheryl, if she had been in charge of the matter herself.

When Roy and Judith are annoyed with Cheryl they accuse her of squeamishness, coldness, high-minded snottiness; they affect to believe that her habitual prudence is a matter of principle rather than temperament; they ridicule her roughly and coarsely, as though to present proof, by contrast, of the defects they attribute to her.

At such times Danny, for his part, seems slightly gratified, as if these allegations were a guarantee of Cheryl's quality. It is the silken coolness of Cheryl's face and hair that he praises; he praises her reserve. He declares that he would marry her on the spot, but this appears to be an axiom, which requires no response. He does not make it necessary for her to examine her feelings about him—as he is the first to point out, she is very young.

"So, Carter back to stay?" Roy asks.

Cheryl shrugs. "He's looking into a few projects," she says, trying out Carter's word. "He might do a play."

"Ho," Roy says. "Greasepaint. Footlights. Very tony. He's looking kind of nervous. He got stagefright already?"

"He's not nervous," Cheryl says.

"He looks nervous. He looks like shit. And no wonder. He hasn't made a decent picture since *Apple Pie*, you realize that? I understand he's got himself a bit of a reputation these days. Fooling around, making demands, and so forth. Very high-handed."

"Guess they keep you pretty well informed about him, Roy."

"Hey. You read things. You hear things."

Evidently Roy is determined to bully her tonight. Cheryl has spent the last few days at Danny's, and it must be that in her absence Judith has been singing her praises, or the praises of some father of Cheryl's that Judith has invented for the purpose of torturing Roy. Well, good. Cheryl wishes her mother were around right now. For once, Judith's rash mockery, her raucous slatternly astuteness would be a pleasurable danger—a relief from Roy's goading prissiness and the indecipherable pressures emanating from Danny. "Is Mother coming in tonight?" she asks.

"I expect she'll show up in due course," Roy says. "To get a load on. At least, she didn't give me reason to presume she had alternative plans. Naturally she would of been here already if she'd known who you and Danny were entertaining."

Judith always snorts at the mention of Carter. Nothing personal—merely that she's bound to be skeptical in regard to the sudden celebrity of a familiar face.

"He come in to score tonight?" Roy asks.

"He came in to see Danny," Cheryl says.

"Uh-huh," Roy says.

"He's clean."

"He's clean," Roy says. "He just likes to hang out in the can 'cause he feels insecure in public. Ah, time was he'd come in, he and his buddies from acting class, the picture of innocence, slumming. Fresh-faced silly-ass kids putting away the beer and shooters, thinking up things to deplore. Seems like no time at all before he's over at Danny's table."

Cheryl sighs. What does she care?

"Speaking of which," Roy says, "you tell that boyfriend of yours I want a word with him. Guess he's forgotten me in all the excitement."

"Take it easy, Roy. If Danny said he'd do something for you he'll do it."

"And you watch yourself, my girl," says Roy, smug and fatherly now that he's managed to exasperate her. "It's a known fact this guy's a demon with women."

"Grab your stuff, sweetheart," Danny tells Cheryl when she returns to the table. "We're going up to Carter's for a bit."

Cheryl hesitates. But Danny seems at ease, perfectly in control, and he is waiting. "You have to be up in the morning?" she asks Carter.

"No, no." Carter speaks with an automatic, beleaguered graciousness. "Be nice if you drop by. It's still early."

"It's *early*," Danny says, putting an arm around her. "We won't stay long."

They stop at the bar on their way out, and Roy extends an enormous hairy arm, spreading a wide but transparent smile over cold appraisal. "Great to see you back again," he says.

"Great, yeah, great to see you," Carter says, abashed.

"Going to stick around for a while?" Roy says.

"Depends on whether a few things work out," Carter says.

"Well, best of luck to you." Roy's smile becomes still wider and more punishing as Carter becomes more uncomfortable. "Don't be a stranger, now." Cheryl can just hear Roy telling Judith later how arrogant Carter has become. She can just see the two of them shaking their heads over it, over life. But why should Carter remember Roy, anyway?

"Here you go," Danny says, handing Roy an issue of *New York*.

"I read this one already," Roy says obtusely.

"Page 38," Danny says. "A terrific article. I saved it for you."

Roy's puzzled frown transmutes into a huge and genuine grin. "My man," he says, and at this moment he and Danny could be father and son, united in the intricate execution of some athletic feat. Danny can always bring out the best in Roy, and sometimes when Cheryl sees them together she is reminded of the time, when she was eleven or so, that Judith discovered Roy behind the bar here and brought him back home with her. What a surprise he'd been—good-looking and boyish. Engaging, genial. Roy: a miracle.

"If my mother comes in—" Cheryl says.

"What, tell her what?" Roy says peevishly.

"Oh, fuck off, Roy," Cheryl says.

"The guy's practically family," Danny explains to Carter on the way uptown. "He lives with Cheryl's old lady—remember? Judith?"

Carter shakes his head. He appears not to be concentrating.

"She's one terrific lady," Danny says. "Very talented. She was Miss New York State one year. You should see some of those old pictures of her. Gorgeous. Looks just like Cheryl in a funny bathing suit. Same eyes, same legs, same hair."

There was a time when people frequently asked if Cheryl and Judith were sisters, but now Judith's kitten face is pouchy with alcoholic malice and sentimentality.

"She's quite a character, quite a lady," Danny says. "She used to be a dead ringer for Cheryl."

"Is that right?" Carter says.

Although Judith is not quite forty, what people now say is "She must have been a good-looking woman at one time."

"Dead ringer," Cheryl says, again disloyal. And when Carter directs to her a slow smile, rich with bitter complicity, she is as shocked and shamed and thrilled as if she herself had voiced some declaration.

As soon as Danny empties a gram bottle onto Carter's shiny dark coffee table, it is Cheryl who digs in, using the tiny gold spoon Danny had given her as sort of a joke shortly after they started going out. "Like getting pinned," he'd said. "You know about that? Like those old-time beach-party movies." Danny loves movies, particularly ones—his *friends*—that date from his early childhood.

Cheryl feels steadier right away, and decides to strike off on her own and explore. It seems that this is a hotel, or something like a hotel. There had been a uniformed man in the elevator, and there were many elevators, or several at least, and downstairs in the lobby other uniformed men, and, distantly, in a dim gilded recess, something like a desk, Cheryl now realizes, and beyond that a huge set of double doors, glassy but dark, possibly leading to a restaurant where there would be heavy white cloths on the tables, and waiters in white jackets.

Cheryl goes from Carter's living room back to his small foyer and chooses one of several doors. Although the building seems old and solid, the rooms in this apartment have an almost abstract regularity, and they flow from one to another—chambers and chambers, Cheryl thinks—in a random manner, as if the phenomena of daily life eluded categorization. The furniture, also stripped of the burdens of particularity, is unused-looking, and here and there is a clean glass ashtray holding a matchbook.

Eventually Cheryl comes across a room where there is an enormous bed, and she stretches out upon it, taking care to keep her shoes from touching the stiff, glossy spread. There are a number of doors in this room, too, and large mirrors on three of the walls. But the wall to Cheryl's left is almost entirely glass.

She is in the sky here, and rolled out beneath her, a spectacular toy, is the Park. At its borders the shadowy towers of toy buildings, flecked with gold windows, rise into the night. And inside the Park pale light from globy lamps coats the branches and trunks of trees in a soft gleam. It is still early enough in the year so that no leaves hide the shapes of these trees. A little car glides through them soundlessly, along a curving drive. There are no sounds here whatsoever, behind the heavy glass, and no motion of air.

What sorts of trees are those, below her, Cheryl wonders. What shapes will their leaves be? Cheryl imagines that she herself is here to make these decisions. She imagines the toy people below looking up expectantly, searching the windows for her face—the giant serious face of the child who is to arrange their toy lives.

Cheryl stands, causing a phalanx of Cheryls, not children at all, to rise in the mirrors. The bedspread retains no impression of her body, and, more strangely, the first door she opens leads directly back into the living room, where Carter and Danny are.

Danny is happily going through a stack of movie cassettes, most of which feature Carter, and Carter has evidently called down for drinks. Danny locates *The Timekeeper*, his favorite of Carter's movies, and puts it on the machine. Harsh splinters of light are flung out into the room, and Danny watches, rapt, as Carter appears onscreen and proceeds, with fever-pitch caution, to break into a safe. The corporeal Carter, however, perches nervously on the arm of the sofa where Danny and Cheryl sit, and from time to time he springs up to range back and forth as if he were tethered to the screen, until a room-service waiter arrives with drinks, releasing him.

The waiter pauses for a moment, watching a tiny wind-whipped Carter climbing down a fire escape, before he sets the drinks down on the coffee table. "That was a terrific film, Mr. Hall."

"Thank you," Carter says. He signs the check and hands the waiter a large tip. "Thanks."

"Thank you, sir," the waiter says, lingering by the sofa. "I admire your work tremendously."

"Oh—" Carter looks around, but as Danny is resolutely staring at the screen, he is forced to assume the role of host. "Please," he says, handing the waiter a book of matches from the ashtray on the coffee table. "Help yourself."

"Don't mind if I do." The waiter produces a beautiful professional smile. Perhaps he, too, is an actor. Deftly and authoritatively he scoops a small portion from the white mound on the coffee table onto the matchbook cover, lifting it to his right nostril, and inhales quickly. Cheryl thinks of him downstairs in the restaurant she has imagined there, tossing salads and carving roasts on a silver trolley. Is this something she has ever seen in real life, she wonders. The waiter repeats the operation, using his left nostril.

"Outstanding," he says. His eyes rest briefly on Cheryl and Danny, who are motionless on the sofa, staring at the screen. Then he puts the matchbook down on the coffee table in front of them with a little click. "Well, thank you, sir," he says to Carter.

"Thank you," Carter says. "Thanks very much." He closes the door behind the waiter and returns to stand behind the sofa.

"Look at that," Danny says to Cheryl, pointing at the screen with proprietary pleasure.

The waiter has left a bottle of Finnish vodka on ice, and a large bottle of soda, and three setups, and although Carter has also requisitioned a frozen Margarita, Cheryl decides in favor of vodka-and-soda. This is one evening she intends to stay high, and it may take a fair amount of alcohol to maintain her current fine equilibrium. She doesn't want to throw a whole lot of sugar on top of that.

"Look," Danny says. "We're coming up to the part on the bridge."

"I can't watch this," Carter says. But what he can't seem to do is turn away.

"How the hell do you do that?" Danny asks as Carter appears, shirtless in a slushy rain, running along a bridge. "You look like you were *dying* of fear."

"I was dying of fear," Carter says. "I was fucking dying of fear. We were all fucking dying of fear. It was probably the coldest day of the last twenty years, the bridge was iced over, no one could agree how to set up the shot. Everybody was slipping around like fish—we almost lost the camera operator a few times."

"Very dedicated guy, huh?" Danny says respectfully.

"On top of that, we all had some kind of flu, but we couldn't slow down—we were already four days behind schedule because the first director turned out to be a bit of a junkie and got himself fired and replaced with this kid who'd never done a feature before, although of course when this came out he was red hot until his second one came out. Now he can't get a job in the mailroom. So there's some bondsman standing around waiting to grab the film if this kid falls one more second behind, and the producer's there, too, and they're watching each other and the director like ferrets and trading antibiotics, and alternating trips to the bathroom to throw up, and everything is one, two takes, and meanwhile—" But

Carter's sentence is fractured by a volley of bullets as well as a loud buzzing. "Excuse me," he says. He looks irritated, but Cheryl thinks there's a note of satisfaction in his voice. "House phone."

Carter disappears into the foyer and returns a minute or so later with a tall woman whose hair is just a bit longer and lighter than Cheryl's. So exaggerated are the slenderness and curvature of this woman's lines that she seems to be on the other side of some distorting lens.

"My, my," the woman says. She drops her jacket on the sofa near Danny. "Home movies."

Carter shrugs, but he walks wearily to the set and turns it off.

"Hey," Danny protests, in a jokey, affectionate manner.

Carter pushes his hair back with both hands. "Suzannah, Danny, Cheryl," he says.

"Pleased to meet you," Danny says.

"You were going to call me, Carter," Suzannah says.

"I forgot," Carter says.

Danny is the first to recover, and he undertakes the task of setting things right. "Help yourself," he says to Suzannah, indicating the mound on the coffee table.

Suzannah seems to have been waiting for this offer. "No, thank you," she says quickly and coldly. She stares at some point embedded in space, but an awful disorder atomizes the room again, and she shifts ground, sitting down next to Cheryl. "I had a brutal day," Suzannah says confidingly to her. "I've simply got to sleep—I have to look halfway decent tomorrow."

Cheryl is happy to fall in with Suzannah's childish amiability. "Are you a model?" she asks.

"I'm an actress," Suzannah says, no longer amiable.

Carter laughs softly, and Suzannah stands up. "How did the audition go?" Carter asks.

"Very well, thanks," Suzannah says. She walks over to the TV and starts the tape again. "I won't keep you. I just came by to pick up a few things."

"Absolutely." Carter's voice is enmeshed in the flickering of the movie. "Go right ahead." Pointedly he picks up the matchbook and hunkers down by the coffee table.

Suzannah pauses at the door to the bedroom. "I thought you had a meeting in the morning," she says.

"I do," Carter says.

"We should go," Cheryl says to Danny.

"Don't leave," Carter says, putting his hand out to Cheryl. His eyes shadow as he looks up at her. Then once again he bends over the table, but this time Suzannah doesn't look— she has gone into the bedroom.

"Can we go back?" Danny says. "We missed a lot on the bridge." He rewinds the tape himself, then sits down again, with his hands behind his head. "Ah," he says as Carter materializes in front of them shirtless and half crazed with panic.

Carter watches with intense concentration from the arm of the sofa, but before his image even reaches the bridge he gets up to replay the beginning of the scene. Danny seems not to mind Carter's intervention, even when Carter stops the tape to stare at a frame, which he does several times. In fact, Danny only nods, as if Carter had carried out an impulse of his own. Danny seems to be growing more and more at home here, at the same time that Carter seems to be growing more and more distressed, held in thrall by the figure on the screen.

In the bedroom Suzannah, with unnecessary energy and commotion, is taking from a closet and a bureau drawer items of clothing which she then folds and puts into a Bloomingdale's bag. Cheryl watches from the doorway, but the mirrors have caught the dense, subtle colors of the Park, and on top of them, in serially reflected planes, the dark bed floats irresistibly. Suzannah continues to stride back and forth as Cheryl enters and lies down on the bed, her hair fanning out. If one of them leaves, Cheryl thinks, there will still be an infinite number of people in the mirrors. But "if two of us leave," she comments aimlessly, aloud, "there won't be any people at all."

"What is the matter with you?" Suzannah says, and slams the bureau drawer. "You're really out there, aren't you?"

"I just wondered if you wanted to talk," Cheryl says, although she hadn't particularly. She feels good, she feels fantastically good. She hadn't particularly wondered anything.

"Well, no, actually, I don't want to talk, thank you." An infinity of Suzannahs toss their hair. "Now that you mention it, I don't want to talk. I'm sure you want to talk, but I haven't just put a month's income up my nose, and I don't actually want to talk."

How often, particularly before the advent of Roy, would Judith dramatize herself in just this way, overstating the indignity of her situation so as to justify to herself her own lack of generosity or affection, forcing the tolerance of those around her in order to elicit a response that would validate her accusations of cruelty or thoughtlessness, defending, at her own expense, the territory to which her appearance entitled her until age shrank the margins of that territory, leaving her stranded (as who could know better than Cheryl) within the confines of her own devalued body?

The brawls that Cheryl has seen! Brawls that Judith's memory seasons to a satirical palatability, so that her persecuting demands and the grudging male objects of them reappear anecdotally, amusing and typological, like shifty cartoon mice armed with bottles and planks, saber-toothed cartoon cats stalking them. Cheryl is enraged by this miniaturization, and she herself has no such power over the past. For her, it rises up with the force of experience and subsides dizzyingly, leaching out all colors, severing gravitational pull, setting everything flying. Recognizable terrain falls away beneath her at these times with a roar, an unstable bluff.

It crosses Cheryl's mind that she is a coward. And certainly she has endured the coward's punishment, waiting, always waiting, while Judith piles on the provocations, for the inevitable rotation toward catastrophe. The two of them, Cheryl and Judith, scamper into Cheryl's focus as an awful comedy act: the panicked child, clutching at every flimsy scrap of junk as the rubble rains down, and the mother, dabbing at a last tear, ready to go out dancing.

Really ridiculous, Cheryl thinks. And in the suppleness of her mood the awful sensations attenuate and slip off. But Suzannah's helpless brutality, treacherously familiar, compels Cheryl's vigilance. "Carter seems like a very emotional person," she commiserates cautiously.

"An emotional person," Suzannah responds with scorching gentility. "An emotional person. Gosh, I appreciate your pointing that out. I don't think anyone has ever—has ever *had* that insight. But you know what, see—all those emotions, those fancy little emotions of his, what they are is little circus tricks. Because that's what Carter is—a fancy little circus animal. And when he gets bored with one trick he tries a new trick, and he practices it until everyone applauds. And when everyone applauds he's sick of that trick, and he drops it. But if he gets scared—well! Three *months* he's been back here straightening himself out, one decent offer and it all falls apart." She wipes with her palm at the teary film glistening on her face, as if a fly had alighted there. "He got tired years ago of the bit he and I worked up together, but he still calls me in from time to time, whenever he's planning to degrade himself in some especially terrific way and he doesn't have a big enough audience." She gives her shopping bag an efficient little shake to settle the contents. "A good enough audience."

Yes, Cheryl thinks, gazing out at her Park as Suzannah cries. Her heady languor is opening out into a great, clear field. It is easy to understand that Carter would become bored with Suzannah. Even Suzannah's flaring beauty leaves no place to rest. Still, as Cheryl understands all too well from Judith's noisy love affairs, self-serving anguish of this sort requires cooperation, and at one time Carter must have fanned the flame. Circumstances sometimes arise in which it is made clear that Danny has no interest in, or talent for, this particular sort of romance, and at these moments Cheryl almost floats with relief. Maybe she's not in love with Danny, she thinks, but she does value him at his worth. He is always polite, always respectful, never intrusive or careless; he believes in behaving correctly and (except for certain terrible occasions to which she has only heard allusions) does not lose control of himself; he is responsible for his actions; and he is amazingly generous. Cheryl knows he helps out Roy from time to time, for instance, and Judith, too, although certainly neither is ever able to pay him back.

Suzannah blows her nose. "O.K.," she says in a tiny, docile voice. "Ready."

Suzannah does not look at anyone as she retrieves her jacket from the living-room sofa, and she knots her scarf with elaborate concentration.

"I'll go down with you," Danny offers. "Sorry, honey," he says to Cheryl. "I got a call. I'll be back in a little while."

"You could give me a lift home," Cheryl says.

"Well, it's the wrong direction," Danny says. "Why not wait for me here? This is a very impatient guy."

"Stick around," Carter says, reaching for Cheryl's hand again. "How come everybody's leaving?"

"O.K., sweetheart?" Danny says, giving Cheryl a little kiss on the cheek. He turns to Suzannah. "If you're going uptown I can drop you."

Suzannah looks at Carter. "No, thank you," she says.

As soon as Danny and Suzannah are out the door, Carter returns to watching himself on tape with complete absorption. Great, Cheryl thinks. Maybe she'll just take a taxi home. Or go back to the bar and hang out with Judith and Roy. This is a frequent source of annoyance; Danny is obliged to carry his beeper everywhere. Even worse, some of his clients consider themselves entitled to a social occasion. Danny of course is sympathetic to this and sensitive to his clients' needs, but Cheryl hopes this particular errand will be a brief one. There is a quick savage rift in her bright frame of mind: naturally Danny, who sincerely loves to be surrounded by people, never would have questioned whether Carter truly wanted her to stay, never would have suspected that he was simply profiting by her presence to dispatch Suzannah.

"Come here," Carter says without turning around. "I want you to watch something." And Cheryl, rocked by an unruly gratitude, sits down in the bleaching glare from the screen, next to him.

Carter fills their glasses again, and they refresh themselves, he by means of the matchbook and she by means of her little gold spoon, and then Carter plays once again the scene on the bridge. "Here," he says after they've watched it several times, "I'll show you something else." He makes several selections from the pile of cassettes on the floor and proceeds to play moments from them. Each scene that he shows features himself, usually in a state of extreme but suppressed tension or elation, and Cheryl marvels at the difference between the man she is sitting next to and the man she is watching; onscreen Carter seems smoothed out—hard and lustrous, his complications forced back into an invisible core that radiates alarmingly into all of his actions. The real Carter, with his exhausted boy's face, his clearly shifting uncertainties, is more interesting to Cheryl.

"You can't see what goes into it, can you?" he says.

She looks at him, waiting.

"I mean you can't see it," he says, gesturing toward the screen. "I can't see it, either. I can't see it any more than you can. They take what I do and they pour it into this huge machine, and the incredible thing is it usually comes out just the way they want it. And that's terrific, I suppose, that's just great, I'm not saying it isn't. I'm proud of it, I'm proud that I can do it. It's difficult, it's scary as hell, hardly anyone can do it very well. I'm amazed every time it works. But the thing I want to say is, the *reason* I'm proud is not because it's a good thing to do, it's just because I can do it, don't you think? I'll tell you what I think. I think that people like to do what they're able to do. People love to do what they're able to do. That's what nature is, right? The expression of itself."

What he means, Cheryl thinks, is— Wait, no, it's obvious. But obvious the way air is obvious, and in fact the air in the room is massing and separating—part breaks off, soaring. Above her, beating dark, then bright, the shadowed undersides, bright top sides, there: she can stabilize it, it melts brightly back . . .

"So of course," Carter is saying, "everyone is grateful to anyone who lets them do what they're able to do. I'm grateful to those people out there for letting me do what I can do. And the confusing part is, those people are grateful to me, but only because I can generate a lot of money for them, and that's a talent that they recognize. They've got a very pragmatic approach to talent. 'Look, look,' they say. 'That looks like *money*. Oops, no, that's a bottle cap. There, hey, *that* looks like money. Oh, whoops, it's a candy wrapper.' And they just throw out anything, they have absolutely no interest in anything, that they don't know just what to do with, that isn't already money. So they're pretty grateful to me. But I'll tell you something else, which is . . . They don't like me! They used to like me, they used to be very interested in my opinions. About the script, about the camera angles, about the caterers, you name it. But at the moment I am persona non grata. Particularly in the editing room, let me tell you —persona non grata. And the reason is, I'm just not so grateful to them as I used to be. Because, wonderful, wonderful, they let me do what I can do, but look what it ends up as. It ends up as *nothing*. And it's the same for all of us—the actors, the directors, the editors, the cinematographers, the designers. We can all do these amazing things, these incredible things, and people let us do them because it all generates money. But look at the final products: not worth spending two hours watching, let alone months and months making. Certainly not worth squandering all that ability on. Ridiculous, hollow, hypocritical, cynical, corrupt trash. And I'm grateful to do it. But the thing is, I'm trying to exert some control finally, trying to hold out for something decent. But, see, there isn't anything decent, so you get into these habits of rationalizing: 'Oh, it's not really so bad, you know; it doesn't actually *glorify* violence, it *depicts* violence.' 'It isn't *actually* pointless, it's a *parody* of pointlessness.' "

"Maybe—" But what? Cheryl's attention has been a bright ribbon threading through this billowing newness. "Maybe you should—"

"I don't know why I'm talking about this," Carter interrupts. "I don't know why I'm saying these things to you. What do you care? You probably *watch* all this shit."

What? Cheryl freezes.

"You probably think it's all fantastic—"

"As a matter of fact," Cheryl says—normally she might not find it worth it to protest, but she feels good; she'll be generous, help him and herself out of this—"I don't happen to think about it at all. You think it's big news those movies are stupid? You think you're the only person that ever noticed?"

"I'm sorry," Carter says. "I'm sorry. You're right, I'm sorry."

"Everybody knows they're stupid. Nobody but you cares, is all."

"You're right. Listen, I'm mortified. I apologize, O.K.? I've got a terrible attitude, I know." He holds up a little peace offering on the matchbook. "It's just that I'm so used to people who take it absolutely seriously—I'm so used to dealing with these very aggressive, very combative people, who act as if this moronic shit was the most important stuff in the world. I don't know any people like you. I'm completely out of touch with the real world."

"You think I'm the real world?" Cheryl says. "Jesus."

"Yeah," Carter says. "Anyhow, the only living inhabitant."

Cheryl shakes her head and smiles provisionally.

"What a smile," Carter says. "And this play—I've sort of said I'll do it, but I don't know. I haven't actually signed anything. I'm supposed to do that tomorrow. Tomorrow, Christ—what time is it? Today. And there are a lot of good reasons to do it. Because, for one thing, it would be something to do. And for another thing, it's O.K. I mean, there's nothing actually criminal about the script. Also, I haven't been near a stage for years, and it's a completely different set of techniques. Very interesting. Working in real time. With other performers. Everybody spinning a web of concentration. Doing the same thing over and over and making it better."

He lies down with his head in Cheryl's lap. "Different techniques." He grins. "Shouting."

"Um," she agrees contentedly.

"What do you know about it?" he says as Cheryl smooths his hair back from his face. "Don't stop, that feels good. And at least there's a real script, you know? Some sort of a text. Even if it's complete shit from beginning to end, at least it's *something*—it was written by an actual human being, not by a million monkeys at a story conference, with everybody else, like me, throwing in their ax to get ground. 'Oh, I don't think that's right for my *character*. *My* character wouldn't do that; my character's a *saint*. He might rob the bank, but he wouldn't shoot the poor old guard, he'd shoot the shitty *cop*, who beats his wife.' Hey," he complains, as Cheryl neglects his hair in order to scoop up a little spoonful from the coffee table. "Me, too, at least. Not that this play's Ibsen, you understand. The guy's a novelist is the problem, not a playwright, but this is his first play, so everybody's falling all over themselves about it. Especially him, you know? All these guys have a play up their sleeve, they all think they can write a play. But it's a special thing, a special set of skills. Not to denigrate this guy—he's an excellent writer. Excellent. But he just can't write for the stage, when you get down to it. He can't write for actors. All very static, very ponderous. Guy doesn't have a clue. So it could be . . . see, you know what—" He raises his glass, looking through it quizzically, with one eye shut, as if it were a prism. Then he drains what remains inside it. "Kind of thirsty," he says, casting his eyes sideways comically at Cheryl. "No. Thing I meant to say is, there are two sides to every issue. Got that?"

"O.K.," she concedes.

"Wait," he says, peering at his glass again and rotating it. "There's one side to every issue, except it's wraparound.

Well, anyhow, never mind, my *point* is, there are a lot of reasons not to do this play, am I right? I mean it's the actors that are left holding the bag, particularly on a stage. No camera, for one thing. And you can't just waltz out onto the stage and play an idea. An idea! Because that's what you look like—print, believe me. But the producers are *crawling*. I'm the only person for this role, I've got to do it, I'm perfect, it was written for me, it would be great for me to do stage work. But the truth is, I'm gonna tell you the truth, which I didn't understand until this second. The truth is, it wouldn't be great for me. It wouldn't be great for me at all, it would be great for them; it would be great for the box office. Unless maybe I can do a little bargaining—talk to them about rewrites, because unless they do something about my part the thing it would be for me is catastrophic, because, see, the entire universe is waiting for me to make the wrong move. 'Did he—could he—oh, no, look, I think maybe he—yes, he—oh, *too bad*, he *sucks*!' So I can't afford to, you know, afford to take something just because it's respectable."

Carter falls silent, while Cheryl drifts along on these considerations.

"You know that girl you met before," Carter says.

"Suzannah," Cheryl says carefully.

"Yeah, Suzannah. She practically had me talked into this thing. She always thinks I should accept offers, just because they're there. Routine challenges. See, that's what she'd do. Course she doesn't have the opportunity to do it, 'cause nobody offers her anything. But that doesn't stop her from having opinions about the way I should conduct myself on every point. Protocol for every possible contingency. What it is is she can't take the strain of constant fluctuation. Which is what life is."

"Maybe that's just how you feel right now," Cheryl says.

Carter sighs. "No," he says, into the sofa.

Cheryl is only briefly ashamed at having caused Carter to dispense with Suzannah this way. After all, Suzannah had been so determined to treat her and Danny like, as if they were—Cheryl doesn't want to think what. To treat them as she had treated them, despite the obvious fact that they were invited guests, friends of Carter's.

"What about you?" Carter says. "Here I am talking and talking. Tell me about you."

But Cheryl's life—a toy life, she thinks—has taken place far below, on an edge of the city which cannot even be seen from up here. "Nothing to tell," she says.

"Come on, no holding out. Tell me—I don't know, tell me about . . . oh, life with Mom, the beauty queen."

Cheryl pauses. She is not equipped! Danny is always far too protective, far too private, to air his concerns. And Judith's exhaustive catalogues of her own calamitous life are vehicles, weapons, ornaments, decoys—anything but confidences. Whereas Carter, she feels, has been so wholehearted, so candid, so sure of her understanding and participation. She longs to offer him an exchange of equivalent value and substance. But how can she present Judith, as a stranger, for inspection? What sound relic can she possibly reclaim from the churning chaos of her own history? She needs some likeness of Judith that she can pull out and hand over, one that will bear up, converting scrutiny to admiration. She concentrates, framing an approximation of Judith, fans it out in aspects, and reaches back, passing over the recurrent scenes, the vanity and pitiable hopes, the violent, precarious gaiety, the carping remorse—far back to when Judith was young and people were eager to give her things, to keep her happy. "It was wonderful when I was little," Cheryl says. She hears her own voice, dropping the words one by one into the huge room.

"My mother made everything into an adventure. Everything was special for her. She loved to have fun, she loved to get presents. Everyone always said that she was the child, really, and I was the grownup. It was sort of a joke. I was a very finicky little girl. Sort of disapproving."

"Disapproving, huh?" Carter says fondly.

"And my mother was absolutely wild. She'd laugh and laugh at me about it." Cheryl is halted suddenly, choked by old horror as Judith twists free, shattering the suffocating confections in which Cheryl has attempted to convey her to Carter, and she is shouting, hoarse and frantic, from the next room, and some man is there shouting, too. And Cheryl keeps watching frozen from the doorway until—so quickly that she sees it happen over and over again—Judith folds inward, as Cheryl's own legs buckle, onto her knees, and covers her mouth with her hands. *No more!* But the blood seeps out through Judith's fingers, and then it is Carter, instead of Judith, that Cheryl finds herself guarding through the clearing screen of blood. She turns away, sickened. What is it that he wants? "It's easy to hurt a person who's like that," she finishes, closing down the commotion. "It's easy to disappoint them."

"Disappoint them," Carter says. "Yeah, I know the sort of person. I've got limited patience for that myself. It's always *their* expectations, *their* ideas about everything, that they impose on you. Like that girl Suzannah. And you're supposed to feel guilty about disappointing them."

Something winds off from Cheryl in a slow coil and slides out of reach. What has happened?

"What's the matter?" Carter says. "I know what it is. You always take care of people, don't you, I bet. And no one takes care of you. You haven't even had anything to eat tonight, you know that? Going to waste away, leading this life. What do you want, a salad? Chef's salad?" Carter picks up the phone. "Steak? How about some chicken? High-caliber protein, very healthy. Too boring, huh? Speak to me, they got a lot of stuff down there. Shark? Roast pig? Your own personalized roast pig, little apple in its mouth? You tell me, they got everything."

Wonderful—the waiter arriving with a silver trolley, covered dishes, the waiter in his white jacket, looking at her, the dealer's girlfriend. Cheryl shakes her head, shaking him away. "I'm not hungry," she says. "Please don't call down."

"O.K., O.K.," Carter says. "No calling down, we won't call down. I don't know what you got against it. Your pig, though. Come on, tell you what—let's check out the archives."

The kitchen is vast and spotless. A frying pan, an insubstantial-looking pot, and a spatula stand out in the dim light with an accusing and vaguely ludicrous purity. "Anyone ever been in here before?" Cheryl says. "It looks like a . . . it looks like . . ."

"Right," Carter says. "It looks like a museum. On the moon, for after it's all over. Kitchen Division of the Moon Museum of Humans. No, hey, I use this place all the time. Look, all sorts of stuff. Cornflakes; milk for cornflakes; orange juice, except it's museum property, probably about a thousand years old; capers. What's this?" He takes a paper bag from the bottom shelf of the refrigerator and peers into it. "Pastrami on rye," he comments, returning the bag to the shelf.

"Keeping that for hard times ahead?" Cheryl says.

"What hard times? No hard times ahead. I'm keeping it for . . . I'm keeping it for a keepsake. Can't just throw a magnificent thing like that into the garbage."

Carter picks up the box of cornflakes and inspects it closely. "Not so fast," he says, holding the box over his head as Cheryl reaches for it. "You don't think I know what I'm doing, do you? Listen, I make these things all the time. All us great chefs are men." He takes two heavy bowls from a cupboard and pours cornflakes into them, finishing with a sommelier's flourish and a glance of sly triumph at Cheryl.

"That's really something." She smiles, waiting for Carter to hand her the carton of milk and the bowl filled with packets of sugar, but he is lost in contemplation of a cornflake. "These things are absolutely incredible," he says, "you know that? These things are insufficiently appreciated. If they cost a hundred dollars a box, rich people would line up for them."

Cheryl draws over to admire the cornflake in Carter's palm, and it does seem an impossible thing, all suspended froth. "How do they make these things, anyway?" she asks. "What are they?"

" 'What are they?' " Carter says magisterially as he puts an arm around Cheryl. "What are they? They are . . . a mystery." The two of them sway slightly, considering the magnitude of things, and Cheryl traces, with slightly drunken precision, the outline of an island on his shirt, that happy sea.

"You like my shirt," he says. "You like my shirt so much I'm going to give it to you."

"You can't give it to me," she says.

"I'm about to experience an anxiety surge. I'm developing severe feelings of competition in regard to my own shirt. I've got to give it to you."

"You can't give it to me," Cheryl says. "It's your souvenir."

"Souvenir," Carter says. "If there's one thing I don't need, it's a souvenir. Come on, I want to show you."

In the bedroom Carter plants himself in front of the closets with a piratical stance. "Booty," he says, flinging open the door from behind which Suzannah had earlier removed her things. "What about this suit? This was when I was a mobster.

Look at those lapels. Could carve a tusk with them, huh? Now, this thing—this was from a duel. Fight over some lady. She was a tart, though, as it turned out." He pauses to raise an admonitory eyebrow at Cheryl. "Fatigues, satin jacket— well, that one wasn't wardrobe, we all got that, from my last movie, still sitting on a shelf somewhere."

Carter continues to ransack the closets, piling costumes and objects on the bed in mirrored splendor. "Powdered wig, motorcycle helmet, pith helmet, space helmet, five-pound jar of Gummy Bears from an A.D., little model Chrysler Building. Yeah, I been in a lot of different time zones, a lot of different incarnations. Oops," he says, remembering, "I was gonna give you my shirt. Turn around. I'm very self-conscious about my chest. I don't want you to see my chest."

"I've seen your chest," Cheryl points out. "I saw your chest about two hundred times tonight. Everybody in the world's seen your chest."

"Ha—" Carter wags a finger. "You're trying to confuse me, trick me into exposing myself. Think I don't know the difference between . . . whoops, the difference between—"

"You win," Cheryl says. She could use a little pick-me-up in any case. "I'll wait for you out there." And she is surprised, upon entering the living room, to see her little gold spoon lying on the coffee table, because she never leaves it out. Never.

In a moment Carter appears, wrapped in a huge black cape. Vampire? Swordsman? And he hands Cheryl the shirt folded small and bright, like a little flag. In return Cheryl holds out for him her spoon, containing almost all that remains of what Danny had deposited on the coffee table.

Silent in the gauzy first light, they sprawl on the sofa, feet to feet. Cheryl is feeling a little ragged. She is usually reg- ulated by Danny's rather sparing intake, she realizes, although she has suspected on recent occasions that Danny is involved with greater quantities than he lets on.

"You're a lovely kid," Carter says. "Lovely kid. Actors always need new life." He sighs. "I'm beginning to be afraid of things, you know? I don't know how that happened to me. When I was your age I used to see people acting out of fear—I never thought it would happen to me. I thought, I'll never get like that. These days I'm so scared I can hardly walk across the room. Sometimes you see people, their life just hasn't worked out. Ever worry that you're going to be one of those people?"

"Sure," Cheryl says. But what does he mean, worked out? She reaches over, pressing at the residue of white on the coffee table, and licks her finger.

"You can really scarf that up, can't you?" Carter says. "You're a real little vacuum cleaner."

"I'm just keeping you company," Cheryl says, stung.

"*You're* keeping *me* company," Carter says. "That's pretty funny. Hey, don't look at me like that. I'm just being honest. It's for your own good. End up on the trash heap, you go on like this."

His foot is jiggling wildly, Cheryl notices. "Want a drink?" she asks. "Or I might have some Valium."

"Shit," Carter says, as tears gather in his eyes. "I'm so fucking sick of being confused."

Cheryl sighs. Danny could have left them one more tiny little eighth or so if he was going to be away this long. He'd certainly know they'd be needing some by now.

"Sorry," Carter says. "I'm sorry, but you don't know what it's like to be frightened. Really frightened, I mean. You're too young to know what that's like. But me, everything I do is motivated by fear now. At least Suzannah's got that part right. I can't even work anymore. I don't have the heart to work. I'm afraid to do this play, I'm afraid to do a movie—"

God, he is *tireless*, Cheryl thinks. And she just isn't interested in some whole new . . . "Do you want her to come
back?" she says reluctantly. New *exercise*.

"What—Suzannah?" Carter says. "Where's that drink you
were going to make me? Truth is, though, at one time she
was a very good friend to me. We took acting class together
years ago, and this'll probably seem pretty strange to you but
I didn't know anyone like her. All I knew was these very
snooty, very convoluted prep-school kids. And at first she
seemed so fresh to me, so clear. Course, all it is is, like a
lot of good-looking women, she's got a stake in appearances.
And that's why she'll never be a good actress, she'll just be
one more dime-a-dozen model. Until they turn her out to
pasture."

Out to pasture.

"What's the matter?" Carter says, sitting up to look at her.
"You don't like me now. You have to like me. I made you
like me."

Cheryl hands him his drink without looking at him.

"You forgot the lime," he says, but she still won't look at
him. "You're fired, you forgot the lime. Hey." He tugs gently
at a lock of her hair, and she closes her eyes. "O.K." He
shrugs. "You don't want to play anymore. I don't know why
everybody's always so pissed off at me."

"She'll come back," Cheryl says. "If you want her to."

"Not this time," Carter says an instant before the house
phone rings, and Cheryl thinks she detects once again a muted
triumph as Carter goes to answer it. "Well, there's the man,
I guess," he says. "Certainly took his time, didn't he?"

Danny is breathless and apologetic.

"Shouldn't have left me alone with your girlfriend," Carter
says. "We're in love, except of course she won't speak to
me."

"I am really sorry," Danny is saying. "Listen, I really didn't expect this. I got very hung up by this guy, and there was absolutely nothing I could do. I mean, he's a very good friend. My broker, actually. But he's had some big problems lately, and he really needed to talk. By the way, if you're looking for a broker, this is definitely a guy to consider. He is very, very sharp. And a very fine person."

Still, Cheryl thinks. At least he means it. He does mean it.

"Hey, sweetheart," Danny says, "you're not mad 'cause I had to work, are you?"

Cheryl glances involuntarily at Carter, who looks quickly away. Surely he couldn't think Danny stayed away intentionally—*how dare he?* "We have to go," she says. "I'm tired, and Carter has a big day ahead of him. Meetings, decisions . . ."

"Right, that's right," Danny says. "Oh, yeah, wait—I promised you something to help you sleep, didn't I?"

"I can't sleep," Carter complains. "I've got to talk to those guys."

"Sleep first," Danny orders soothingly. "It'll do you good. These little green ones are for that, and here's something to get you back up again. Help you with your ordeal."

Carter makes no acknowledgment of the few capsules and the new little glass bottle Danny places on the coffee table.

"Oh, wow," Danny says to Cheryl, seeing her gold spoon lying there. "Don't forget this."

"Or this." Carter doesn't look at her, but he stands to hold out the garish folded shirt, and when Cheryl makes no move to take it from him he tucks it directly into her purse. "What do I owe you?" he asks Danny quietly. "For this stuff?"

"Please," Danny says. "Absolutely not. Not this time. Say, that's some— What do you call that thing—a cloak?"

"What a character," Danny says as the doorman holds the door open onto the bright, noisy street. How loud everything is out here! "Literally gave you the shirt off his back, huh? If he decides to stick around, we'll probably be seeing a lot of him. Look, I got a parking space right here. Is that luck, or what?" His face is an impenetrable mask of sweetness, well disposed and as satisfied as if he'd just rolled the evening up and tucked it back into his pocket. He reminds her of someone, Cheryl thinks. Oh, yes: he reminds her of Danny.

Cheryl climbs into the car next to him. A ride home, why not? She is fantastically tired, truly exhausted, and it won't be much fun, later, to wake up. She closes her eyes, and Danny bobs up in the pitching dimness and away. All her surroundings are coming loose, peeling off as the dimness balloons—her antecedents, chunks of her life crumple like Danny and blow past. There is nothing she recognizes, no one even to wave to! What a pity—she smiles slightly, and an instant before she is engulfed by a blissful wave of fatigue she opens her eyes and sees the man who was Danny smiling, too—what a pity that she so eagerly handed Judith over, in a version as diminutive and harmless as Judith ever rendered herself, to serve the transient purposes of a stranger. It would have been so simple just to let Judith out, all ravenous and fractured and appalling, to make some splendid uproar in commemoration of this departure. She thinks her mother might have done that, for her, with pleasure.

THE

CUSTODIAN

FOR YEARS AFTER ISOBEL LEFT
town (was sent from town, to live with an aunt in San Francisco) Lynnie would sometimes see her at a distance, crossing
a street or turning a corner. But just as Lynnie started after
her Isobel would vanish, having been replaced by a substitute,
some long-legged stranger with pale, floaty hair. And while
Lynnie might have been just as happy, by and large, not to
see Isobel, at those moments she was felled by a terrible
sorrow, as though somewhere a messenger searching for her
had been waylaid, or was lost.

It was sixteen years after Lynnie had watched Isobel disappearing from view in the back seat of her father's car when
Lynnie really did see her again. And then, although Isobel
walked right into Lynnie's shop, several long, chaotic moments elapsed before Lynnie understood who Isobel was.
"Isobel," she said, and, as the well-dressed customer brows-
ing meditatively among the shelves and cases of expensive
food turned to look full at Lynnie, the face that Lynnie had
known so well—a girl's face that drew everything toward it
and returned nothing—came forward in the woman's.

"Oh," Isobel said. "It's you. But Mother wrote me you were
living in Boston. Or did I make that up?"

"You didn't make it up," Lynnie said.

"Well, then," Isobel said, and hesitated. "You're back."

"That about sums it up," Lynnie said. She let her hand bounce lightly against the counter, twice. "I hear you're still in San Francisco," she said, relenting—they were adults now.

"Mmm," Isobel said. "Yes." She frowned.

Lynnie cleared her throat. "And someone told me you have a baby."

"Oh, yes," Isobel said. "Two. And a husband, of course. All that sort of thing." She and Lynnie smiled at one another—an odd, formal equilibrium.

"And you," Isobel said, disengaging. "What are you doing these days?"

"This—" Lynnie gestured. "Of course, I have help now."

"Heavens," Isobel remarked unheatedly.

" 'Heavens,' " Lynnie said. "I know." But either more of a reaction from Isobel or less would have been just as infuriating. "Heavens" or "How nice" was all that anyone had said when Lynnie retreated from Boston and managed, through effort born of near-panic, to open the store. All her life Lynnie had been assumed to be inadequate to any but the simplest endeavor; then, from the moment the store opened, that was something no one remembered. No one but her, Lynnie thought; she remembered it perfectly.

"Isn't it funny?" Isobel was saying. "I drove by yesterday, and I thought, How nice that there's a place like that up here now. I'll have to stop in and get something for Mother, to cheer her up."

"I'm sorry about your father," Lynnie said.

"Yes," Isobel said. "God. I was just at the hospital. They say the operation was successful, but I don't know what that's supposed to mean. It seemed they might mean successful in the sense that he didn't die during it." Her flat green glance found Lynnie, then moved away.

"Hard to think of him . . . in a hospital," Lynnie said. "He always seemed so—" He'd seemed so big.

"Strong," Isobel said. "Yes, he's strong all right. He and I are still on the most horrible terms, if you can believe it. It's simply idiotic. I suppose he has to keep it up to justify himself. All these years! You know, this is the first time I've been back, Lynnie—he came out for my wedding, and Mother's made him come with her twice to see the boys, but I haven't been back once. Not once. And there I was today—obviously I'd decided to get here before he died. But did he say anything—like he was glad I'd come? Of course not. Lynnie, he's riddled with tumors, he can't weigh more than a hundred pounds, but he behaved as though he were still sitting in that huge chair of his, telling me what I'd done to him."

Lynnie shook her head. How easily Isobel was talking about these things.

"So," Isobel said.

"Well," Lynnie said.

"Yes," Isobel said.

"I'll wrap up some things for your mother if you want," Lynnie said. "I've got a new pâté I think she'll like. And her favorite crackers have come in."

"Lovely," Isobel said. "Thanks." She pushed back a curving lock of hair and scanned the shelves as though waiting for some information to appear on them. "So Mother comes into your store."

"Oh, yes," Lynnie said.

"Funny," Isobel said. Isobel looked like anyone else now, Lynnie understood with a little shock. Very pretty, but like anyone else. Only her hair, with its own marvelous life, was still extraordinary. "How's your mother, by the way?" Isobel said.

"All right," Lynnie said, and glanced at her. "So far."

"That's good," Isobel said opaquely.

"And at least she's not such a terror anymore," Lynnie said. "She's living up north with Frank now."

"Frank . . ." Isobel said.

"Frank," Lynnie said. She reached up to the roll of thick waxed paper and tore a piece off thunderously. "My brother. The little one."

"Oh, yes," Isobel said. "Of course. You know, this feels so peculiar—being here, seeing you. The whole place stopped for me, really, when I went away."

"I'm sure," Lynnie said, flushing. "Well, we still exist. Our lives keep going on. I have the store, and people come into it. Your mother comes in. Cissy Haddad comes in. Ross comes in, Claire comes in. All six of their children come in. . . ."

"*Six*—" Isobel stared at Lynnie; her laugh was just a breath. "Well, I guess that means they stayed together, anyway."

"Mostly," Lynnie said. But Isobel only waited, and looked at her. "There was a while there, a few years ago, when he moved in with an ex-student of his. Claire got in the van with the four youngest—Emily and Bo were already at school—and took off. It didn't last too long, of course, the thing with the girl, and of course Claire came back. After that they sold the stone house. To a broker, I heard."

"Oh," Isobel said. Absently she picked up an apple from a mound on the counter and looked into its glossy surface as though it were a mirror.

"They're renovating a farmhouse now," Lynnie said. "It's much smaller."

"Too bad," Isobel said, putting down the apple.

"Yes."

"Was she pretty?" Isobel asked.

"Who?" Lynnie said. "Ross's girl? Not especially."

"Ah," Isobel said, and Lynnie looked away, ashamed of herself.

Isobel started to speak but didn't. She scanned the shelves again vaguely, then smiled over at Lynnie. "You know what else is funny?" she said. "When I woke up this morning, I looked across the street. And I saw this woman going out the door of your old house, and just for an instant I thought, There's Lynnie. And then I thought, No, it can't be—that person's all grown up."

For a long time after Isobel had left town, Lynnie would do what she could to avoid running into Ross or Claire; and eventually when she saw them it would seem to her not only that her feeling about them had undergone an alteration but that they themselves were different in some way. Over the years it became all too clear that this was true: their shine had been tarnished by a slight fussiness—they had come to seem like people who were anxious about being rained on.

Newcomers might have been astonished to learn that there was a time when people had paused in their dealings with one another to look as Ross walked down the street with Claire or the children. Recent arrivals to the town—additions to the faculty of the college, the businessmen and bankers who were now able to live in country homes and still work in their city offices from computer terminals—what was it they saw when Ross and Claire passed by? Fossil forms, Lynnie thought. Museum reproductions. It was the Claire and Ross of years ago who were vivid, living. A residual radiance clung to objects they'd handled and places where they'd spent time. The current Ross and Claire were lightless, their own aftermath.

Once in a while, though—it happened sometimes when

she encountered one of them unexpectedly—Lynnie would see them as they had been. For an instant their sleeping power would flash, but then their dimmed present selves might greet Lynnie, with casual and distant politeness, and a breathtaking pain would cauterize the exquisitely reworked wound.

It is summer when Lynnie and Isobel first come upon Ross and Claire. Lynnie and Isobel live across the street from one another, but Isobel is older and has better things to do with her time than see Lynnie. And because Lynnie's mother works at the plant for unpredictable stretches, on unpredictable shifts, Lynnie frequently must look after her younger brothers. Still, when Lynnie is free, she is often able to persuade Isobel to do something, particularly in the summers, when Isobel is bored brainless.

They take bicycle expeditions then, during those long summers, often along the old highway. The highway is silent, lined with birchwoods, and has several alluring and mysterious features—among them a dark, green wooden restaurant with screened windows, and a motel, slightly shabby, where there are always, puzzlingly, several cars parked. Leading from the highway is a wealth of dirt roads, on one of which Lynnie and Isobel find a wonderful house.

The house is stone, and stands empty on a hill. Clouds float by it, making great black shadows swing over the sloping meadows below with their cows and barns and wildflowers. Inside, in the spreading coolness, the light flows as variously clear and shaded as water. Trees seem to crowd in the dim recesses. The house is just there, enclosing part of the world: the huge fireplace could be the site of gatherings that take place once every hundred, or once every thousand, years. The girls walk carefully when they visit, fearful of churning up the delicate maze of silence.

For several summers, the house has been theirs, but one

day, the summer that Lynnie is twelve and Isobel is just turning fourteen, there is a van parked in front. Lynnie and Isobel wheel their bicycles stealthily into the woods across the road and walk as close as they dare, crouching down opposite the house, well hidden, to watch.

Three men and a woman carry bundles and cartons into the house. Bundles and cartons and large pieces of furniture sit outside, where two small children tumble around among them, their wisps of voices floating high into the birdcalls and branches above Lynnie and Isobel. The woman is slight, like a child herself, with a shiny braid of black hair down her back, and there is no question about which of the men she, the furniture, and the children belong to.

Lynnie squints, and seems to draw closer, hovering just too far off to see his face. Then, for just a fraction of a second, she penetrates the distance.

The sun moves behind Lynnie and Isobel, and the man to whom everything belongs waves the others inside, hoisting up the smaller child as he follows. Just as Lynnie and Isobel reach cautiously for their bicycles, the man looks out again, shading his eyes. They freeze, and for a moment he stands there peering out toward them.

Neither Lynnie nor Isobel suggests going on—to town, or to the gorge, or anywhere. They ride back the way they've come, and, without discussion, go upstairs to Isobel's room.

Isobel lies down across her flounced bed while Lynnie wanders around absently examining Isobel's things, which she knows so well: Isobel's books, her stuffed animals, her china figurines.

"Do you think we're the first people to see them?" Lynnie says.

"The first people *ever*?" Isobel says, flopping over onto her side.

Lynnie stares out Isobel's window at her own house. She

doesn't know what to do when Isobel's in a bad mood. She should just leave, she thinks.

From here, her house looks as though it were about to slide to the ground. A large aluminum cannister clings to its side like a devouring space monster. "Do you want to go back out and do something?" she asks.

"What would we do?" Isobel says, into her pillow. "There's nothing to do. There's not one single thing to do here. And now would you mind sitting down, please, Lynnie? Because you happen to be driving me insane."

As she leaves Isobel's, Lynnie pauses before crossing the street to watch her brothers playing in front of the house. They look weak and bony, but the two older boys fight savagely. A plastic gun lies near them on the ground. Frank, as usual, is playing by himself, but he is just as banged up as they are. His skin is patchy and chapped—summer and winter he breathes through his mouth, and even this temperate sun is strong enough to singe the life out of his fine, almost white hair. She looks just like him, Lynnie thinks. Except chunky. "Chunky" is the word people use.

Inside, Lynnie's mother is stationed in front of the TV. At any hour Lynnie's mother might be found staring at the television, and beyond it, through the front window, as though something of importance were due to happen out on the street. The television is almost always on, and when men friends come to visit, Lynnie's mother turns up the volume, so that other noises bleed alarmingly through the insistent rectangle of synthetic sound.

Lynnie brings a paper napkin from the kitchen and inserts it between her mother's glass of beer and the table. "May I inquire . . . ?" her mother says.

"Isobel's mother says you should never leave a glass on the furniture," Lynnie says. "It makes a ring."

Lynnie's mother looks at her, then lifts the glass and crumples the napkin. "Thank you," she says, turning back to her program. "I'll remember that." A thin wave of laughter comes from the TV screen, and little shapes jump and throb there, but Lynnie is thinking about the people from the stone house.

Lynnie's mother can be annoyed when she knows that Lynnie has been playing with Isobel; Isobel's father works for the same company Lynnie's mother works for, but not in the plant. He works in the office, behind a big desk. Whenever Lynnie is downstairs in Isobel's house and Isobel's father walks in, Lynnie scuttles as though she might be trodden underfoot. In fact, Isobel's father hardly notices her; perhaps he doesn't even know from one of her visits to the next that she is the same little girl. But he booms down at Isobel, scrutinizing her from his great height, and sometimes even lifts her way up over his head.

Isobel's mother is tall and smells good and dresses in neat wool. Sometimes when she sees Lynnie hesitating at the foot of the drive she opens the door, with a bright, special smile. "Lynnie, dear," she says, "would you like to come in and see Isobel? Or have a snack?" But sometimes, when Lynnie and Isobel are playing, Isobel's mother calls Isobel away for a whispered conference, from which Isobel returns to say that Lynnie has to go now, for this reason or that.

When Lynnie looks out the window of the room she shares with Frank, she can see Isobel's large, arched window, and if the light is just right she can see Isobel's bed, too, with its white flounces, and a heavenly blue haze into which, at this distance, the flowers of Isobel's wallpaper melt.

One day, doing errands for her mother in town, Lynnie sees the woman from the stone house coming out of the bakery with the children, each of whom carefully holds a large, icingcovered cookie. The woman bends down and picks up one of the children, smiling—unaware, Lynnie observes, that people are noticing her.

Lynnie sees the woman several times, and then one day she sees the man.

She has anticipated his face exactly. But when he smiles at her, the little frown line between his eyes stays. And the marvelousness of this surprise causes a sensation across the entire surface of her skin, like the rippling of leaves that demonstrates a subtle shift of air.

When Lynnie sees Isobel she can't help talking about the people from the stone house. She describes variations in their clothing or demeanor, compiling a detailed body of knowledge while Isobel lies on her bed, her eyes closed. "Should we give them names?" Lynnie says one afternoon.

"No," Isobel says.

But Lynnie can't stop. "Why not?" she says, after a moment.

" 'Why not?' " Isobel says.

"Don't, Isobel," Lynnie pleads.

" 'Don't, Isobel,' " Isobel says, making her hands into a tube to speak through. Her voice is hollow and terrifying.

Lynnie breathes heavily through her mouth. "Why not?" she says.

"Why *not*," Isobel says, sitting up and sighing, "is because they already have names."

"I know," Lynnie says, mystified.

"Their names," Isobel says, "are Ross and Claire."

Lynnie stares at her.

"They had dinner at Cissy Haddad's house one night," Isobel says. "Ross is going to be teaching medieval literature at the college. He's in Cissy's father's department."

" 'Department'?" Lynnie says.

"Yes," Isobel says.

Lynnie frowns. "How do you know?" she asks. How *long* has Isobel known?

Isobel shrugs. "I'm just telling you what Cissy said." She looks at Lynnie. "I think Cissy has a crush on him."

"What else did Cissy say?" Lynnie asks unhappily.

"Nothing," Isobel says. "Oh. Except that he's thirty-five and Claire's only twenty-three. She used to be one of his students."

"One of his students?" Lynnie says.

" 'One of his—' " Isobel begins, and then flops down on the bed again. "Oh, Lynnie."

One day Lynnie sees Cissy Haddad in the drugstore. Lynnie hurries to select the items on her mother's list, then waits until Cissy goes to the counter. "Hi," she says, getting into line behind Cissy. She feels herself turning red.

"Oh, hi, Lynnie," Cissy says, and smiles wonderfully. "Are you having a fun summer?"

"Yes," Lynnie says.

"What're you doing?" Cissy says.

"Just mostly looking after my brothers," Lynnie says. She feels bewildered by Cissy's dazzling smile, her pretty sundress. "And riding around and things with Isobel."

"That's good," Cissy says. And then, instead of saying something useful about Isobel, which might lead to Ross and Claire, she asks, "Are you coming to high school this year? I can't remember."

"No," Lynnie says. "Isobel is."

Cissy peers into Lynnie's basket of embarrassing purchases.

"What are you getting?" she asks.

"Things for my mother," Lynnie says, squirming. "What about you?"

"Oh," Cissy says. "Just lipstick."

One fall day when Lynnie gets home from school, her mother summons her over the noise from the TV. "You got a phone call," she says shortly. "The lady wants you to call her back." And Lynnie knows, while her mother is still speaking, whom the call was from.

Lynnie dials, and the soft, dark shadow of Claire's voice answers. She is looking for someone to help with the children on a regular basis, she explains, several afternoons a week. She got Lynnie's name from Tom Haddad's daughter. She knows that Lynnie is very young, but this is nothing difficult—just playing with the children upstairs or outside so that she can have a couple of hours to paint. "I thought I would be able to do so much here," she says, as though Lynnie were an old friend, someone her own age, "but there's never enough time, is there?"

"I'll need you just as much with the boys," Lynnie's mother says later. "And you'd better remember your homework."

"I will," Lynnie says, though, actually, beyond a certain point, it scarcely matters; however hard she tries, she lags far behind in school, and her teachers no longer try to stifle their exclamations of impatience. "I'll do my homework." And her mother makes no further objections; Lynnie will be earning money.

Claire leads Lynnie around in the house that used to be Lynnie and Isobel's. Now it is all filled up with the lives of these people.

Everywhere there is a regal disorder of books, and in the biggest room downstairs, with its immense fireplace, there are sofas and, at one end, a vast table. A thicket of canvases and brushes has sprung up in a corner, and Lynnie sees pictures of the table on whose surface objects are tensely balanced, and sketch after sketch of Ross and the children. "What do you think?" Claire says, and it is a moment before Lynnie realizes what Claire is asking her.

"I like them," Lynnie says. But in fact they frighten her —the figures seem caught, glowing in a webby dimness.

In the kitchen huge pots and pans flash, and a great loaf of brown bread lies out on a counter. Claire opens the door to Ross's study; stacks and stacks of paper, more books than Lynnie has ever seen breed from its light-shot core.

Upstairs Bo and Emily are engrossed in a sprawling project of blocks. Emily explains the dreamlike construction to Lynnie, gracefully accepting Bo's effortful elaborations, and when Lynnie leaves both children reach up to her with their tanned little arms.

Twice a week Lynnie goes to the stone house. Bo and Emily have big, bright, smooth wooden toys, some of which were made by Ross. Lynnie strokes the toys; she runs her hand over them like a blind person; she runs her hand over the pictures in Bo and Emily's beautiful storybooks. But then Claire counts out Lynnie's money, and Lynnie is to go. And at the first sight of her own house she is slightly sickened, as upon disembarkation—not by the firm ground underfoot but by a ghostly rocking of water.

When Claire finishes painting for the afternoon, she calls Lynnie and Bo and Emily into the kitchen. For a while, although Bo and Emily chatter and nuzzle against her, Claire seems hardly to know where she is. But gradually she returns, and makes for herself and Lynnie a dense, sweet coffee in a little copper pot, which must be brought to the boil three times. They drink it from tiny identical cups, and Lynnie marvels, looking at Claire, that she herself is there.

Some afternoons Ross is around. He announces that he will be in his study, working, but sooner or later he always appears in the kitchen, and talks about things he is reading for his book.

"What do you think, Lynnie?" he asks once. He has just proposed an idea for a new chapter, to which Claire's response was merely "Possible."

Lynnie can feel herself blush. "I don't know," she says.

Amusement begins to spread from behind his eyes. "Do you think it's a good idea?" he asks.

"Yes," she says, wary.

"Why?" he says.

"Because you just said it was," Lynnie says, turning a deeper red.

He laughs happily and gives Lynnie a little hug. "You see?" he says to Claire.

When the snow lies in great drifts around the stone house, students begin to come, too, and sit around the kitchen. They drink beer, and the girls exclaim over Bo and Emily while the boys shyly answer Claire's gentle questions and Lynnie holds her coffee cup tightly in misery. Now and again, as he talks to them, Ross touches the students lightly on the wrist or shoulder.

Late one Saturday afternoon, Lynnie is washing dishes in her own house when her mother walks in with several large grocery bags. "I was just in town," she announces unnecessarily, and grins an odd, questioning grin at Lynnie. "Now, who do you think I saw there?"

"I don't know who you saw," Lynnie says, reaching for a dishcloth.

"The man you work for," her mother says.

"How do you know who he is?" Lynnie says.

"Everybody knows who he is," her mother says. "He was in the stationery store. I just went in to get some tape, but I stuck around to watch. Muriel Furman was waiting on him. She almost went into a trance. That poor thing." Lynnie's mother shakes her head and begins to unload groceries. "Homeliest white woman I ever saw."

"Mother," Lynnie says. She stares unhappily out the little window over the sink.

"I've seen the wife around a few times, too," Lynnie's mother says. "She's a pretty girl, but I wish her luck with him."

Lynnie has not been to Isobel's house once this year. Isobel comes and goes with Cissy Haddad and other high-school friends. From across the street Lynnie can sometimes see their shapes behind the film of Isobel's window. At night, when Isobel's light is on and her window is transparent, Lynnie watches Isobel moving back and forth until the curtain closes.

One afternoon as Lynnie is arriving home, she almost walks into Isobel. "Wake up, Lynnie," Isobel says. And then, "Want to come over?"

"Lynnie, dear," Isobel's mother says as Lynnie and Isobel go upstairs. "How *nice* to see you."

It has been so long since Lynnie has been in Isobel's room that Isobel's things—the flouncy bed and the china figurines and the stuffed animals she used to see so often—have a new, melancholy luster. "How's high school?" she asks.

"It's hard," Isobel says. "You won't believe it."

But Lynnie will. She does. Almost every day she remembers that that is where she is going next fall—to the immense,

tentacled building that looks like a factory. She has reason
to suspect that she will be divided from most of her classmates
there, and put into the classes for people who won't be going
on to college—the stupid people—with all the meanest
teachers. No one has threatened her with this, but everybody
knows how it works. Everybody knows what goes on in that
building.

Lynnie picks up a stuffed turtle and strokes its furry shell.

"How's school?" Isobel asks. "How's old Miss Fisher?"

"She doesn't like me," Lynnie says. "Miss Fish Face."

"Oh, well," Isobel says. "So what? Soon you'll never have
to see her again." She looks at Lynnie and smiles. "What
else have you been up to?"

Lynnie feels slightly weak because of what she is about to
tell Isobel. She has been saving it up, she realizes, a long
time. "Well," she says slowly, "I've been babysitting for the
kids at the stone house."

"Have you?" Isobel says, but as she says it Lynnie understands that Isobel already knew, and although Isobel is
waiting, Lynnie cannot speak.

"You know what—" Isobel says after a moment. "Lynnie,
what are you doing to that poor turtle? But do you know what
Cissy's father said about that man, Ross? Cissy's father said
he's an arrogant son of a bitch." She looks at Lynnie, hugging
her pillow expectantly. "I heard him."

Lynnie and Claire and three students watch as Ross describes various arguments concerning a matter that has come
up in class. The students look at him with hazy, hopeful
smiles. But not Lynnie—she is ashamed to have heard what
Isobel said to her.

Ross glances down at her unhappy face. "Apparently Lynnie disagrees," he says, stroking a strand of her pale, flossy

hair behind her ear. "Apparently Lynnie feels that Heineman
fails to account for the Church's influence over the emerging
class of tradesmen."

The students laugh, understanding his various points, and
Ross smiles at Lynnie. But Lynnie is ashamed again—doubly
ashamed—and leans for comfort into the treacherous hand
that still strokes her hair.

Lynnie has two Rosses who blend together and diverge
unpredictably. Many mornings begin drowsily encircled in
the fleecy protection of one, but sometimes, as Lynnie continues to wake, the one is assumed into the other. He strokes
Lynnie's hair, inflicting injury and healing it in this one
motion, and she opens her eyes to see her own room, and
Frank curled up in the other bed, breathing laboriously, susceptible himself to the devious assaults of dreams.

In the fall, Lynnie is put, as she had feared, into the classes
for the slowest students. Had anyone entertained hopes for
her, this would have been the end of them.

A few of her old schoolmates are confined to her classes,
but most have sailed into classes from which they will sail
out again into college, then marriage and careers. She sees
them only in the halls and the lunchroom and on the athletic
fields. Every day they look taller, more powerful, more like
strangers.

Most of those in her classes really are strangers. But in
some ways they are as familiar as cousins met for the first
time. Their clothes, for instance, are not right, and they are
the worst students from all the elementary schools in the area.
The boys are rough or sly or helpless, or all three, like her
brothers, and the girls are ungainly and bland-looking. They
stand in clumps in the halls, watching girls like Isobel and

Cissy Haddad with a beleaguered envy, and trading accounts of the shocking things such girls have been known to do.

Oddly, Isobel is friendlier to Lynnie at school, in full view of everyone, than she is out of school, despite Lynnie's stigma. "Hi, Lynnie," she calls out with a dewy showpiece of a smile, not too different from her mother's.

"Hi," Lynnie answers, facing a squadron of Isobel's friends.

One afternoon as Lynnie approaches her house a silence reaches for her like a suction. Her brothers are not outside, and the television is not on. No one is in the kitchen or upstairs. She sits without moving while the winter sky goes dark. Across the street Isobel turns on the light in her room and sits down at her little desk. After a while she leaves, turning off the light, but Lynnie continues to stare at the blank window. By the time Lynnie hears her mother's car, her arms and legs feel stiff. She waits for a moment before going downstairs to be told what has happened.

Frank is in the hospital with a ruptured appendix, her mother says; her face has a terrible jellylike look. If she could see her own face, Lynnie wonders, would it look like that?

There will be no more going to the stone house; she will be needed at home, her mother is saying, staring at Lynnie as though Lynnie were shrinking into a past of no meaning —the way a dying person might look at an enemy.

The next day, Lynnie seeks out Isobel in the lunchroom. "A ruptured appendix," Isobel says. "That's really dangerous, you know."

"My mother says Frank is going to be all right," Lynnie says doggedly.

"Poor Lynnie," Isobel says. "So what are you going to do if Ross and Claire hire someone else?"

Lynnie puts her head down on the lunch table and closes her eyes. The sweet, unpleasant smell of the lunchroom rises up, and the din of the students, talking and laughing, folds around her.

"Poor Lynnie," Isobel says again.

Later that week, Lynnie brings Isobel to the stone house. Claire makes coffee, and when she brings out a third tiny china cup, Lynnie is unable to hear anything for several seconds.

Ross comes in, whistling, and lets the door slam behind him. "What's this?" he asks, indicating Isobel. "Invader or captive?"

"Friendly native," Claire says. "Isobel's going to be our new Lynnie."

"What's the matter with our old Lynnie?" Ross says. He looks at Isobel for a moment. "Our old Lynnie's fine with me."

"Oh, Ross." Claire sighs. "I told you. Lynnie's brother is sick."

"Hmm," Ross says.

"He's in the hospital, Ross," Claire says.

"Oh, God," Ross says. "Yes, I'm sorry to hear that, Lynnie."

"First day of the new semester," Claire says to Lynnie. "He's always disgusting the first day. How are your new students, my love?"

"Unspeakable," Ross says.

"Truly," Claire says. She smiles at Isobel.

"Worse than ever," Ross says, taking a beer from the refrigerator. "There isn't *one*. Well, one, maybe. A possibility. A real savage, but she has an interesting quality. Potential, at least."

"I used to have potential," Claire says, "but look at me now."

Ross raises his beer to her. "Look at you now," he says.

Ross holds the door as Lynnie and Isobel leave. "I've seen you in town," he says to Isobel. "You're older than I thought."

She glances up at him and then turns back to Claire. "Goodbye," she says. "See you soon."

"See you soon," Claire says, coming to join them at the door. "I do appreciate this. I'm going to have another baby, and I want to get in as much painting as I can first."

"You're going to have another baby?" Lynnie says, staring.

"We're going to have hundreds of babies," Ross says, putting his arms around Claire from behind. "We're going to have hundreds and hundreds of babies."

Afterward, Lynnie would become heavy and slow whenever she even thought of the time when Frank was sick. Their room was desolate while he was in the hospital; when he returned she felt how cramped it had always been before. Frank was testy all the time then, and cried easily. Her family deserved their troubles, she thought. Other people looked down on them, looked down and looked down, and then when they got tired of it they went back to their own business. But her family—and she—were the same whether anyone was looking or not.

Isobel's mother stops Lynnie on the sidewalk to ask after Frank. The special, kind voice she uses makes Lynnie's skin jump now. How could she ever have thought she adored Isobel's mother, Lynnie wonders, shuddering with an old, sugared hatred.

At night Lynnie can see Isobel in her room, brushing her hair, or sometimes, even, curled up against her big white pillows, reading. Has Isobel seen Ross and Claire that day? Lynnie always wonders. Did they talk about anything in particular? What did they do?

At school, Isobel sends her display of cheery waves and smiles in Lynnie's direction, and it is as though Ross and Claire had never existed. But once in a while she and Isobel meet on the sidewalk, and then they stop to talk in their ordinary way, without any smiles or fuss at all. "Claire's in a good mood," Isobel tells Lynnie one afternoon. "She loves being pregnant."

Pregnant. What a word. "How's Ross?" Lynnie says.

"He's all right." Isobel shrugs. "He's got an assistant now, some student of his. Mary Katherine. She's always around."

Lynnie feels herself beginning to blush. "Don't you like him?"

"I like him." Isobel shrugs again. "He lends me books."

"Oh." Lynnie looks at Isobel wonderingly. "What books?" she says without thinking.

"Just books he tells me to read," Isobel says.

"Oh," Lynnie says.

It is spring when Lynnie returns to the stone house. She is hugged and exclaimed over, and Emily and Bo perform for her, but she looks around as though it were she who had just come out of a long illness. The big, smooth toys, the wonderful picture books no longer inspire her longing, or even her interest.

"We've missed you," Claire says. Lynnie rests her head against the window frame, and the pale hills outside wobble.

But Claire has asked Isobel to sit for a portrait, so Isobel is at the stone house all the time now. The house is full of people—Lynnie upstairs with Emily and Bo, and Ross in his study with Mary Katherine, and Isobel and Claire in the big room among Claire's canvases.

In the afternoons they all gather in the kitchen. Sometimes Mary Katherine's boyfriend, Derek, joins them and watches Mary Katherine with large, mournful eyes while she smokes cigarette after cigarette and talks cleverly with Ross about his work. "Doesn't he drive you crazy?" Mary Katherine says once to Claire. "He's so opinionated."

"Is he?" Claire says, smiling.

"Oh, Claire," Mary Katherine says. "I wish I were like you. You're *serene*. And you can *do* everything. You can paint, you can cook . . ."

"Claire can do everything," Ross says. "Claire can paint, Claire can cook, Claire can fix a carburetor . . ."

"What a useful person to be married to," Mary Katherine says.

Claire laughs, but Derek looks up at Mary Katherine unhappily.

"*I* can't do anything," Mary Katherine says. "I'm hopeless. Aren't I, Ross?"

"Hopeless," Ross says, and Lynnie's eyes cloud mysteriously. "Truly hopeless."

Now and again Ross asks Isobel's opinion about something he has given her to read. She looks straight ahead as she answers, as though she were remembering, and Ross nods soberly. Once Lynnie sees Ross look at Mary Katherine during Isobel's recitation. For a moment Mary Katherine looks back at him from narrow gray eyes, then makes her red mouth into an O from which blossoms a series of wavering smoke rings.

One day in April, when several students have dropped by, the temperature plummets and the sky turns into a white, billowing cloth that hides the trees and farmhouses. "We'd better go now," one of the students says, "or we'll be snowed in forever."

"Can you give me and Lynnie a lift?" Isobel asks. "We're on bikes."

"Stay for the show," Ross says to her. "It's going to be sensational up here."

"Coming?" the student says to Isobel. "Staying? Well, O.K., then." Lynnie sees the student raise her eyebrows to Mary Katherine before, holding her coat closed, she goes out with her friends into the blowing wildness.

"We should go, too," Derek says to Mary Katherine.

"Why?" Mary Katherine says. "We've got four-wheel drive."

"Stick around," Ross says. "If you feel like it." Mary Katherine stares at him for a moment, but he goes to the door, squinting into the swarming snow where the students are disappearing. Behind him a silence has fallen.

"Yes," Claire says suddenly. "Everybody stay. There's plenty of food—we could live for months. Besides, I want to celebrate. I finished Isobel today."

Isobel frowns. "You finished?"

"With your part, at least," Claire says. "The rest I can do on my own. So you're liberated. And we should have a magnificent ceremonial dinner, don't you think, everybody? For the snow." She stands, her hands together as though she has just clapped, looking at each of them in turn. Claire has a fever, Lynnie thinks.

"Why not?" Mary Katherine says. She closes her eyes. "We can give you two a ride home later, Isobel."

Bo and Emily are put to bed, and Lynnie, Isobel, Ross, Claire, Mary Katherine, and Derek set about making dinner. Although night has come, the kitchen glimmers with the snow's busy whiteness.

Ross opens a bottle of wine and everyone except Claire

drinks. "This is delicious!" Lynnie says, dazed with happiness, and the others smile at her, as though she has said something original and charming.

Even when they must chop and measure, no one turns on the lights. Claire finds candles, and Lynnie holds her glass up near a flame. A clear patch of red shivers on the wall. "Feel," Claire says, taking Lynnie's hand and putting it against her hard, round stomach, and Lynnie feels the baby kick.

"Why are we whispering?" Ross whispers, and then laughs. Claire moves vaporously within the globe of smeary candlelight.

Claire and Derek make a fire in the huge fireplace while Ross gets out the heavy, deep-colored Mexican dishes and opens another bottle of wine. "Ross," Claire says. But Ross fills the glasses again.

Lynnie wanders out into the big room to look at Claire's portrait of Isobel. Isobel stares back from the painting, not at her. At what? Staring out, Isobel recedes, drowning, into the darkness behind her.

What a meal they have produced! Chickens and platters of vegetables and a marvelously silly-looking peaked and scroll-rimmed pie. They sit at the big table eating quietly and appreciatively while the fire snaps and breathes. Outside, the brilliant white earth curves against a black sky, and black shadows of the snow-laden trees and telephone wires lie across it; there is light everywhere—a great, white moon, and stars flung out, winking.

Derek leans back in his chair, closing his eyes and letting one arm fall around Mary Katherine's chair. She casts a ruminating, regretful glance over him; when she looks away again it is as though he has been covered with a sheet.

Isobel gets up from the table and stretches. A silence falls around her like petals. She goes to the rug in front of the fire and lies down, her hair fanning out around her. Lynnie follows groggily and curls up on one of the sofas.

"That was perfect," Claire says. "Ideal. And now I'm going upstairs." She burns feverishly for a moment as she pauses in the doorway, but then subsides into her usual smoky softness.

"Good night," Lynnie calls, and for full seconds after Claire has disappeared from view the others stare at the tingling darkness where she was.

Ross pushes his chair back from the table and walks over to the rug where Isobel lies. "Who's for a walk?" he says, looking down at her.

Mary Katherine stubs out a cigarette. "Come on," Ross says, prodding Isobel with his foot. Isobel looks at his foot, then away.

Ross is standing just inches from Lynnie; she can feel his outline—a little extra density of air.

"Derek," Mary Katherine says softly. "It's time to go. Lynnie? Isobel?"

"I can run the girls home later," Ross says.

"Right," Mary Katherine says after a moment. She goes to the closet for her coat.

"Come on, you two," Ross says. "Up. Isobel? This is not going to last—" He gestures toward the window. "It's tonight only. Out of the cave, lazy little bears. Into the refreshing night."

Ross reaches a hand down to Isobel. She considers it, then looks up at him. "I hate to be refreshed," she says, still looking at him, and shifts slightly on the rug.

"I don't believe this," Mary Katherine says quietly.

Lynnie sits up. The stars move back, then forward. The

snow flashes, pitching her almost off balance. "Wait, wait," Isobel says, scrambling to her feet as Mary Katherine goes to the door. "We're coming."

In the car Derek makes a joke, but no one laughs. Next to Lynnie, Isobel sits in a burnished silence. Branches support a canopy of snow over them as they drive out onto the old highway. Three cars are parked in front of the motel. They are covered with snow; no tire tracks are visible. All the motel windows are dark except one, where a faint aureole escapes from behind the curtain. Isobel breathes—just a feather of a sigh—and leans back against the seat.

Lynnie wakes up roughly, crying out as though she were being dragged through a screen of sleep into the day. Frank is no longer in his bed, and the room is bright. Lynnie sits up, shivering, exhausted from the night, and sees that the sun is already turning the snow to a glaze.

"You got in late enough," Lynnie's mother says when Lynnie comes downstairs.

"I tried not to wake you," Lynnie says.

"I can imagine," her mother says. "You were knocking things over left and right. I suppose those people gave you plenty to drink."

"I wasn't drunk, Mother," Lynnie says.

"No," her mother says. "Good. Well, I don't want you staying late with those people again. You can leave that sort of thing to Isobel. She looked fairly steady on her feet last night going up the drive."

Lynnie looks at her mother.

"I wonder what Isobel's parents think," Lynnie's mother says.

"Isobel's parents trust her, Mother," Lynnie says.

"Well that's *their* problem, isn't it?" her mother says.

———

Isobel has stopped coming to the stone house, and her portrait leans against the wall, untouched since she left. But one day, at the beginning of summer, she goes along with Lynnie to see the new baby.

"He's strange, isn't he?" Claire says as Isobel picks him up. "They're always so strange at the beginning—much easier to believe a stork brings them. Did a stork bring you, Willie? A stork?"

Through the window they can see Ross outside, working, and Lynnie listens to the rhythmic striking of his spade and the earth sliding off it in a little pile of sound. "We're planting a lilac," she hears Claire say. Claire's voice slides, silvery, through the gold day, and Ross looks up, shading his eyes.

The sun melts into the sky. Lynnie hears Claire and Isobel talking behind the chinking of the spade, but then once, when there should be the spade, there is no sound, and Lynnie looks up to see Ross taking off his shirt. When had Claire and Isobel stopped talking?

Isobel stands up, transferring Willie to Lynnie.

"Don't go," Claire commands quietly.

"No . . ." Isobel says. Her voice is sleepy, puzzled, and she sits back down.

The room is silent again, but then the door bangs and Ross comes in, holding his crumpled shirt. "Hello, everyone," he says, going to the sink to slap cold water against his face. "Hello, Isobel." He tosses back dripping hair.

"Hello," Isobel says.

Lynnie looks up at Claire, but Claire's eyes are half closed as she gazes down at her long, graceful hands lying on the table. "Yes," Claire says, although no one has spoken.

"Ross," Isobel says, standing, "I brought back your book." She hands Ross a small, faded book with gold on the edges of the pages.

He takes the book and looks at it for a moment, at the

shape of it in his hand. "Ah," he says. "Maybe I'll find something else for you one of these days."

"Mm," Isobel says, pushing her hair back.

Willie makes a little smacking sound, and the others look at him.

"When's good to drop things by?" Ross says.

"Anytime," Isobel says. "Sometime." She pivots childishly on one foot. "Saturdays are all right."

Claire puts her hands against her eyes, against her forehead. "Would anybody like iced tea?" she asks.

"Not I," Isobel says. "I have to go."

The students have left town for the summer—even Derek. At least, Lynnie has not seen him since the night it snowed. And Mary Katherine herself is hardly in evidence. She comes over once in a while, but when she finishes her work, instead of sitting around the kitchen, she leaves.

Lynnie might be alone in the house, except for Bo and Emily. Claire is so quiet now, sealed off in a life with Willie, that sometimes Lynnie doesn't realize that she is standing right there. And when Lynnie and the children are outside, the children seem to disappear into the net of gold light. They seem far away from her—little motes—and barely audible; the quiet from the house muffles their voices.

Ross is frequently out, doing one thing and another, and his smiles for Lynnie have become terribly kind—self-deprecating and sudden, as though she had become, overnight, fragile or precious. Now that Isobel has finally gone away, Ross and Claire seem to have gone with her; her absence is a vacuum into which they have disappeared. Day after day, nothing changes. Day after day, the sky sheds gold, and nothing changes. The house is saturated with absences.

———

Now Lynnie sees Isobel only as she streaks by in the little green car she has been given for her sixteenth birthday, or from the window in her room at night before she draws the curtain. One Saturday afternoon when Lynnie is outside with her brothers, Ross pulls up across the street. He waves to Lynnie as he walks up Isobel's drive and knocks on the door. Lynnie watches as Isobel opens the door and accepts a book he holds out to her. Ross disappears inside. A few minutes later he reemerges, waves again to Lynnie, and drives off.

These days Lynnie's mother is more irritable than usual. There have been rumors of layoffs at the plant. Once, when Lynnie is watching TV with her they see Isobel's father drive up across the street. "Look at that fat bastard," Lynnie's mother says. "Now, there's a man who knows how to run a tight ship."

Even years and years later, just the thought of the school building could still call up Lynnie's dread, from that summer, of going back to school. Still, there is some relief in finally having to do it, and by the third or fourth day Lynnie finds she is comforted by the distant roaring of the corridors, and the familiar faces that at last sight were the faces of strangers.

One afternoon the first week, she sees Cissy Haddad looking in her direction, and she waves shyly. But then she realizes that Cissy is staring at something else. She turns around and there is Isobel, looking back at Cissy. Nothing reflects from Isobel's flat green eyes.

"Isobel—" Lynnie says.

"Hello, Lynnie," Isobel says slowly, and only then seems to see her. Lynnie turns back in confusion to Cissy, but Cissy is gone.

"Do you want a ride?" Isobel asks, looking straight ahead. "I've got my car."

"How was your summer?" Isobel asks on the way home.

"All right," Lynnie says. The sky is a deep, open blue again. Soon the leaves will change. "I was sorry you weren't around the stone house."

"Thank you, Lynnie," Isobel says seriously, and Lynnie remembers the way Cissy had been staring at Isobel. "That means a lot to me."

Lynnie's mother looks up when Lynnie comes into the house. "Hanging around with Isobel again?" she says. "I thought she'd dropped you."

Lynnie stands up very straight. "Isobel's my friend," she says.

"Isobel is not your friend," her mother says. "I want you to understand that."

On Saturday, Lynnie goes back to her room after breakfast, and lies down in her unmade bed. Outside it is muggy and hot. She has homework to do, and chores, but she can't force herself to get up. The sounds of the television, and of her brothers playing outside, wash over her.

A car door slams, and Lynnie gets up to look out the window—maybe Isobel is going somewhere and will want company.

But it is not Isobel. It is Ross. Lynnie watches as Ross goes up Isobel's front walk and knocks on the door. The sound of brass on brass echoes up to Lynnie's room.

Isobel's car is in the driveway, but her mother's and father's are gone. Lynnie watches as Isobel appears at the front door and lets Ross in, and then as dim shapes spread in Isobel's room.

Lynnie returns to her bed and lies there. The room bears down on her, and the noise; one of her brothers is crying. She turns violently into the pillow, clenched and stiff, and for a while she tries to cry, but every effort is false, and unsatisfactory. At certain moments she can feel her heart beating rapidly.

Later, when she gets up again, Ross's car is gone. She turns back to the roiling ocean of sheets on her own bed, and reaches out, anticipating a wave rising to her, but it is enragingly inert. She grabs the unresisting top sheet and tries to hurl it to the floor, but it folds around her before it falls, slack and disgusting. The bottom sheet comes loose more satisfyingly, tearing away from the mattress and streaming into her arms like clouds, but a tiny sound bores into the clamor in her ears, and she wheels around to see Frank standing in the doorway with his hand on the knob. He looks at her, breathing uncomfortably through his mouth, before he turns away, closing the door behind him.

That night Lynnie's mother sits in front of the television in the dark, like a priestess. The cold, pale light flattens out her face, and craterlike shadows collect around her eyes, her mouth, in the hollows of her cheeks. "And what do you think of your employer visiting Isobel?" she says.

Across the street, Isobel's window blazes. "He lends Isobel books," Lynnie says.

"I see," her mother says. "Quite the little scholar."

The next day, Lynnie rides her bicycle to the stone house to say that she will not be working there any longer. Pedaling with all her strength, she is not even aware of reaching the edge of town, though afterward she can see every branch of the birchwood along the old highway as it flashes by, every cinder block of the motel, even the paint peeling from its sign.

Claire stands in the doorway while Lynnie talks loudly, trying to make herself heard through the static engulfing her. She has too much homework, she tries to explain; she is sorry, but her mother needs her. Her bicycle lies where she dropped it in her frenzy to get to the door, one wheel still spinning, and while she talks she sees dim forms shifting behind Isobel's window, a brief tumbling of entwined bodies on the damp leaves under the birches, the sad, washed light inside the old motel, where a plain chest of drawers with a mirror above it stands against the wall. In the mirror is a double bed with a blue cover on which Ross lies, staring up at the ceiling.

"Yes . . ." Claire is saying, and she materializes in front of Lynnie. "I understand . . ." From inside, behind Claire, comes the sound of Ross whistling.

It is the following week that Isobel leaves. Lynnie watches from her window as Isobel and her mother and father load up her father's car and get into it. They are taking a trip, Lynnie thinks; they are just taking a trip, but still she runs down the stairs as fast as she can, and then, as the car pulls out into the street, Isobel twists around in the back seat. Her face is waxy with an unhealthy glow, and her hair ripples out around her. Lynnie raises her hand, perhaps imperceptibly, but in any case Isobel only looks.

So nothing has to be explained to Lynnie the next day or the next or the next, when Isobel does not appear at school. And she is not puzzled by the groups of girls who huddle in the corridor whispering, or by Cissy Haddad's strange, tight greetings, or by the rumor, which begins to circulate almost immediately, of an anonymous letter to Isobel's parents.

And when, one day soon after Isobel's departure, Isobel's mother passes her on the sidewalk with nothing beyond a rapid glance of distaste, Lynnie sees in an instant what Isobel's mother must always have seen: an impassive, solid, limp-haired child, an inconveniently frequent visitor, breathing noisily, hungry for a smile—a negligible girl, utterly unlike her own daughter. And then Lynnie sees Isobel, vanishing brightly all over again as she looks back from her father's car, pressing into Lynnie's safekeeping everything that should have vanished along with her.

HOLY WEEK

SUNDAY

Everything as promised: Costumes, clouds of incense—processions already begun; town tingly with anticipation. Somber, shabby brass bands. Figures of Christ, the Virgin Mother—primitive, elegant—on wooden float-type-things (*anda*, word McGee used). Men in purple satin churning around them. From wooden-shuttered hotel window can see people crossing square with armloads of palm. Truly pleased Zwicker decided to send me. (Shd. make up for Feb. issue/ Twin Cities!)

Square in middle of town, town little dish set in ring of mountains, high under the sun. Air glimmery, uncertain; clouds draping mountains, colors diffusing into soft sky. Soft sun. Walls like cloud banks, pretty colors fading, wearing down to stone. Decay subtle, various. Ruins of earthquake (1770s? Check). Shattered arches, pediments, columns—huge. Grasses taking root in the tumbled stone, sprouting tiny white flowers. Churches: lush stone vines, stone fruit. In square, stone fountain with stone shells and mermaids.

Crowds lining the streets—tourists, Indians. Mostly Ladinos (McGee explained: mixed race, Span. + Indian). Indians impenetrable as they watch Jesus pass by, ribs showing through white plaster skin, trickling red plaster blood; they watch so intently, holding their babies up to look. Unnerving, the way they watch, way they walk, gliding along in those fantastical clothes of theirs. Silent emissaries from a vanished world, stranded in ours—gliding through the streets with baskets of flowers on their heads, through the square, through these new centuries of ruins. Squat on their heels at the corners selling hallucinatory textiles or tiny orchid trees, letting the happy tourists haggle. Barefoot, dirt-poor, dressed like royalty—incredible. Only thing: poor judgment to have brought Sarah?

Had awful morning in capital, waiting to hook up with McGees. Awful city. Diesel fumes up your nose. Big black puffs of dirt—soot, or something. Hang there in the air, then whisk over and deposit themselves on your face and clothes. Sarah and I sat in big hotel, shiny and gloomy, full of dark, heavy-faced men in suits and sunglasses. Many mustaches. Daughters in prom dresses, limp sons. Some Americans, too. Prob. business—don't look like tourists. Hotel bar very dark, suit/mustache people gazing over their drinks at Vietnam movie showing on enormous screen. Movie mesmerizingly vile—machine guns, gore, etc., Vietnamese girl, U.S. soldiers in camouflage swarming all over her.

Sarah glowering at screen, running her hands impatiently through her hair, making it fluff up like little yellow chick feathers. Offered to go for walk with her. She said, "Thanks, Dennis. Out there?"

Vietnamese girl ripped down middle. Sarah (very loud): *Shit*. Men glancing at us through currents of black and greenish air. What to do? Had warned Sarah not to drink Margaritas until she got used to the altitude.

Two clean, hardy U.S. types, mid-sixties approx. abruptly confronting us. McGees, of course. "I'll bet you're our man," Mrs. (Dot) said. "The Desk told us you'd be in here."

Clearly Zwicker had not mentioned Sarah. Husband (Clifford) produced expression of aggressive blandness, Dot underwent violently shuttling succession of reactions. How well
I've come to know the looks! Might as well be back in Cedar
Rapids.

Sarah stared, affronted, as Dot nodded with pity at her tiny
skirt, patted her arm. "*Lovely* to meet you," Dot said.

"So," McGee said. We all stood, looked at the screen. A
bomb exploded over a small village. McGee snorted, shook
his head. Said, "All set, everyone? Luggage up front?"

Filthy little eateries by the side of the road. Harsh dust,
like grains of concrete, all over everything. Leaves, trees,
caked with harsh, pale dirt. Buildings rotting, people streaming along—so many, so poor—bellying out into the road in
the clouds of black exhaust, receding behind us, big, glossy
cars shooting past them. Buses swaying on the sharp curves,
top-heavy with cargo, clinging passengers.

Tried to monitor conversation in back between Sarah and
Dot. Truth is, was very nervous about what Sarah might say,
in her mood. Now, this is the *actual* problem about being
involved with someone twenty-odd years younger. A trade-
off, in my opinion. On the one hand, the intensity, the clarity
(generally) of Sarah's reactions. On the other, her impatience,
stubbornness, unwillingness to see the other point of view.
Fundamentally youth's refusal to acknowledge the subtlety,
complexity of a situation; at worst, adds up to a sort of
insensitivity.

Still, Dot admittedly hard to take. Could hear her enum-
erating, at some length, flaws in local postal system. Glanced
back, saw Sarah in glaze of boredom, rousing herself to nod
sanctimoniously. Frowned warningly, and she shot me elec-
trifying little smile.

McGee pleasant enough. Seemed to enjoy driving. Said
he'd been delighted to meet Zwicker when he was up in the

States in the fall: *delighted*. Told McGee how highly Zwicker had spoken of him; said that it was entirely due to him that Zwicker was so eager to get piece on town for supplement (true). McGee offered to help in any way he could. Asked what sort of thing I was after—hotels, restaurants, Easter celebrations? All of it, told him, though supplement particularly interested in food.

He nodded. Said, "We'll see to it." Said he would be more than happy to take me around to restaurants, introduce me to important local grower (could give me interesting regional recipes). Said it would mean a lot, good press coverage in the States. Said tourist revenues had fallen off catastrophically in past decade.

Stark landscape; droopy gray sky. Pines. Long, dark, sad hills. Billboards (all Span., of course) advertising herbicides, pesticides, fungicides, etc. Another: Cement Is Progress. Antlike figure in valley, tiny beyond billboards, giant load of wood on his bent back. Just like ant with giant leaf, or some other impossible burden.

The sight was timeless, stonily beautiful—solitary peasant in the field. The man's life curved out behind him in a pure, solid arc. Tried to imagine how it felt to have such a life— I mounted the arc, swooped up, then down along it. *Atomized* on contact with the man at the bottom; shards of my life flew all over the car—son, ex, house in Claremont. Dorm all those years ago in Princeton, bank where I worked for so long, new office at the supplement. Waking in my sunny Cedar Rapids bedroom, sometimes Sarah next to me. Other women I've been involved with, movies I've seen, opinions I've held—a burst sackful of items flying all over the car.

Glanced back at Sarah again to reincorporate myself, but her clear eyes were directed out the window, and her piratical earring gleamed—a signal! Meaning? Sarah's earring, my son, my office—all *signals*, incoherent fragments, of which I ought to be the unifying principle; encoded dispatches from my own life! Too loud, too bright to decipher—the urgent, jagged flashing: a messenger shouting across a chasm. A knife lying on the counter. A ditch by the side of the road . . .

MONDAY

Was in strange state yesterday. Better now. Odd how that happens—everything completely inscrutable, intractable, portentous; then everything completely fine. Like having two abutting brains, one of them utter chaos; sickening sensation of slipping through some membrane. Perhaps triggered yesterday by psychobiological response to unfamiliar foods? Pollens?

In any case, over. Hotel first-rate, good night's sleep. Dinner, just Sarah and I, at ex-convent (Santo Tomás, daily except Tues. Spectacular. Must write up, despite food). This morning breakfast in hotel courtyard—flowers, darting hummingbird; fruit, rolls, coffee. Impossible not to feel happy. Sarah clearly blissful. Stretching, reaching over to run her finger along my wrist. Waiter (Ricardo) utterly charmed by her. Had to smile at his expression when she ordered third portion of fruit and rolls.

How could I have doubted, yesterday, it was right to bring her? Of course it was. I think. (Joke.) Ah, so hard to sort out, me and Sarah. What can we really have with one another, ultimately? Occurs to me sometimes that, for all her wildness, restlessness, she wants something more from me than I (obviously) can give.

Have to remind myself always she's at an odd point in life. Hard to remember the terror—a sort of swampiness, feeling of wandering around in a swamp, while some awful *fait accompli* is preparing to drop on top of you.

Looked up and saw her watching me—eyes elongated, sparkling. "You're thinking, Dennis."

"Not really," I said. That look of hers! "I was wondering why you picked me up that night at the Three Chimneys, actually."

"I did that?" Sarah said. "Whoops. Well, gosh, Dennis—I must have thought you'd be fun."

A bit of pineapple lodged in my throat.

"Cheer up, Dennis," Sarah said as I coughed. "A lot of men would be thrilled to be considered a sex object, you know."

"Oh—now, actually, Sarah," I said. "To be serious for a moment, I know the McGees aren't the world's most fascinating people, but it's by their good offices, really, that we're here."

"Yup," Sarah said, patting her stomach as she glanced at it fondly. "Your point?"

"Well," I said, "the fact is, there are certain ways in which everyone is sensitive. For instance, everyone can tell when they're being mocked."

Sarah burped daintily and looked pleased with herself. "Almost everyone," she said.

Sarah gone out for a walk. Can just see from window her tiny bright skirt disappearing around corner. Processions continue. Men in purple satin (Jerusalemites, McGee says) carrying *andas*. Takes dozens to carry each one. Sweat streaming down their faces. Occasionally one stumbles on the cobblestones, slight panic in his eyes. Forcefully primitive representations of Adam and Eve, the world; funny little artificial flowers and flamingos, Christ with loaves, fishes. Tourists darting about with cameras.

Extraordinary activity taking place right outside window.

People with immense baskets of flowers, using stencils to make a big rectangular picture with the petals, right on the street. Birds, butterflies, a basket of flowers, all made out of flower petals, appearing on the cobblestones outside. Such a poor country, such impassioned profligacy!

Town even more crowded than yesterday. Young Scandinavians, Americans, Germans, tall and vain, lounging in the square, stretching out bare, tanned legs, trading information, chatting up the Indians, selling each other drugs; Europeans on the balconies of posh vacation homes, drinking from glasses of wine or iced tea as the incense drifts up past them.

Amazing sight on the porticoes of the municipal building across from square—huge families spreading out blankets, starting up little fires in front of the Cathedral to cook corn, stockpots. Children running up and down, playing on the steps, lifting one another to drink from the disease-bearing fountain in the square. Confusing, people like these. Hard to tell who's Indian, who's Ladino. McGee explains many Indians want to pass (status thing, I presume—should have asked). You cut your hair, stop wearing that amazing clothing, speak Span rather than own languages (of which there turn out to be 22!!!!), and bing! Just like that, you're Ladino.

Sarah glorious in knot of Indian children. No question they are cute—what eyes, what smiles! Those ragged, princely little outfits, runny noses . . . Like nesting dolls, in series —each taking care of an even tinier child. They play with Sarah's hair, combing it, fascinated, with her comb (which trust she will wash).

> *Hotel Flor*. Daily 7:00 a.m.—9:30 p.m. After a morning of browsing through town, the Flor is a delightful stop for the weary traveler. A

large *sala* to the rear of the hotel, with its
peaceful garden well-hidden from the bustling
street, is an ideal spot for a refreshing meal.
A "typical plate" is available at lunch or dinner, which includes beef accompanied by gua-
camole, succulent fried plantains, silken
black beans, and *chirmol*—the favored regional sauce, sparkling with lightly cooked tomatoes, green onions, and cilantro. Or, for
the homesick, the menu offers baked chicken,
and a satisfying array of steaks.

Others might prefer to settle into one of the
generous chairs ranged along the leafy courtyard just within the high hotel walls, to linger
over a snack and a frosty drink while listening
to the music of a live marimba band, intermingled with the calls of the brilliant red,
green, and blue parrots, permanent residents
of the huge, gnarled trees in the center of the
courtyard. Etc., etc. Mention rooms? Large,
airy, clean; waitresses in native dress.

Tried to persuade Sarah to order chicken (always safe),
though her *plato típico* turned out to be O.K., I think. Gua-
camole looked delicious, but warned Sarah off it when I saw
little bits of uncooked green stuff—herbs? chives?—peeking
out. Had drinks there later with McGees, though, in courtyard, and they said guac. sure to be safe in a place like the
Flor. Watched them polish off two orders of chips slathered
with it. Sarah had some, too. Can't blame me if she gets sick!
McGees have been down here so long they must have all
kinds of protective antibodies.
Was glad I'd had talk with Sarah in morning about the

McGees—she was charming with them over drinks. Serious, respectful, asking them how long they've been living down here, etc. Dot explained they still kept home in Virginia, to be near son, daughter-in-law. Had come down frequently for work during seventies and eighties, she said. Fell in love with town. Sarah managing very creditable rendition of rapt attention.

Marimba band started up jarringly. Odd sight—musicians in ceremonial (McGee said) clothing, staring straight ahead, the little mallets bouncing all over the keyboards. Played "I Love Paris." Eerie, uninflected instrument—bit nerve-racking after a time. Band angry about something?

Sarah asked McGee what his job had been. Tactfully avoided word "retirement." McGee said he had been in government for forty years. "Yes"—he said; looked like he was savoring the memory of a marvelous wine—"I was with the Department of Agriculture."

Something squawked, causing Dot to heave like a wave. "Oh, look," she said, subsiding. "Aren't they fun?"

Loutish parrot fussing in the tree above us. Sarah got up to talk to it. "Say something, bird," she said. "Something interesting, please."

Her yellow hair was right next to the bird's red plumage. Its crazy little eyes were rolling around like beads in a dish. "Be careful," I sai... "They can take your finger off just like that."

Sarah sighed. Sat back down. Was looking incredibly pretty. Noticed that the courtyard, strangely, was rather lugubrious. All that shade! Marimbas playing "Happy Birthday" over and over—aimless, serpentine version.

Noticed Sarah goggling in the direction of hotel gate. Turned, myself, to chilling vista: line of soldiers marching past, rifles held out at the ready. It took me a long, choppy instant to understand that I was looking at young boys—they were practically children, but their boots and uniforms had transformed them into something toylike and fathomless, and their eyes were hard with rage. "Is there some kind of trouble here in town?" I said to McGee, when I could speak.

"Not at all," McGee said. "Simply routine."

"You know, they just don't get the point down here," Dot said. " 'Happy Birthday' has a *point*. It must have been a request."

McGee chuckled at Sarah, who was still wide-eyed and greenish. "Not to worry," he said. "Just a symbolic prelude to negotiations." Told us that the town is a national showpiece, so army stays away, for the most part. Evidently, though, have been rumors since Feb. about guerrillas in the surrounding villages. But, McGee said, no actual fighting.

Sarah and I had gotten guidebooks, of course, before leaving, and I had tried to tell her whatever I knew about the region. Not easy to remember what's happening where, though. Who we support and why. All these countries! Veritable stew of armies, guerrilla groups, death squads, wobbly emerging democracies, etc. "A strong military, isn't it?" I said.

Then—oh, so much. So much. How to remember? Careful—get down *just as happened*.

"Well, the reports of abuse tend to be sensationalized in the States," McGee said. "Although it's true these boys can make a mighty nuisance of themselves. Foreigners are perfectly safe, of course, but the tourists don't like the look of it one bit," he added, just as I overheard Dot asking Sarah if she liked to shop.

"Do I like to shop," Sarah said musingly. "Well, now, there's a—"

"What are you two saying over here?" I asked hurriedly.

"Girl talk," Dot said, with a smile to Sarah of pained for-giveness. "I was asking your young friend if she liked to shop. Because, seriously, for those of us who do enjoy such things, this is the town for it. If I were you, in fact, I'd do some collect-ing now, while it's still possible. Because they're beginning to use synthetic pigments and machines. And even here in town the people don't know what the old things are worth."

Sarah opened her mouth, but I preempted her. "Sarah will have to budget her shopping time," I said. "We won't always be able to count on her company—she's brought along a lot of reading for her thesis."

"Thesis," Dot said. She and McGee exchanged some mi-nute eyebrow work as Sarah made a quick face at me. "I'm impressed."

"Well, well," McGee said. "What field?"

"Art history," I said. "Sarah plans to write about Van Meegeren, the forger."

McGee picked an insect from his drink. "A subject well worth pursuing, I'm sure," he said.

Sarah tilted her head modestly, as though McGee had con-ferred a great honor. "Let me ask you, Cliff," she said. "Is this army one of the ones we like, or one of the ones we don't like?"

" 'We?' " McGee said. Sarah's expression! Poor, unsus-pecting McGee. "The United States? Nothing's ever that sim-ple, is it?"

Sarah smiled at him. "Well," she said.

"Oh, *no*—" I said. "That is, do you believe it? They're playing 'My Funny Valentine.' "

"You have to remember, dear," Dot said to Sarah, "the function of the army is to protect people. The army protects the people who own farms from the guerrillas. The army protects the president."

Sarah nodded. "Except in the case of a military coup, I guess," she said sympathetically.

"I de*test* 'My Funny Valentine,' " I said.

But Dot was gurgling delightedly. "*You*," she said, and shook her finger at Sarah.

"Unfortunately—" McGee frowned. "The army is necessary whether we like it or not. This place is teetering on the brink."

Sarah was gazing at McGee with a terrifyingly detached interest.

"Tired?" I said to her. "Time for a nap?"

"Brink of what?" Sarah said.

McGee looked away impatiently. " '*Brink of what?*' she says."

"Well, I could use a nap," I said. "If nobody else could."

"Listen to me, dear," Dot said. She leaned forward and looked into Sarah's eyes. "We may not love the army, but you should understand that everyone hates the guerrillas, now. Even the people they claim to represent. There was a time, of course, when those people put their trust in the guerrillas, but now it's clear to everybody that the guerrillas only cause misery for innocent people."

"Misery how?" Sarah said. "Innocent of what?"

"Sarah," I said.

"After all," Dot said. "There are bound to be—"

"Well, now," McGee said. He gestured around the courtyard full of laughing foreigners. "Every place has its problems. All right, then?" He smiled at Sarah. "Enough said."

"No, Cliff," Dot said. "I think everybody here should understand that where people are behaving suspiciously—if there's any reason for the army to suspect that a village or a family has been tainted—there are bound to be reprisals."

"Naturally. Everyone understands that." McGee turned to Sarah. "Dorothy's only . . ."

"I'm just—" Dot began.

"Dot's only *saying*," McGee said, "that people here have to be more cautious about their affiliations than we at home do."

"For God's sake," I said, much more loudly than I'd intended, just as the marimbas stopped, "what *is* all that screaming?"

Sarah and the McGees turned; stared at me from under a dome of silence while the parrot screeched and cackled hellishly on its dark branch.

> *El Sombrerito.* Lunch and dinner, Mon.–Sat.
> Clean, Amer.-owned. Wide variety of steaks,
> roast chicken. Desserts baked on premises.
> Pleasant ambiance, rotating shows of local art
> (paintings, macramé, etc.). Mango mousse a
> standout—luxurious, satiny, etc.

TUESDAY

> *La Marquesa.* Breakfast, lunch, and dinner,
> Mon.–Sat. Moderately priced. Dramatic view
> of volcano, mountains. Courtyard, waitresses
> in native dress. Eggs, pancakes, steaks. Ice
> creams (not rec.).
> Must look into Sabor de China and
> Giuseppe's.

Sarah and the hotel maid fascinated with one another, despite the fact that they can't talk to each other at all. María a round, humorous-looking girl. Indian, I surmise (despite maid's uniform) from the long hair, the measuring, satirical expression, the lofty, graceful, telltale walk (saw her in street yesterday carrying trays of toilet paper stacked on her head).

Also, Spanish seems not much better than mine. Surely not her first language. She and I communicate with one another by shouting (Procession this morning?!? Yes!?! Nice??! Good!!!).

Since Sarah speaks no Spanish whatsoever, she and María have managed with a much more dignified vocabulary of gestures and smiles. But this morning, as María was changing our bed, Sarah enlisted me as interpreter. "Come on, Dennis. Ask her something."

"What thing?" I said.

"I don't know," Sarah said. "Ask where she lives."

"Don't you think that's prying?" I said.

"No." Sarah looked at me. "Why would that be prying?"

"Well, it isn't, really," I said. "But, after all. She may not want to talk about her private life with strangers. Tourists. She may feel sensitive about that sort of thing. She might very well feel she was being patronized. After all, she's not just a curiosity—she's as real as you or I."

Sarah made a loud snoring sound, which caused María to shake with laughter.

So, after a few garbled exchanges, I was able to tell Sarah that María lived in one of the villages outside town with her husband, her mother, and her children, about an hour's walk away.

"An hour's walk!" Sarah said. "That's a big commute. Do you think she really walks?"

"¿Qué dice?" María said.

When I told her what Sarah had said, more or less, she leaned toward me, widened her eyes theatrically, and lowered her voice. "I don't really walk!" she confessed. "I *run*."

"You run?" I asked her. (Wanted to say, Why on earth, something like that, indicating amazement, but couldn't think how. Surely not literally *on earth*.) "Why?" I said.

She lowered her voice even further. "*Cafetales!*" she said, and launched into a confidential torrent of chatter.

"What's she talking about?" Sarah asked.

"I don't know," I said.

"But what's she *saying*?" Sarah said.

"I don't *know*," I said. "Her Spanish is peculiar. All I can tell is she's saying something about someone *being* somewhere. In the coffee plantations she goes through to get here. I don't *know*."

Just then María took it into her head to ask if Sarah and I had any children. "*¿Qué?*" I said. "No."

"No, what?" Sarah said.

"No, nothing. No, you and I don't have any children."

Sarah laughed. "Relax, Dennis," she said. "Ask her how many children she has."

But María seemed to have anticipated the question. "Tell the señora," she was already saying, solemnly and proudly, "I have seven children. Four of them are living and three of them are dead."

Rest of morning very nice. Sarah hauled me right back into the bed María had just made. Then the market for about an hour with the McGees, after which they dropped us off for lunch at La Mariposa, introduced us to owner. Place very agreeable, will be able to write up nicely. (Daily except Sun., 12 p.m.–10 p.m.) Gardens, fountain. Very popular with Americans, like ladies at table nearby wearing outfits made from native textiles. "Have you ever *seen* anything so beautiful," they kept saying to one another.

Perhaps can find tactful way to suggest house wine less than ideal. Also meat. (Sarah's baked chicken might have been nice, but somewhat raw, alas.)

Sarah began very funny imitation of the beauty-loving ladies at the table near us. Had to shush her—probably friends of the McGees. Owner cruised by to talk with us for a few minutes. Said how hard things are for restaurants now, prices increasing geometrically, value of currency plummeting, everything grown for export. Told us that price of black beans ("the traditional food of our poor") has almost doubled in recent months. Sarah: "So, what are your poor eating now?"

Couldn't help smiling. Owner smiled, too—with hatred. "I really wouldn't know," he said.

Actually, town might be most beautiful thing I've ever seen myself. Gets more beautiful as eye adjusts. So high, so pale, so strange. Flowers astonishing—graceful rococo shapes, sinuous, pendant, like ornamentations on the churches. Every hour of the day, in every changing tint of air, new details coming forward. The ancient stillness. All the different ancientnesses—Spain, Rome, themselves so new compared to the Indians. All converging right here in the square. Concentrated in the processions, in every dark eye.

Sarah, for all her snootiness to Dot about shopping, can't resist stopping at every corner and every market. Our room now draped with astounding textiles, bits of Indian clothing —crammed with flowers and little orchid trees. (María shakes her head, amused, all indulgence with Sarah.)

Early this evening processions of costumed children all over the place. Sarah enthralled. Flower-petal pictures appearing everywhere—*alfombras* (carpets) McGee tells me they're called. Put down only to be trampled within hours by the processions—celebration of the suffering of Christ.

Saw a man lifting a mesh sack of mangoes about twice his size. Bent way backward over it, slipped its strap around his forehead, then drew himself forward so that the mangoes rested on his back, as though he were a cart. Sarah stopped in her tracks and stared.

I put a comforting arm around her, tried to move her along. Think it must be particularly humiliating to be stared at if you're doing uncongenial work. "It certainly does look awful to us," I said. "But it must be different for people who do it every day."

"Sure," Sarah said. "The difference is that they do it every day."

I held Sarah away from me and looked at her. "Sarah?" I said. "Are you angry at me?"

"No," she said tentatively.

The group of ladies from the table near us at lunch walked by and waved as though we were all old friends. One called over to us: "How are you enjoying it? Gorgeous, aren't they, the processions?" Shaded her eyes, flashed a toothy smile. "*Thought*-provoking!"

Sarah waved absently, then frowned and nestled against me. I stroked her hair, and the perfume of incense and flowers rose up around us. "Dennis," she said meditatively, "don't you like me?"

"Don't I like you?" I said. I held her away from me and studied her, but she was serious. "What do you mean? I adore you."

I smiled and gave her a squeeze, but it was a few moments before she spoke. "So then, listen, Dennis. Why did you have to trot out my—my *credentials* for the McGees?"

"I thought you'd be pleased," I said, amazed. Explained that I'd only been trying to provide her with an excuse not to see them. "Besides," I said. "Why shouldn't I be proud of you?"

She drew away from me. "Dennis, who are these people to demand respectability from me? I don't *like* these people. These people are idiots."

Felt oddly stricken. Can't really blame Sarah—that's how

she feels. But, still, McGees are clearly doing their best to be hospitable, pleasant. "Of course, the McGees might not be our favorite people," I said. "But why should they be?" Tucked an unruly label back inside Sarah's T-shirt. "And, after all, they're perfectly harmless."

Sarah stared sadly into the lively crowds.

"Besides," I said. "They're getting on." I stooped over, quavered. "I'll be like that soon myself, I suppose."

Sarah frowned again, then laughed. "Oh, *Dennis*," she said, but her hand crept over and curled into mine, like a pliant little animal.

Buen Pastor. Lunch, dinner, Tues.–Sun. Of the many beautiful restaurants in town, perhaps the loveliest is *Buen Pastor*. Enjoy a cocktail of platonic perfection outside in the moonlit garden. Or, if the evening is cool, in the bar, where a fire may be roaring at the massive colonial hearth. There are likely also to be fires in each of the several beautifully proportioned dining rooms. It has to be said that the menu, though worthy, is not particularly inspired, but each of its few items is carefully prepared (the steak *au poivre* is sure to please) and the wine list is adequate. The staff is happy to assist you in your selections (all speak English here), and despite the luxury of the surroundings, a memorable evening with cocktails, wine, and a full meal for two will put hardly a dent in your wallet. The atmosphere is relaxed, intimate, and romantic.

WEDNESDAY

"Relaxed, intimate, and romantic!" was the first thing I heard
this morning— Woke up to see Sarah reading the notes about
Buen Pastor I'd started to slam together last night when we
got in from dinner, which I'd imprudently left right in the
typewriter. (No more of that, you can be sure! From now on,
everything gets put away immediately. Locked up.) Sarah
laughed incredulously. "You call that place relaxed, intimate,
and romantic?"

"For God's sake," I said. "That's just a draft! I hadn't even
finished."

"Well, when you get around to 'revising your draft,' " Sarah
said, "you might mention that the first thing you see when
you get to the door is some kind of *butler* with a machine
gun."

"Submachine gun," I said. "Machine guns are larger."

"Oh, well, then," Sarah said.

"Besides," I said. I rubbed my eyes. "I can't just put that
into my piece, can I, Sarah?"

"Why can't you?" she said. She sat down next to me on
the bed. "Dennis."

"Because," I said. "Sarah, please. I'm supposed to be
writing about people's *vacations*."

Sarah stuffed a corner of the pillow into her mouth.

"I'm sorry," I said. Couldn't suppress a sigh. "I wasn't
aware, last night, that the guard upset you."

"Naturally he upset me." Sarah said. "I assumed he upset
you, too."

"Of course he did," I said. "Naturally he upset me." (Naturally I was upset when I went to give my name to the maître
d' and saw that thing pointing at me. But it isn't as though
restaurants at home don't have their own security systems.)
"Sarah—" I took her hand. "What's happened? Has some-

thing happened? Have you been having an awful time here?"

Gloomy, theatrical pause. "The truth is, Dennis," she said, "I've been having a terrific time."

That sound ominously familiar; that muted, baffled, fragile tone designed to censure. Can't understand it—some sort of curse hovering over me that makes women sad? The women who are attracted to me are active, capable women. Women with interesting and demanding careers. Women, sometimes, with reasonably happy marriages, families. (Which, granted, can have its drawbacks, but one expects it, at least, to ensure a certain degree of stability.) Yet how rapidly these self-sufficient women become capricious and sulky. Absolutely unglued. Even the perky, adventurous wives who come my way (unsolicited, unsolicited!) simply *transform* themselves. And these women, who, I think it's fair to say, engage me for nothing more than, to use Sarah's (rather crude) word, *fun*—these same women—invariably begin to accuse me, in the most amorphous terms, of some unsubstantiated crime. It's a strange thing. It is. All these women, showing up on my doorstep, demanding my attention and affection. And then, when I've given them every bit of attention and affection I've got, insisting that I've failed them in some way. "Self-absorption," one of them said. "Shallowness of feeling," said another. As though I were some kind of broken *vending* machine!

Margaret S.? Who actually claimed I was "rejecting" at the very moment *she* was leaving *me*? Even Cynthia—my own wife—so happy when I married her, so confident; the way she became self-pitying and tremulous in front of my very eyes! Implored her to tell me what was the matter. Huge error. The matter was me, naturally; I was not really interested in her. Not *interested!* And the way, when I pointed out the irrefutable demonstrations of my interest, she would become incoherent: "Not that, not that! You know that's not what I'm talking about."

"Sarah," I said, "when we were in San Francisco you told me you loved traveling. That's what you said. You said you *loved traveling*."

"When we were in San Francisco," Sarah said, "and I told you I loved traveling, we were in San Francisco."

"Well, but travel is travel," I said. "One sees new things."

" 'New things!' " Sarah said. "Guys in uniforms with automatics?"

"Now, that's not fair," I said, gently. Waited for a moment so she would hear the whining tone of her own voice, see the roomful of her happy purchases, see out the wooden-shuttered window, where a jaunty little halo of cloud sat over the peak of a volcano, and women padded silently by with their black-eyed babies bundled on their backs.

"I'm sorry, Dennis," she said. Clambered over into my lap. Twined herself around me. "I just feel so strange. I don't know what's going on. The thing is, I really *am* having a terrific time."

Faint sounds of a brass band and the fragrance of incense were beginning to filter into our room with the buttery sunlight. Persecuting loveliness. Rubbed the tender edge of Sarah's ear. Pointed out that the restaurant was something like an airport, if you thought about it: protection irrelevant to most of the travelers.

"Well, I *know*," Sarah said. "But who's all the protection *from*, here? I mean, look, Dennis, who is the enemy?"

Snuggled her against me. Reminded her that we've all read about such things; pointed out that we're overreacting, she and I, simply because we're *here*.

Made me think: How tempting it is to put oneself into the drama—"It's awful; *I've* seen it." Unattractive, self-aggran-

dizing impulse. Reminded Sarah of the morning we were
having breakfast at her place and Karen stormed in, ranting
about factory farming, and we kept saying, "We know, Karen,
we know, it's really awful." Lifted Sarah's chin and was rewarded with a reluctant smile. "But Karen couldn't stop talking, remember? Because she had just *seen* it the day before.
So, to her, it seemed just incredibly *real*?

"The thing is," I said, "we could go around sniffling all
the time, but terrible things are going to happen whether
we sniffle or not. Yes, the lives some people lead are hor-
rifying, but if you accept the idea that it's better for some
people to be fortunate than for no people to be fortunate,
then it's preposterous to make yourself miserable just because *you* happen to be one of those fortunate people. I mean,
here we are, in an amazingly beautiful place, witnessing
possibly the most lavish Easter celebration in the whole of
the New World. Wouldn't it be morally reprehensible not to
enjoy it?"

Sarah sighed. "I know," she said. "You're right."

"We could reject that out of principle," I said. "But what
would the principle *be*?"

"All right, Dennis." Sarah jumped up and fluffed her hair.
"I already said I agree."

Came back to the room later, tempers restored by breakfast.
María there, putting a jug of fresh water on the table. Said,
"Procession now?! Nice!!"

"Tell me something, Dennis," Sarah said when María left.
"*Do* you ever think about having another child?"

"Of course not," I said. "I mean, I think about it, of course,
but I don't think about actually doing it."

"Take it easy," Sarah said. "I was just wondering."

"I already have one perfectly good child," I said. "An
adult, now, actually, almost. It doesn't make sense to start

all over at my age. For someone your age—well, that's a different story. You *should* have children."

"I didn't say I wanted children," Sarah said, crossly.

"You have every right to want children," I said. Looked at her closely—a bit puffy? Due for her period any minute now, I think. "You're one of those women who can do it all, you know. Career, family—"

"Hey," Sarah said. "I didn't say I wanted *children*. I was just asking how you feel."

"I know," I said. "Goodness." I was just *saying* how I feel.

Especially hot today; was noticing it very suddenly—room darkened swoopingly. Put my head in my hands, then Sarah was speaking: "Listen, Dennis—are machine guns, like, a *lot* bigger than submachine guns?"

"Some of them," I said. The fact is, David is much more vivid to me as I imagine him now, playing basketball with his friends, strolling away from the house in Claremont on his way to a movie, spinning along in his rattly little car, than he seems when he's sitting across from me in some padded restaurant, waiting patiently for our visit to be over. "Why?"

"Because I think maybe that's one out there."

"Good Lord," I said. Sat up to look out the window and saw a wooden platform coming down the street. It looked amazingly like one of the *andas*, except that it was accompanied by a convoy of soldiers in uniform instead of towns-people in purple satin, and in place of Christ or the Virgin Mary, it displayed a mounted machine gun. "Yup, that's what it is, all right," I told Sarah.

The soldiers—the hard-eyed, ravenous-looking boys—surged up beyond the window, and in their midst the lordly, searching weapon reigned. A plunging shame weakened my hands and my knees as though at any second that instrument

of terrible destruction might swing around toward me, dis-
covering the foolish incidentalness of my body, its humili-
atingly provisional life. No one on the street appeared to
notice the entourage. A path cleared apparently by casual
occurrence; only sign of anything out of the ordinary: a
barely perceptible slowing, a thickening of motion as it
passed.

Sarah and I stood at the window, watched until the entire
retinue, with its platform and its sickening gleam of metal,
turned the corner. Within an instant nothing left but the soft
bustle of the street.

I put my arm around Sarah, and the small intimacy con-
ducted away my panic. Tried to reassure her: "If there were
anything out of the ordinary occurring, someone would tell
us."

"Someone did tell us," Sarah said.

"Who?" I said.

"María," she said.

"The maid?" I said. "I mean someone who actually knows."

"Like who?" Sarah said.

"Like a journalist, for example."

Sarah stared at me. "Dennis," she said. *"You're* a
journalist."

"All right, Sarah," I said. "Please."

Does Sarah know how cruel she is sometimes? Obviously
there's no way in the world I'd be doing something of this
sort if the bank hadn't gone the way banks tend to go these
days. "But you know what I mean. Obviously I'm not saying
María doesn't know what's happening to her. Obviously she
does know what's happening to her. All I'm saying is that
she has no way of *understanding* it. In context, that is. If I
were you, I really wouldn't worry about María. She has quite
a little flair for drama, but the truth is that her attention is

on the Easter celebrations. Festivities. Frivolous matters"—
I smiled and pushed a strand of hair from Sarah's eyes—
"just like ours is."

"Dennis," Sarah said. "The *maid* is afraid to come to *work*.
There's a mounted *machine* gun rolling down the street."

"I am not disputing that," I said. "Obviously. It's only
that— Sarah, tell me something frankly. Are you embarrassed
by what I do?"

"Embarrassed!" Sarah said, and actually blushed. "By
what you do? Of course not, Dennis."

"Look, Sarah," I said. "This travel/restaurant business is
every bit as much a joke to me as it is to you. And I would
certainly never dream of calling myself a *journalist*—"

"Well, of course you're a—"

"I would never dream of calling myself a journalist *at this
point*," I said. "But it's an easy target, isn't it? It's easy to
be snobbish about this, just because it doesn't seem 'important' in some superficial way. And who knows, it's not impossible, that in a few years I could be—well, I could hardly
hope for anything like the foreign desk, I suppose. But I won't
be *anywhere* if I'm not reasonably—and, besides, it's only
fair to Zwicker, who, quite frankly, took *pity* on me, no matter
what you might think of his half-witted—"

"No, you owe him a lot, Dennis," Sarah said.

"No, I owe Zwicker a lot. He's giving me a rather decent
salary, he's given me a job that some people might consider
cushy, even prestigious, so the fact is that—"

"No, it's terrific, Dennis. Look. He sent you to San Francisco, he's going to send you to London. And we would never
in a million years be here if it weren't for—"

Etc., etc., as I remember. But somewhere around that
ridiculous point I slightly crumpled up a bit. Heat, and actually I don't think either of us is exactly used to the altitude

yet, either. And then Sarah was really very sweet for a long, long time. And afterward she seemed quite pleased. But the strange thing about sex (tho. maybe it's different for a woman) is that if you start off feeling a little bad sometimes, sometimes when it's over, you can really feel awful.

> *El Lomito Borracho.* 12:00 p.m.–9:30 ₁ m. This cheerful steak house with its white-washed walls and posters of Indians draws a young crowd, mostly Germans. The sirloin with grilled onions is probably your best bet here, but be sure to ask for your meat—as anywhere in the region—*bien asada* (well done).

THURSDAY

> *Café Bougainvillea.* Hours subject to change. Juices, coffee, milk shakes, cakes. Pleasant. Hygiene questionable.

Town at fever pitch today and yesterday. Air sharp and bright—mountains entirely revealed, like a crown tossed around us. Crowds larger, aboil. More people arriving by foot or bus to camp across from the square with their little bundles of possessions, blankets. Flowers furiously blooming. *Alfombras* spread out for the boot. Chilling roll of drums, sepulchral brass, sun flashing in the air like swords. This morning Christ in scarlet robes, rocking down the streets in an ocean of incense; swarms of purple-gowned Jerusalemites. Sweat pouring from the faces of men bearing the *andas*. McGee bobbing in and out of the crowd, snapping pictures.

"Do you see those men in shackles, walking next to the

cross?" Dot said. "Those are the thieves. Do you see? The amazing thing is, they use real criminals. Just petty thieves, probably, or poor drunks. But this afternoon, when the procession goes by the square, the whole town will sing an anthem about forgiveness, and one of the thieves will be untied and released into the crowd, just the way they did it in Jerusalem."

"That's beautiful," Sarah said.

"Yes . . ." Dot said, frowning. "Oh, it's a lovely holiday. The painted eggs, the mystery of spring, the little candies hidden on the lawn for the children. And here! My goodness. The flowers, the processions . . ."

Sarah inscrutable; peering out at the procession, working away absently at a ragged nail with her teeth.

"It's just that they take it all so *literally*," Dot said. She sighed. "Like this business with the thief. I mean, this is something that happened almost two thousand years ago— do you see what I mean? It's a *holiday*. But they are so literal-minded. You'll see. On Saturday, Sunday—nothing. No processions, no *alfombras* . . . They're not interested in the Resurrection at all, really. Today and tomorrow are the big days. The Crucifixion is the part of it they relate to." She nodded admonishingly at Sarah. "*Martyrdom.* You see, they pick so at the story—the Crucifixion, the poor, the rich. That sort of thing. The imperial authorities. The soldiers."

The crowd was jostling around us, Dot serenely accustomed to it—burbling on, unfazed. "We used to go out to the little villages. Santa Catarina and so on. But no more. They've taken the wonder right out of it, haven't they? Of course, they *are* very poor—no one would deny them that. Still, it's just tempting fate, isn't it? To glorify it the way they do?

"When Cliff was still with the Department of Agriculture we had a place out by the lake, and we would go to the celebrations there. The people are mostly seasonal labor on the plantations, so, as you might imagine, it's been a fertile area for guerrilla activity; and now, of course, the people bring politics into simply *everything*.

"And the priests can be just as bad. There was one, just about ten years ago, in the village across the lake from us. An American, if you please. Who should have known better. It's a terrible story, really. It makes me *sick* to tell it—I'm sorry the whole thing came up. You see, it was what he allowed them to do, some of these people in his parish. He let them dress up the figures of the saints—the figures of Christ, even—as Indians." Dot nodded as she looked from Sarah to me. "Well, not just *Indians*—actually as guerrillas, do you see? With the little masks and so forth? And they did it right in that great big church of theirs, which is practically the only real building in that town. Father Tobin thought he could get away with it, I suppose, because he was American. But he might have stopped to think how he was endangering his parishioners. What sort of priest is that, I ask you? His parishioners were disappearing by the score."

The pavement swiped briefly up at me, and I reached out to steady myself against Dot's arm. "No hat?" Dot said. She gave me a penetrating look, and steered us through the crowd to a shady spot. "Reckless creature. Anyhow, it made us just as mad as anything. But of course I'm not Catholic myself, so to my mind the whole *thing* is a bit—there, look! Executioners!"

Group filed by dressed in black, black conical hats, but faces eerily covered by flaps of white fabric with holes cut out for the eyes. Saw a Pontius Pilate—pointed him out to Sarah: "Do you see the sign he's carrying? It says, 'I wash my hands of the blood of this innocent man.' "

"This is just the sort of thing I mean," Dot said.

"What's what sort of thing?" Sarah said. But Dot was gazing out with displeasure.

Felt unaccountably nervous—started chattering at Sarah: "Well, it's complex, isn't it? Because the thing is that the local people said to Pilate, 'Look. You've got to get rid of this fellow Jesus. He's got this whole mob of crazy hillbillies behind him, and they're saying his claims supersede the claims of Rome.' And *Pilate* said, 'Well, I don't happen to think Jesus is guilty of anything, but I can't stop you from doing whatever you want to him, can I? Because I can't intervene in local affairs.' So who knows who was using who? After all, you could say that it was very much in Pilate's interest, as well as the interest of the local authorities, that Jesus be killed, because, after all, Jesus was certainly fomenting unrest in Pilate's province."

Sarah turned to me. "So you mean the guy with the sign—"

"Well, *no*," I said. "I'm just trying to point out various ironies of the situation . . . And it's interesting to remember that that's where those phrases come from. You know: 'I wash my hands of it.' 'My hands are clean.' And so on. They come from the Bible."

"As do so many," Dot said vaguely. "Oh, there he is—" She waved as McGee appeared from the crowd, coughing from incense. "I thought we were going to have to send out the Romans! Did you get some good ones?"

"Indeed I did," McGee said. "Ought to have some beauties."

"Clifford left the lens cap on last year," Dot explained.

"By the way," Sarah said to her. "What happened to the priest?"

"Excuse me?" Dot said.

"The priest in the village near the lake," Sarah said.

"Well," Dot said. "Do you mean— I mean, no one knows, exactly, do they? That is, they came in a van, as usual. But the windows were smoked glass, of course, and they weren't wearing uniforms. The van slid up behind him, they say. Just the way those vans do. I'm afraid they got him just outside the church." Dot shook her head. "You can still see the bullet holes. And it took quite some time to scrub down the wall and the street, we were told . . . Well. But no one recognized them. No one knows who they were."

FRIDAY

Sabor de China and Giuseppe's both awful. Best to skip.

Last night, after all the wooden shutters were closed and the town was quiet, Sarah and I went out. Above the encircling mountains the sky was bright with stars; down on the ground the night was pouring back and forth, glistening over the cobblestones and churches. Sarah and I walked around for a bit, then sat down in the square next to a pale-trunked palm.

Was terribly aware how quickly it would be over, sitting with her there in the fragrant night. Thought of her ten years hence: a dinner party, high over some sparkling city, Sarah in a wonderful little dress, more beautiful, even, than now. Gazing out the window, next to someone—a colleague, an admirer . . .

Could feel the future forming in embryo—the sort of longing that sleeps watchfully in one's body through time and separation. Could imagine so clearly—Sarah at this future party, confiding to this admirer: Her first involvement with a mature man, her introduction to so much that was new . . . No, she and I won't have meant *nothing* to each other . . .

The shine of her hair like a little light around her as she absorbed the night, breathing it into her memory for that moment in the future. Raised her hand and stroked it, spread-

ing out the fingers; kissed her palm. Asked what she was
thinking.

"I'm thinking, Thank God we're rid of the McGees for
once." She laughed.

I looked down at her hand.

"What's the matter, Dennis?" she said.

Said I was sorry about the McGees. Sorrow, in fact, had
fallen over me like a gentle net. "They really are idiots."

"Well, they're not *idiots*," Sarah said.

I looked at her. "That was *your* word," I said.

"Yes? Well, I was wrong, then," Sarah said. "Wasn't I."

Across from us the people in the shelter of the porticoed
municipal building slept, cradling the town in the mesh of
their breathing.

" '*Tainted*,' " Sarah said. "I mean, *Jesus*."

Noticed that the people in front of the municipal building
were stirring, rousing themselves in a dreamlike way, rolling
back the blanket of sleep, sitting up—first one or two, then
several more, shaking others gently by the shoɹ.der until,
soon, they were all awake, getting to their feet, smoothing
out their rumpled clothing.

In moments they were in the square with us, talking in
low, eager voices. Some were speaking Spanish, some were
speaking languages I'd never heard. Were paying no attention
to us at all; leaned over the basin of the fountain to splash
themselves or their babies with water, or to reach up with tin
cups for its less polluted streams.

But then—as unexpectedly as they'd appeared in the
square, they filed out again. Absolutely weird. Sarah and I
paused a moment, then followed. Soon we were in a part of
town we'd never seen before. Lanterns swaying from stone
arches, heavy shutters swinging open as we passed by—
behind them women in black staring out at us from candlelit
rooms or patios.

Crowd led us to a churchyard dense with people, tiny stands selling food, wooden toys, shiny whirling things. No tourists, no wealthy Ladinos, none of the Europeans who keep houses here in town. All the people ragged and thin—surroundings incredibly festive, but their faces, as they milled about, were serious. Abstracted.

The sky was scattered with stars, balloons, plumes of incense. Above a long flight of wide, shallow steps a scrolled church (such delicate adornments! carved fruit, carved vines) floated like a dove, pale pink in the moonlight. Candles alight everywhere, flickering, converging into a flickering river at the huge, open church doors.

Tantalizing aromas: food frying in vats or simmering in huge kettles or roasting on sticks over fires. Sarah pulling me from one culinary spectacle to another in an agony of cupidity. "Look, Dennis—can you believe it? There's real food in this country!"

"Don't even think of it," I said.

"Please," she said. People were eating patiently, without greed, as though they were preparing themselves for something. Men were so thin it was hard not to watch them as they ate—so frail. Several had what looked like a band of hair shaved from the top of their heads—worn away from hauling loads by a strap, I suppose. Sarah hovered longingly by a woman frying huge disks of tortilla, then using them to scoop up a bright, chunky sauce. "I can't stand it!"

"Out of the question," I said. At our feet a flock of tiny children chewed solemnly at the dirty treat. "Do you imagine I'd let you do something like that to yourself? But listen. The minute we get home I'm taking you to the Red Fox Inn for a decent meal."

"Do you promise?" Sarah said as the crowd carried us with them into the floating church. Was just making me swear it, but then she gasped and took my arm.

We were at the front of the crowd—the entire floor between us and the altar was a picture, a picture carpet, made of flower petals, like the *alfombras*, but vast: Jesus, all of flowers, white-robed on a mountaintop with waves of power radiating from his raised hands. And beneath him, pouring out toward us, becoming us, a flower multitude—the poor, the mourning, the meek, the hungry, the pure in heart, the persecuted . . .

Behind us, people were pushing their way forward. I glanced back and saw that the crowd was not flowerlike at all, but thin and dry as tinder, their eyes alight with a fanatical, incendiary ecstasy of poverty.

My God. Who *were* these people? Their legs were ulcerated, their feet were bare and thickened, their backs were bent from hauling wood or fruit or coffee, but what act of madness might they not be capable of? The guerrillas in the neighboring villages dozing tensely under the dark trees, the children who work the raging fields, the maids, the porters, the farmers, curled up on their beds or straw mats, alert in their sleep, dreaming their dangerous dreams. People who can't afford a newspaper. People in whose languages no paper will ever be printed, people who couldn't read one if one *were* printed in their languages—these people who don't even know there's a world out there, it's these people who could burn the world to the ground. Stunted and sloe-eyed, with the delicate, slanting planes of their faces, their brilliant clothing, their ancient, outlandish languages, they seem like strange, magical creatures. But, no! These people have lives that go from one end of the day to the other. They eat or go hungry. They have conversations behind closed doors—

As Sarah and I were thrust out the side door we saw a small knot of soldiers dispersing in the courtyard below us, blending into the crowd. My hands felt weak again, and damp. *Tainted*, I thought; *tainted*. Next to me Sarah picked up a wobbly child who was steadying himself against her knees, and nuzzled his soft, black baby hair, through which I could absolutely *see* the columns of lice tramping. But when I opened my mouth to warn Sarah I could hardly croak.

The baby waved his new little hands for balance—his new little enemy hands. His swimming black baby eyes reflected for an instant, in exquisite miniature, the thousand or so candles, the floating church, the thick, blest, kindled crowd. Which of the reflected men could that baby hope soon to be? Which of the frail old enemy men?

A little girl tugged urgently at Sarah's skirt and held out her arms to claim her brother as a noise manifested itself at a distance. The noise came toward us slowly, solid and tidal, but separated, as it approached, and we were engulfed in shouts, hoofbeats, chanting, as lanterns and torchlight wavered through smoke and incense.

Facing us, at the head of the mob, two Roman centurions reined in their huge horses to a nervous, hobbled trot. Around them surged the Jerusalemites in their purple satin and Roman foot soldiers holding lances, as well as hundreds of town dwellers in ordinary clothing.

A trumpet sounded, and the edgy crowd fell silent. The sky gleamed black, the moon was streaking through the clouds. Sarah's pale face narrowed and flashed like a coin, and I had the sensation that if I concentrated I would be able to remember all the events that were to follow—every detail . . .

And, yes, one of the centurions was already holding out a scroll: *Jesus of Nazareth was condemned to die by crucifixion!* The pronouncement rang out against the stone of the church like something being forged; its echo pulsed in a cataract of silence.

SATURDAY

> *Hotel Buena Vista.* Breakfast, lunch, and din-
> ner daily. The *Buena Vista* offers probably the
> best lunch deal in town. Help yourself to the
> unlimited buffet, complete with tortillas made
> fresh in front of your eyes by Indian women in
> full dress, take a swim, and if you've hap-
> pened to come on the right day, view a fash-
> ion show around the pool, all for about the
> price of a hamburger and fries back home.
> Exotic birds wander the grounds, and caged
> parrots enliven the scene, as well. The fare is
> standard, but the steaks are flame-grilled, and
> tasty.

Clouds below us, plane not too crowded. Sarah sitting with
a book on her lap, gazing out the window, at nothing.

This morning, as we were leaving, it was just as Dot had
said it would be. No *alfombras*, no processions, tourists thin-
ning out. No trace whatsoever of the pilgrims in front of the
municipal building. Just women in black, privately lamenting
Mary's murdered child. But yesterday—Friday—processions
were volatile, grief-stricken, unrelenting: Christ in black,
prepared for his death, then Christ on the cross, broken.

Felt v. peculiar—ill-tempered, rattled—all yesterday
morning. Suppose from my disorientation of Thurs. night +
looming lunch with McGees.

And then—the *Buena Vista* itself! *¡Dios!* Curvy Ladino
girls modeling hideous clothing around the pool, children
streaking between them, landing in the water with loud
splashes, bloodcurdling shrieks. Indian women making tor-

tillas, watching with expressionless sentry eyes. Well-to-do visitors from the capital dispatching slender, olive-skinned sons to the parking lot with little plates of rice and beans for the maids. A species of splotchy, knobby tourists (Evangelicals, apparently; McGee says they get a big price break at the *Buena Vista*) sunning themselves in plastic lounge chairs, laughing loudly and nervily, as though they'd just hoodwinked their way out of prison.

Sarah struggled with her little sink stopper of a steak for a few minutes, then got up and ambled around the lawn, looking unusually pensive. When she sat back down, she started telling the McGees about something she'd seen a few days ago. Had she mentioned it to me? Don't think so. Said she'd seen three big guys grab a boy as he walked out of a store—nobody was paying attention except for one lady, who was yelling. Then the men bundled the boy up, put him on a truck. "I didn't really think much about it at the time," Sarah said. "It was like a tape playing too fast to make any sense of." She looked from Dot to Cliff. "I suppose I just assumed it was a kid getting picked up for a robbery . . ."

"Oh, Lord," Dot said with a sigh.

"Now, Dorothy," McGee said.

"No, Cliff." Dot's voice trembled slightly. "I don't care. Their poor mothers. You know"—she turned to Sarah—"after the boys are trained, they're sent to other parts of the country, because it does work out better if they don't speak the language, doesn't it? Oh, I know that it's all necessary, but it's terribly hard for the families. Their families love them. Their families need them to work." She turned back to McGee. "I think it's disgusting, Clifford, frankly."

McGee lifted his hand for peace. "I never said—" he began, but just at that moment a tall man of thirty-five or so approached. His thatchy hair and matching mustache were the color of dirty Lucite. A large, chipped tooth might have given his smile an agreeable, beaverlike goofiness except for an impression he gave of the veiled, inexhaustible rage you see in certain ex-alcoholics. "Excuse me," he said. "Do you happen to be Clifford McGee?"

"I am he," McGee said judiciously, extending his hand.

"My name's Curtis Finley," the man said. "I work with your old outfit, and you were pointed out to me once at the Camino."

"So, they've got you down here, do they?" McGee said. "Have a seat. We're just—what is it they say?—*improving the shining hours*."

Sarah stood up suddenly, then flopped back down into her chair. Finley glanced at her. "Thank you, sir," he said to McGee. "Yes, I've been here for a bit, now. I'm on my way to supervise a project up north."

"Really," McGee said. "A lot going on up there. You'll have to come by when you get back, let me know how things went. I like to keep up."

"I imagine you do, sir," Finley said. "They still talk about you at the office." The two men smiled at each other, and a faint smell of sweat imprinted itself on the air.

Dot nodded toward Sarah, who was splayed out glumly in her chair. "*This* young lady saw a recruitment the other day," Dot said.

"Dorothy," McGee said, as Finley looked sharply at him.

"Those cretins," Finley said. He turned to me and Sarah, showing his teeth to indicate friendliness. "So, what brings you folks down here?"

"Dennis is a journalist," Sarah said. She drew herself together and smiled primly.

Finley looked away from her legs. "Recruitments are very unusual here in town," he told me. "And technically against the law. In fact, as I understand it, something's being done about them now."

"I'm not really a *journalist*," I assured him hurriedly. "I'm just doing food. Hotels, Easter celebrations in a general sort of way . . ."

"I see . . ." Finley said.

"Actually," I said, "I'm a banker."

"Oh." Finley looked at McGee.

"No," Dot said. "You see, Dennis is doing the most marvelous thing—he's writing a nationally syndicated article about Holy Week. Isn't that wonderful?"

Finley frowned. "Oh." He showed his teeth again. "Well, how are you enjoying it? Beautiful town, isn't it?"

McGee shifted in his chair. "We're taking these two to the de Leóns' tonight, for dinner," he said. "They're old friends, and the cook does wonderful things with regional produce."

"Oh, yes." Finley looked at me with vague bitterness. "Interesting fellow, de León. Never met him personally. Good morning, isn't he?"

"Pardon?" I said.

"Good morning," McGee said. "You've seen them in the supermarkets. Oranges, grapefruits. Even some bananas with the little sticker that says—"

"Oh, yes," I said. "Of course. Good Morning!"

"Yes," McGee said. "that's de León. Good Morning! Oranges, Good Morning! Grapefruits. Coffee's his main thing, but he's all over the place now, really."

"Had some trouble with a son, I remember hearing," Finley said.

McGee nodded. "A bad patch. Over now."

"Kid had one wicked case of red-ass, as I heard it," Finley said. He turned to Sarah. "If you'll pardon me."

"Excuse me?" Sarah said with a misty smile. "Sorry, I

wasn't really . . . Oh, Mr. Finley, do you happen to know
what this pretty vine is?" She pointed to an arborlike construction above us.

"Curtis," Finley said. He peered overhead, then looked at
Sarah. "Vine?"

"I think," Dot said, squinting distantly, "that the rain is
going to come early this year. Last night I saw lightning from
over by the coast."

McGee smiled comfortably. "Same family as the Japanese
wisteria," he said.

Later Sarah hunched over in the big chair in our room,
hugging her knees while I walked back and forth.

"Just because a fellow doesn't happen to recognize one
particular plant," I said, "does not mean he's some kind of
impostor."

Sarah sighed noisily.

"Well, after all," I said. "But, besides. I think one has to
ask oneself what, in all honesty, are the alternatives."

"What on earth are you saying, Dennis?" Sarah said.

Mustn't let Sarah force me into positions—her willful na-
ïveté, threat of shrillness. Always have to remember to relax,
keep perspective. Allow her to relax. Tried to point out calmly
that, whatever one thinks of this method or that, people's
goals tend to be—on a certain basic level—the same. "We
all want life to improve for everyone; we're all struggling, in
our own ways, to make things better. Yes, even people who
differ from us can be sincere, Sarah—I mean, unless you're
talking about a few greed-maddened dictators. Psychopaths,
like Hitler, or Idi Amin. Sociopaths, I guess, is what the
word is now. Is that what they say in your classes, 'sociopaths'?"

Sarah gazed down at her sandled toes and wiggled them.

"But it's funny," I said, perching next to her on the arm of the chair. "Isn't it? The way terminology can change like that. It must reflect a wholesale shift in the way moral reasoning, or whatever, is perceived to work. I think it's so interesting, that, don't you? They used to say 'psychopaths' when I was young."

Sarah wiggled her toes again. "Isn't it wonderful," she leaned down to say to them, "the way that bogus agronomists are crawling all over the place, struggling to improve life for everyone?

"Oh, yes, Sarah," she answered herself in a crumply little voice. "Deeply heartwarming. But that word 'agronomist'— I think the word you want is 'agriculturalist,' interestingly. You know, when I was just a *little* toe—"

"Oh, Sarah," I said.

"Ex*cuse* me, Dennis." Sarah looked at me icily. "I was talking to my *foot*."

For the rest of the afternoon, we were very, very cautious with one another. Was dreading dinner. But Sarah was on her good behavior, or a variant of it. Was weirdly tractable, polite. Just as well, especially because the de Leóns turned out to be exactly what one would have expected—exactly what one would have feared.

The Sra. steely in linen and small gold earrings. The Sr. somewhat more appealing. Handsome, very Spanish, melancholy. Obvious habit of power; cordiality engineered to infinitesimal degrees of correctness. Daughter, Gabriela, petite like mother. Pure, unclouded face, whispery clothing— quite taken with Sarah; many limpid smiles. Missed the States, she said, her friends from boarding school in Connecticut. Threatened "So much to talk about." All three excellent English.

Maids, passing out hors d'oeuvres and cocktails—rum + Good Morning! fruit juices. Gigantic house, huge collection of antique Indian textiles, pre-Columbian artifacts, splendid colonial furnishings, etc. Evening inexplicably slippery at first—odd tides of dusk from the series of enclosed patios and gardens flowing around the bulky forms inside. Everyone floating a bit, like particles dislodging themselves from something underwater, which was my mind.

Found Sarah in a hallway, staring at a row of photographs. From behind, I watched her examining the face of a beautiful young man, pale, black-haired, who was staring into the camera with an expression of sardonic resignation.

"That's my son Rubén," said Sra. de León, who had come up quietly next to me. "We're very proud of him. He's living in Paris, now. He's been a great help to his father in the last few years." She gave Sarah a frosty, slightly challenging smile.

Eventually we were all moored around the table. Dinner excellent. Amazed by quality. Sadly, though, was unhungry in the extreme. Throughout parade of courses McGees and de Leóns conversing with the informal amiability of old friends: an archaeological site just uncovered nearby, then lurid local gossip—a nun from the U.S. who claimed to have been abducted from a convent in town and tortured. Though eventually, de León told us, the Embassy revealed that the cigarette burns all over the nun's back had been inflicted by a lesbian lover.

"It's always in small places that the most incredible things happen, isn't it?" Dot said. "New York City can't compete with this story."

De León turned to Sarah with a brief burst of male charm. "This government is a collection of amateurs," he said obscurely.

"Vicente is sentimental about the old days," Sra. de León said. "When less was required of us."

"I will not walk around my own property armed," Sr. de León said, his warmth disappearing in the frozen wastes of his wife's smile.

There was a small silence as Sra. de León looked at her napkin with an amused, measured loathing. "Ah," she said, as maids brought in trays of dessert and coffee. "Here we are."

The McGees appeared to be accustomed to the climatic shiftings between the de Leóns. "Vicente"—McGee waved his fork—"Angélica has outdone herself tonight."

"A triumph," I said, gently pedaling Sarah's foot. "And I never would have dreamed it was possible to do something like this with a banana."

"Oh, nor I," Sarah said, withdrawing her foot.

"Very simple," Sr. de León said. "Just caramelize lightly, add a little orange, a little rum, and flame." He handed me a small stack of cards; turned out he had had all the recipes from dinner typed up.

Gabriela laughed. "Daddy is so shy, isn't he," she said.

"Yes, ha," I agreed. Consommé with Tomato, Avocado, and Cilantro, I read. Sole with Good Morning! Grapefruit. Carrots with Zest of Good Morning! Orange. Volcano Salad. Good Morning! Bananas with Juice of Good Morning! Oranges and Rum. Dark Roast Good Morning! Coffee and Cardamom Chewies. "I hardly know how to thank you," I said. "These will really *make* my article—"

"It is my great pleasure," de León said.

"And it will be nice to have some decent press up there for a change," Gabriela said.

"Gaby," Sra. de León chided.

"No, but it's true," Gabriela said. She turned to Sarah.

"You know, it happens all the time. Some reporter, who knows nothing about this country, who doesn't care anything about it, who only cares about making a reputation for himself, comes down and says he wants to write an objective story about life here. And the next thing you know, you open up some magazine and read the most fantastic stuff. As if the country were one big concentration camp—as if all we ever did was bomb the villages."

Sarah put down her fork.

"I *know*," Gabriela said. "Never one word about the *wonderful* things—"

"Gaby," Sra. de León said, and put down her own fork, "why don't you show our new friends the garden."

It was a great relief to leave the table. Gabriela led us through the pungent floral riot, and cut some elegant little lilies for Sarah. Sarah thanked her; asked how far the plantation extended. Gabriela looked puzzled for a moment, then laughed. Explained that we weren't on the plantation at all —that it was hours and hours away, over terrible roads. Said, "Of course, these days if we were to go we would use helicopters, and it would only take minutes. But we never do anymore. Even Daddy hardly goes."

Sarah silent, considering. Then asked who was it, that being the case, who saw to the planting, harvesting, etc.

Gabriela mercifully innocent—entirely impervious to offense potential of Sarah's question.

"Oh, we have what amounts to a rather large village living up there," Gabriela said. "And some very reliable overseers. But we always used to go out at harvest time ourselves, anyway."

Frankly, was very touched by her regretful tone. "You enjoyed it," I observed.

"Oh, yes," she said. "I loved it. We all did. We loved to

watch the harvest, to ride around the countryside on our horses
. . . Well, it was a long time ago, when we could do that—
that was back when our Indians still had their own little plots
of land up north, and we had them brought down on trucks
for the harvest, big trucks, from their tiny villages. And they
were all from different villages, so they wore different colors
and patterns in their clothes, and they spoke all sorts of
different languages. They were so strange, so beautiful. I
used to love to listen to them, and to watch them. To watch
them harvesting the coffee . . ."

"Harvesting coffee," I said. "You know, I never think of
coffee as a legume, but, of course—*coffee beans!*"

Gabriela smiled and shook her hair. In the moonlight she
had a newborn look. "Coffee isn't really a bean at all," she
said. "It's a berry. It's very nice to look at—it turns bright
red. But it's a nuisance to pick. You really have to watch
what you're doing or you can strip the plant. Still, at least,
it's not heavy, as long as you're not hauling the sacks. So it's
one thing that small children can learn to do. Fortunately for
the families."

Sarah started to speak, and stopped.

"It was so beautiful," Gabriela said. "I wish I could show
it to you as it was then . . ." She sighed. "You have to forgive
me for talking and talking like this. But there are so few
people who would understand what it's like for me. People
here can't really understand because most have never lived
in the States or Europe, and my friends in the States can't
understand, because they've never been here."

"Do go on," I said. I glanced reprimandingly at Sarah.

"Oh, I don't know . . ." Gabriela smiled faintly, as though
she were watching something across the garden. "Well, it's
been so long since I've been back, hasn't it. I was about
twelve, I suppose, the last time. That's right—because my

brother, Rubén, who's in Paris now, was sixteen. It's incredible to think about that time, really. It was very confusing. It was very hard, particularly for my parents, because it was just when things were at their worst in this country, and the guerrilla movement really had some strength. And Rubén had picked up some funny ideas. He was just at that age, you know, when children are very susceptible. And I suppose some older boys had gotten hold of him because our family, well"—she smiled sadly—"because our family is very well known. And Rubén began to go around saying things he couldn't possibly even have understood—talking about giving land away, 'returning it,' was how he put it. And ruinous increases in wages. Things that would absolutely destroy his own family. And Mommy and Daddy tried to reason with him. They were very patient—they kept telling him, Rubén, you know, certain people own the land. They have legal title to it. You can't just snatch it away from them, can you? And if we're to drink coffee, if we're to eat fruit, someone is going to have to pick it. And it's a tragedy, of course, that you can't just pay the laborers anything you'd like, but it's a fact. It's simply a fact. Because what do you think would happen to the world if we did? And a banana cost ten dollars? Or a cup of coffee cost twenty dollars? But Rubén would always just slam out of the house. So it was a very hard time for us all. And of course that was the period when the workers had to be watched very, very closely, because, you can imagine— if it was possible to contaminate Rubén, imagine how much easier it would be with a poor, uneducated Indian."

Gabriela reached out to touch a pink rambling rose. "So," she said, "we were all up for the harvest one year, and there was a morning when I woke up very, very early. Before the sun rose. I woke up to this delicious smell, this absolutely delicious smell, of roasting coffee. And I thought, well, now it's time to get up. And then about one thousand things happened in my mind all at once, because I realized it wasn't time to get up—it wasn't time to get up at all, and something was happening that couldn't possibly be happening. And so, before I even knew what I was doing or why, I rushed over to my window. And the window was black and red—black with night and red with fire, wave after wave of fire in the black sky. And the whole storehouse, all our coffee, was up in flames."

"Oh—" Sarah said. She sat down on the rim of an old fountain from which cascaded tiny weightless white flowers.

"Yes," Gabriela said. She seated herself next to Sarah and drew me down beside her. "It was terrible. And after that I never really went back. Mommy and Daddy felt it would be too dangerous, and of course it wasn't nearly as pleasant, because security was tightened up a lot, too. The army came—there are still hundreds of soldiers living there, in fact." She laughed. "Daddy doesn't like that at all. He says it's more of a—what do you call it?—protection racket, than protection, and that the army is bleeding us worse than the workers. But what can you do, after all? And there are guard towers now, and the landing strips, and those awful, you know, *fences*. So it's not so nice anymore.

"But Rubén went back once again with my father. And instead of bringing him to his senses, it all just seemed to make him worse—angrier and wilder and more unhappy. My parents wanted him to go away to school. To Harvard, or perhaps to Oxford. But he wanted to stay in the country, and it turned out to be a very bad thing for everyone that he did. Because then he really became involved with all these crazy student groups. It was so sad. They were so young—they thought they were idealists, but, really, they were just being used. Rubén had been such a sweet boy, such a wonderful brother, but he became very hard. It was just this hard, awful propaganda all the time."

Gabriela frowned at a petal she was smoothing between her fingers. "He said terrible things. He said that we were thieves, you know, and so on. And it's not as though any of us are thrilled with the way things are, of course, but after all—it is people like our parents who generate the entire economy here." She sighed. "He said that people were starving. Heavens! You have to be *stupid* to starve in this climate, don't you?" She turned to Sarah for confirmation and smiled gently. "The fruit simply drops off the trees.

"Anyhow, during the next year, several of our workers and some of the other students—friends of Rubén's—got killed and were found by the side of one road or another. So, even though none of them was from important families, we were all terrified for Rubén. And in fact it was late that same year that the first letter arrived."

Inside, in the soft light, we could see Gabriela's parents and the McGees sipping their coffee and chatting contentedly. I closed my eyes and raised my face to the tiny white flowers above us, as though they were a spray of cool water.

"And the letter stated it all in no uncertain terms— They knew who he was, they knew *where* he was, and so forth. Well, my father got on the phone right away, and started sending my brother to see important people. My father had friends in the police, and friends in the army. And he even had several friends in the Embassy—your embassy here— so we thought we could take care of it quickly enough. But every day went by, and everyone my brother talked to said they didn't know anything about it—they couldn't find out who was sending the letters. And one day Rubén went to see a colonel in the army, whom Rubén and I had known since we were *babies*—my father is the *god*father of one of this man's children. And Rubén came back from that meeting looking like a corpse."

A little leaf spiraled down through the air and landed on Gabriela's dress. She picked it off and looked at it affectionately before she let it flutter away. "Because the Colonel said, you know, right away, that of course he'd help, and he made a phone call while Rubén was sitting right there in his office. The Colonel explained the situation over the phone to whoever it was he'd called, and then he just sat there on the phone, listening, for about twenty minutes, Rubén told us later. And when he hung up, Rubén asked what the other person had said, and the Colonel said, 'Nothing.' "

Gabriela stopped speaking for a moment, and as she resumed, Sarah's cold hand rested briefly on mine. "So the Colonel stood up to walk Rubén to the door, and at the door he burst into tears. And he said, 'I'm sorry. I can't help you. But now, listen to me, please—there's something I have to say to you.' He put his hands on Rubén's shoulders and looked into his eyes, and said, 'When you leave your house, be sure to tell somebody where you're going. Always walk in the direction of traffic' "—Gabriela leaned up for a moment, as I had, into the cool spray of white flowers—" 'and be very, very careful when you cross the street.' "

This morning particularly blue and bright. Ricardo's greeting, María's smile, the roses, the hummingbirds—everything bright, large, standing out in the blue air as though I'd been far away for a long time. Woke up famished. Couldn't eat enough. Melon, grapefruit, pineapple, banana—I ate and ate. Thought of all that fantastic food last night, just sitting in front of me. Laughed slightly. "Horrible, wasn't it?" I said to Sarah. "Thank God we'll never have to do that again." My fork scraped startlingly against my plate. "Sarah?" I said.

Saw she hadn't touched her fruit or her juice or her coffee. I speared a piece of banana and held it out to her. "No?" I said. Waved it temptingly. "All right, but you'll be starving by the time we get to the airport."

She looked at me, then slammed her napkin down onto the table and stalked off.

Made an embarrassed farewell to Ricardo, hurried to our room, where I found Sarah sitting, staring at me accusingly from the unmade bed—the geological record of the aeons of our horrible night, our tense, mid-sleep lovemaking during which the ghouls from Gabriela's wild story rubbed their wicked little numbing dream hands and waited.

"Oh, for heaven's sake," I said, as it dawned on me. "All right. I apologize, Sarah, all right? I'm a brute. I'm insensitive. I'm a white male." Sarah folded her arms. "But frankly, my dear, it *is* a common expression. A manner of speaking. I rather imagine you've used it yourself upon occasion—"

Sarah interrupted. "But guess what, Dennis? I'm the person who's never going to *be* starving. Because that's the person I am, as it turns out. I'm the same person as Dot, Dennis, the same person as Gabriela—"

"Oh, come, now," I said.

" '*Oh, come now,*' " Sarah said. She kicked savagely at the mattress. "Because don't you get it? I mean this is a *war*, Dennis. We're soldiers, *and that's our uniform.*" She started to cry with a thin, infuriating animal anguish. "See, I don't understand why I didn't *know* that. I don't understand why I haven't read about all this in the newspaper."

"In the newspaper!" I said. "You don't understand why you haven't read about this in the *newspaper*? About what, please, Sarah—why you haven't read about what?" Felt I was wading through a dark, cold river. An ashy river clogged with garbage and bones. "You don't know why you haven't read about who you *are*? In the newspaper? Do you consider that a front-page story? Sarah, listen to me. What are you trying to do to me? Are you trying to spoil all the *good* things? Yes, I suppose I should rush off to Zwicker and say, 'Stop the presses, chief, there are some problems out there—rich people make more money than poor people. Life is unfair and people suffer.' God knows, Sarah—it's not as though I don't agree with you, but think about it for a moment, please; use your head. You don't read about yourself in the newspaper because that's not what a newspaper is for. And you don't read in the newspaper about the things that go on here, because *the things that go on here aren't news.*"

God, it was awful. Mortifying. Sarah sobbing, me ranting —was *profoundly* mortified by my outburst. Got blue in the face apologizing, while Sarah sniffled and hiccuped and packed her beautiful textiles, sneaking beleaguered glances over her shoulder at me as though I had forced her at gunpoint to buy them. Made me feel literally like the Gestapo.

Thankfully, by the time we got to the airport she seemed to have exhausted herself—was just sleepy and absentminded, like a child after a tantrum.

On the plane Sarah stared at her closed book as a thin shield of cloud glided beneath us, but I peered across her out the window to watch the little country beneath us vanish.

Oh, the ravages of traveling. Poor Sarah. Unfamiliar rules, disturbance of one's biological rhythms. Whole populations of new microbes . . . The plane went blood-dark for an instant; pale skin boiling up into sticky black welts, slow lines of black-windowed vans patrolling the pale mountains . . .

Hadn't even occurred to me before—I'm *sick*! Bet we both are. Bet we've both picked up some sort of parasite. Damn, damn! Well, God knows I tried to be careful.

Oh, so much to do this week. Doctor. Work up a piece for Zwicker, of course. Unpack. Phone calls. Stacks of mail, naturally—naturally most of it catalogues. It's funny, I always intend to throw them right out, but when it comes down to it I can never resist leafing through, to see all the idiotic junk—programmable toasters, telephones disguised as footballs—that someone has spent time dreaming up and someone will spend money to buy. Shook my head and forced a chuckle, but Sarah continued to look out the window. "Hey," I said, tugging playfully at her sleeve. "I promised I'd take you to the Red Fox Inn tonight, remember?"

"The Red Fox Inn?" Sarah looked at me, then a veil dropped over her expression, and she turned back to the window.

All right. Yes, the planet is littered with bodies. No one's going to dispute *that*—and the bodies are surrounded by clues. But what those clues mean, and where they point— well, that's something else altogether, isn't it?

Took Sarah's unresisting hand, and for a moment feared I was going to burst into loud, raucous weeping. Strange airplane light showing the fatigue behind her closed eyes; showing the age, deep within her, boring its way to her surface.

But will it improve, the world, if Sarah and I stay in and subsist on a diet of microwaved potatoes? Because I really don't think so. I really don't think—and this is something I'll say to Sarah when she's herself again, I suppose—that by the standards of any sane person it could be considered a crime to go to a restaurant. To go someplace nice. After all. Our little comforts— The velvet murmur, the dimming of the street as the door closes, the enfolding calm of the other diners . . . that incredible moment when the waiter steps up, smiling, to put your plate before you . . .

IN THE

STATION

SOUNDS STRETCH OUT IN THE
station—footsteps, crackling announcements, rag ends of instructions and goodbyes echo and balloon, tangle in a mass
that hangs high up under the sooty vaulting of transoms and
girders. Far below, where a thin scurf of yellow electric light
drifts among the newsstands and plaintive groups of benches,
Dee Dee clutched her ticket and inspected rows of shiny
candy bars and magazines. In the distance the station dis-
solves into a watery daylight where points of darkness appear,
and swell, hissing, into trains.

Dee Dee reached, then hesitated, as though she were
choosing cards from a gypsy's pack. "Pardon," a man said
shortly, jostling her as he plucked a newspaper from in front
of her. The train, she remembered; the important thing was
getting on the train.

But where were Carl and Márta? Just a moment ago they
had been walking toward the gate. She looked frantically at
the flow of people—the line was already beginning to form:
unhealthy-looking English families, ladies in twos, the occasional pampered businessman of the sort Dee Dee had seen
in the restaurants, and, because it was summer, throngs of
students, Americans especially, talking and lounging theat-

rically. Everyone wore the resolute, slightly exaggerated expressions of people beginning a journey, as though, fearing irremediable dislocation, they were determined to stamp themselves upon their own futures.

The line collected, and swayed with an absent fretfulness as Dee Dee searched it for Carl and Márta. Ah—there they were, standing a little off to one side. And something was wrong: Márta shook her short, dark hair; her hands flew up. Carl shied as if she were bombarding him, in her pretty accent, with little pellets.

Dee Dee started forward, then stopped. As though signaled by her panic, Carl and Márta turned. Dee Dee smiled uncertainly and waved with her bag of new magazines and candy. For a moment they simply looked at her.

She went light with dread—she was a scrap of something blowing away from them, tumbling away in Márta's somber, lashy gaze. Carl's hair gleamed like stiff filaments of silk. Then he raised his hand in a false little wave of reassurance, and Dee Dee was standing in place again.

Carl and Márta turned back to each other. "Carl," Márta said, and Carl looked at her with terror, as though, Márta thought, she were some beast poised to destroy him.

How enraging. How *enraging*; was he trying to make her say something terrible to him? Well, she just might; if Dee Dee didn't show up soon to stop her, heaven only knew what she might say.

Márta had been in a vicious mood since waking. She'd opened her eyes onto the freezing damp the English affected to consider summer, only to discover that her flatmate, Judit, had drunk the last of the coffee. "No more at all?" Márta demanded, ransacking the cupboard.

"Not unless you remembered to pick some up," Judit said,

unmoved. "It was on your list. Oh, by the way, István called this morning."

Márta shut the cupboard doors with wonderful composure. "Why didn't you tell me?" she said.

"You were asleep," Judit said. "Remember?"

Márta sat. She ran her hands through her hair and listened to Judit's spoon tinkle in her coffee cup. What a day for István to call. "What did he want?" she asked.

"István?" Judit shrugged. "I could hardly interrogate him, could I?"

The instant Judit disappeared into the bathroom to deplete the hot-water supply Márta dialed István. A courtesy; just to tell him she would be away for several weeks. With Carl. But István was out, of course. Or in—behind the sunny, mendacious message on his machine. Márta's heart blackened; in with some girl, doubtless. Márta hung up without leaving a message.

She'd hurried to the station, but Carl and Dee Dee had not arrived yet. How grim it was, dirty and glum—and, with all the rushing strangers, treacherously neutralizing; she could hardly remember who she herself was. So István had decided he wanted to see her again. Too late; too bad, for him.

The air around her was stale with discarded hopes, angers, attitudes no longer useful to those who were traveling. She huddled on a bench to wait, beset by tales, half-heard in her childhood, of cold, of deportations, of police—events that filtered down like ineradicable pollutants from filthy times.

When she saw Carl and Dee Dee coming toward her she merely looked at them, her chin lifted. While Dee Dee hung back, goggling and dawdling like a child, Carl greeted Márta with a crisp little kiss on each cheek. She was not charmed. Did he not see how she felt? Did he not care?

She watched him as they waited in line for tickets. That

limpid, meditative look of his! It was like a steel door, behind which he crouched, hiding.

He handed Dee Dee her ticket. "Is there anything you want before we get on the train?" he said. "It won't be so easy to find things in English, remember."

Dee Dee looked at him and put her hand over her mouth, then shambled off to a newsstand, leaving Márta to go to the train with Carl.

Something was bothering Carl. That, at least, was obvious. Márta looked at him, but his studied air of reverie enforced her silence. Still, the trip had been his idea; he had wanted her to come along. At least, he had pretended to. "Carl," she said.

"Yes!" He turned to her with the transparently fraudulent expansiveness of someone forced to replace a tempting book on a shelf. "What is it?"

She stared at him, searching his face. He *didn't* want to go. *Carl did not want to take this trip.* It was true; Márta was certain—she had the curse of being right. "Tell me, Carl, please," she said, "why we are doing this."

He flinched. "What do you mean?" he said, and then they both turned as though they'd been prodded from behind. Far down the station, Dee Dee stood in her bulky yellow slicker, a lost little lump, looking at them.

Márta had met Carl some weeks earlier at a party she'd attended with István and Judit. István was being suspiciously attentive and delightful; many attractive women were present. István loved parties. He rose to the occasion of being admired, and his paintings were beginning to sell.

Márta had been talking to István when a woman of fifty or so approached. She wore large pieces of ocher-smeared abalone on a thong around her neck and was known to collect paintings. "I don't believe we've met," she said to Márta in a voice like an electric drill, and turned her back.

Her adornments, she was explaining to István, had once served as the currency of some now-impoverished coastal tribe. Márta began to drift away. István plucked at her sleeve, smiling merrily. She looked at him. He shrugged, and turned back to the woman.

In the hot, lively room, Carl was conspicuous for his satiny blond melancholy. Márta placed herself on the arm of a sofa not far from him and gazed out the window at the brooding houses across the street.

Carl drifted next to her and spoke easily, as though they shared some delicate and slightly sorrowful information. Was István watching? If so, certainly he would be jealous. Márta concentrated on sparkling empathetically up at Carl, but then understood that Carl was expecting her to respond to something. To what? she wondered. She made a modestly self-disparaging gesture. It served; Carl began to talk again.

He was truly handsome, she realized. Her sparkle lapsed as she stared. Carl lowered his eyes; his smile was clearly involuntary.

"Do you know many people here?" Márta asked stubbornly through her blush. Over Carl's shoulder, she saw István talking to a girl. The girl was as fragile and responsive-looking as a fawn. She had lovely, trustful eyes, and István was talking to her with the earnest concern that Márta recognized as the hallmark of his most gluttonous moments. Poison squirted into her veins. "Excuse me," she said to Carl. "I have a simply splitting migrane."

Carl brought her to her flat. She was pale and silent. She had let István treat her too badly for too long; he expected her to put up with anything. And tonight, as she had peeked back into the party on her way out with Carl, István had glanced at her with cold dismissal.

Carl settled her on the sofa. He wrapped a blanket around her feet, found aspirin and a glass of water, and stood back uncomfortably. How cramped and shabby the flat looked! In Carl's impeccable Occidental presence Márta saw it clearly. When she looked up at Carl he brushed away the tiny tears that hung ornamentally from her lashes. "You must rest," he said.

Could she have bored him? "No, no," she complained. "Sit and talk to me." And he settled gingerly in a straight-backed chair. She hoped Judit would come in.

But by the time Judit returned, Márta was alone, still curled up on the sofa with the blanket around her feet, reading a novel to nurse a frail feeling of well-being.

Judit glowered. Judit and István had known each other from childhood in Budapest, and Judit took István's side in everything. Márta had heard, from others of course, how for years Judit had tagged along after István, defended him, run errands for him; how she'd been ignored by him, except when he was sick or bored or wanted to meet one of her friends. "He isn't going to call you again," Judit said.

Márta looked up from her book, raising her eyebrows in pleasant inquiry. "István?" she said.

Judit snorted.

Poor Judit. All those girls, and never Judit. And it never would be Judit.

But despite Judit's pronouncement, István did call. He called the very next day. Judit handed the phone silently over to Márta and left the room with a look of gratified persecution.

"Did you get home all right last night?" István said. His voice was silvery with sarcasm.

"Yes, thank you," Márta said. "I was accompanied."

"I am aware of that," István said.

"I felt ill," Márta said. "When I got home I had to lie down."

In the silence she felt a little giddy—István was supposed to have been apologizing by now. "I didn't like to interrupt you," she said. "You were having such a good time."

"I know what this is about," he said. "This is about nothing. I don't even know that girl. I only wanted her to meet you—that's why I was talking to her."

"What girl?" Márta said.

"Don't be ridiculous," István said. "She's only just arrived. You would be able to help her so much if you would only think of someone besides yourself for a change."

"How can you even—" Márta began.

"If only you would dare to be a little kind to someone. A little friendly. Eva has no job yet, she has no friends here—"

Márta stared at the phone in incredulity. What about *her*? She had arrived alone and almost penniless only eight months before. The only reason she had survived was that she had taken the trouble to plan, painstakingly, from Budapest, so that she would not have to exploit other women's escorts at parties. And for all her trouble, what did she have? What she had was, yes—a jealous flatmate, a shiftless roué of a lover, and a dull job in the store of a Hungarian goldsmith. Hardly enough to be tossed out in handfuls to passing girls. She hung up loudly and waited, but the phone was silent.

No matter, she thought, her eyes stinging.

But the days went by and István still didn't call. So then, when Carl did, relief transformed her terror into a tremulous elation.

Carl took Márta to dinner in a pretty French restaurant. The china was thin, milkily luminous in the candlelight, gold-rimmed. On their table were a few flowers so exquisite they seemed about to perish with a little cry. And all around them from the other tables was a soothing rustle, like that of foliage, or money.

Outside, too, was the London Márta had come to but had never before entered. The great green floating parks, the pantherlike cars, the lofty ivory-colored crescents and terraces, the darkly shining shop windows, behind which salesgirls who looked like whippets showed one jewel-like dress, then another, to customers with excellent shoes and handbags.

Márta had begun to think that London might close her inescapably into the brittle émigré life she dreaded, some contemporary version of the lives of relatives she'd heard about in Paris and New York, great-aunts and distant elderly cousins whose apartments were like satellites crammed with dried old bits of uprooted finery. They drank streams of tarry coffee in tiny cups, they ate those few local pastries to which they could resign themselves, as they waited to be orbited back to prewar Budapest.

But, no— Deliverance was everywhere. Márta closed her eyes in thanks, then directed at Carl a smile of gratitude so forceful it almost knocked over a passing waiter.

The smile Carl returned was somewhat puzzled. Indeed, he seemed not to be saying anything much of interest. His firm, he was telling Márta, manufactured machine tools. It was based in Stuttgart but exported goods all over Europe, the United States, and Canada. He would prefer to be on the theoretical rather than the applied end of things, but—he shrugged—this was not bad for now. He enjoyed the irregular schedule, the travel, the flexibility . . . He picked up the saltcellar and examined it, frowning.

"And how is it that you're working for a German company?" Márta asked.

"Why not?" He glanced at her. "After all, I am German
. . . Of course it's rather . . . That is, technically I did grow
up there"—he hesitated—"as I think I was saying to you the
other evening . . ."

The other evening! At the party? At her flat? She'd had so
much on her mind! "My father and stepmother . . ." Carl
coughed. "But I spent all that time here, of course—school,
university. Those holidays at Andrew's . . . Actually, people
do tend to take me for English."

"How wonderful it must be," Márta said, throwing a hasty
cover over her confusion, "to be as much at home one place
as the other."

Carl laughed sadly. " 'As much at home.' Indeed . . ."

"But to travel, as well," she added encouragingly. Perhaps
he didn't appreciate his own good fortune; she herself would
love to travel, to be able to travel, to be able just to delve
into this new, this real, London. Not to have to worry, always,
about money.

"Yes," Carl was saying. "It's good, isn't it, traveling. Some-
times you get a feeling that things could change. Or open up.
You thought it was an endless dark tunnel, but then . . ."
He picked up the saltcellar again.

"But yes," Márta said. "Oh, I would like so much to see
things the way you have seen them. Places that you can see
so easily. France, Italy— Perhaps even this summer I will
take a little time from my job . . ."

"Yes?" Carl said quietly.

A couple brushed by on their way to a table, glancing at
Márta and Carl with interest, admiration. Márta smiled at
Carl, and his eyes, as he smiled back, were moist. Oh, how
could she have expended so much longing on someone like
István, who had such a low opinion of her?

In the morning the London she opened her eyes onto
was Carl's—the blue sky, the serene green-and-ivory city.

But all that week Carl didn't call. That week and the next and the next. What on earth could have happened? Dinner had seemed so . . . *special*. A special, private atmosphere had embraced them. But perhaps, she thought, it embraced Carl and everyone—the person from whom he bought his toothpaste, the parking-lot attendant . . . Still, when he'd put her in a taxi to go home and kissed her caressingly on the cheek, she had the sensation of dissolving beautifully, like some sugary confection.

Perhaps he was working—he could have been called away unexpectedly.

Or perhaps he'd spent the evening with her out of pity. For the hideous foreigner.

The mirror told her one story, then another, while from one day to the next the lovely façade of Carl's London wore slowly away. Behind it, the dirty brick industrial city squatted, waiting to entrap Márta.

"By the way," Judit said one evening. "I happened to see István today."

"Yes?" Márta said, turning away to steady herself.

"He was with that girl from the party," Judit said. "They were talking together so seriously."

At work, Márta flirted recklessly with the men who came in to buy necklaces or rings for women. The men were sickeningly receptive. She smiled as she put their jewels into boxes, and amused herself by seeing them stuffed into hateful pink hunting coats, sailing off big nervous horses, and hurtling clumsily through the air.

At the end of the third week Carl did call. And Márta was astonished to find, at that moment, that she wasn't angry. On the contrary, she experienced, as she held the phone, a bridal gravity, as though the entire period of Carl's silence had been a preparation of some kind.

When Carl came to pick her up, he, too, was subdued, almost quizzical. He stood in the doorway, his hands in his pockets, looking at her. New calm began to emanate from her like light; Ah, yes. Clearly something had altered and intensified between them since they'd seen one another.

That evening's restaurant was sleek and Italian. Márta sipped her wine with contentment, beautiful again, safe again in London. Carl leaned back languidly while she talked; he seemed to take in what she was saying through his eyes, rather than his ears. Freed by his attention, she talked easily. Her life seemed to her to be pleasurable, and of interest. "Will you stop back for a drink?" she asked, and blushed.

Judit was in the sitting room when they came in. As Carl took her hand Judit's sullen expression transmuted into one of canine grief. "Please excuse me," she said, standing. "I must sleep."

Carl had gone to the window, where he stood looking out. "Yes," he said after Judit's door closed behind her. "Well." He glanced delicately in the direction of Judit's room. "Am I staying?" he asked.

He was sculptural, fastidious, ritualistic, consecratory. His silky hair slid through Márta's fingers. Oh, those blind combustions with István! Márta cried out briefly in regret and then forgot István altogether. In the morning when she woke, Carl's eyes were already open. He lay on his back with his hands behind his head. "Birds," he observed, and ran his thumb lightly along her collarbone. She listened: Yes, birds! How marvelous.

She lay wrapped in the sheet, watching as Carl dressed. Already he seemed far away. "My sister will be arriving on Thursday," he said, adjusting his shirt. "It's been a very long time since I've seen her. Would you come meet her? I'd like that so much."

Carl's sister. Márta saw her perfectly. A tall girl in a fluid dress, pale blond and lovely. She and Carl strolled together, reunited, through sun-splashed green. A flock of pigeons lofted before them. Márta shivered—a little familiar chill of exclusion. "How splendid," she said. "I long to meet your sister."

A few evenings later Márta found her way to the address Carl had given her on the phone. It was a large white house that faced a silent square. Not a breath of air disturbed the shrubbery. Behind the door, maple and silver glimmered. The walls were covered with something dark and precious. Carl led Márta up a flight of stairs and into the recesses of the house, where there was a smallish kitchen. A tall girl with long, lion-colored hair turned to Márta, resting a red nail against her mouth.

Márta stepped forward as though magnetized, her legs trembling slightly. She felt terribly unhappy. "You're very pretty," she was dismayed to hear herself saying reproachfully.

The girl swept her hair back as though it were a burden. "You are, too," she said in a swooping English drawl. Her eyes narrowed and gleamed as she smiled. "Very pretty . . ."

"Márta," Carl said, "Jane. And this is my sister, Dee Dee." Márta swiveled in the direction Carl indicated: a girl of indeterminate age—fourteen or fifteen possibly, Márta guessed —sat at the table, scowling through a fringe of preposterously black hair. Márta started to speak, and stopped. No one could say this girl was pretty.

"The poor child's been sleeping," Jane said. "She just got in this morning, and she's disorientated."

"I'm tired," Dee Dee corrected inattentively. "Sort of. Not every minute." The flat American assertions were like a series of little shoves. "Where are you from?" she said to Márta. "You have an accent."

"An accent," Márta said faintly. How could this girl be Carl's sister? "Really."

"Oh, yeah," Dee Dee said. "I get it. Well, I'm from Long Island."

" 'Long Island.' " Márta inclined her head. Whatever that might be.

"Would you like some tea?" Carl asked.

"No," Dee Dee said. "Yes. But I want some food."

"Thank you," Márta said. Where was she? She sat down across from Dee Dee and rubbed her forehead.

Jane reached into the refrigerator and held out at arm's length a white cardboard carton. "Disgusting," she said, and tossed it into the garbage. "Poor pet. Oh, why is there never anything to eat around here?"

"I'm *starving*," Dee Dee said. She sighed noisily and put her head down on the table in an apparent access of self-consciousness.

"Andrew will be here soon," Carl said. He spoke gently. "And then we'll go."

"Someplace fun, I hope," Jane said. "I'm going up to change."

"Jane—?" Dee Dee said.

"Yes, sweet," Jane said vaguely. "I'll be down soon."

Out the window a rain began to fall, as fine as dust. In the silence, Dee Dee slurped her tea.

"Hello," a man said from the doorway of the kitchen. He directed an odd little smile at Carl. "Hello, love," he said to Dee Dee. His handsomeness was like a thrown gauntlet. "You've had some sleep, I trust."

"Uh huh," Dee Dee said. She smiled, then frowned. Her glance swept the sink, the man's face, the ceiling. She opened her mouth and pretended to yawn.

"Andrew," Carl said. "I'd like you to meet Márta."

"Ah, yes." Andrew turned to Márta as though he hadn't seen her before. "So very pleased to meet you." Irony, conspicuously absent from his greeting to Dee Dee, leaked now into his smile.

"Hello," Márta said. They looked at one another for a minute before Andrew turned away. "Good," he said. "Well, is everybody ready? Where's Jane? Jane the drain?"

The restaurant was a solid block of noise, around which chrome and glass flashed harshly. At the bar, women pulsating with jewelry and men in suits as voluptuous and dark as storm clouds snagged one another on heated, gloating, scornful glances. Several turned to look, Márta noted by means of the mirror, as she passed by. No, to look, more likely, at Jane—Jane in her bare green reptilian dress. Márta smoothed down her little skirt and sniffed.

At the table Andrew handed Dee Dee the wine list. "Preferences?" he said.

Dee Dee looked at him dubiously.

"I forgot," he said. "Americans only drink champagne. Champagne it is, then."

How long was it exactly, Márta wondered as she sipped at her champagne, since Carl had seen this sister of his? She looked at the two of them. There was no resemblance. Well, actually, though, there was the faintest resemblance—subterranean, impossible to pinpoint. And at the moment, in fact, Carl looked just Dee Dee's age. No, younger than Dee Dee. Lost. His elegance had reduced into the elegance of a privileged and neglected child. "Are you here on holiday?" Márta leaned over to shout at Dee Dee.

"Holiday?" Dee Dee shouted back. "Oh, vacation. Well, that's one way to look at it, I suppose. I mean, I don't have to be back at school until September, but basically Mother's just dumped me on Carl." Carl raised a languid hand in demurral, but Dee Dee was in full swing. "She wants to romp around with her new boyfriend in private. Actually, she just got furious because I pointed out a few facts. Like the fact that she's old enough to be Kevin's—well, I don't know how old he is exactly, but probably about a quarter of her age. And the fact that she kicked my father out of the house, but I mean who actually *paid* for it, if you see what I mean. Not that my father's the most—but on the other hand, she married him, I didn't. And he does have his good points. Like, for example, he's not a gigolo."

Carl was gazing dreamily toward the larval roiling at the bar. "Strange," he said. "I always think of her as very young. Of course, I can't picture her with any precision—to me she's just a sort of princess with the face smudged out."

"You don't—" Márta began, not loudly enough. Talking here was like pitching something over a fence. "You don't remember your mother?"

"Well, she wasn't my mother for very long," Carl said absently.

"Yeah, but that's exactly what she looks like anyhow," Dee Dee said. "A princess with the face smudged out. 'Nightmare on Elm Street Part Seventy.' When she and her friends are sitting around there are so many face lifts that if someone tells a joke there's this tearing sound. Her hair still looks exactly like yours, Carl. Isn't that amazing, har har? And you should see the house. Thank God I've only got one more year before college. Brass everywhere. Little marble stuff. Chandeliers. It looks like a whorehouse."

The waiter loomed over them threateningly. "Partridge for me," Jane said.

"Yes, yes," Márta said hurriedly. "For me, too." If Jane were just to reach out and swat her, Márta thought as Carl and Andrew conferred over Dee Dee's order, she would be sent sprawling.

A silence rocked unsteadily in the wake of the departing

waiter. Everyone frowned, except Dee Dee, who smiled. Smirked, Márta thought. And why not? She had succeeded in stupefying all of them.

Americans seemed to feel the need to talk, Márta had observed before. And yet theirs was a country into which the concept of conversation seemed never to have penetrated. Dee Dee! So charmless, so graceless, yet she evidently considered it perfectly appropriate to crawl out to the center of the stage and wave her rattle, as though she were of special interest simply by virtue of her parents' shortcomings; astounding to think that she actually must be near seventeen! She spoke of the ordinary confusion of her private life with respect, even awe, as though she were describing the play of monumental cosmic forces. But *obviously* life was grotesque —there was no personal credit to be extracted from that, Márta thought; if life progressed in a natural fashion she herself would be alone somewhere now with Carl.

The waiter refilled Dee Dee's glass for the third—Márta counted—time. Madman. Soon he would be hauled off in chains, to prison, where he belonged.

Jane was delicately picking her partridge to pieces with her fingers, working away at the little bones with her teeth. On Márta's own plate a carcass lay horrifyingly mauled. Besides, so what if Dee Dee's mother had had a little tuck here or there—obviously she could afford it! Did Dee Dee consider herself entitled to some shrunken old saint in a babushka? Surely no one was supposed to believe *Dee Dee's* hair had come into the world black like a telephone.

The swelling foreignness of the evening, the noise—Márta was shrinking into a darkness from which she could only peer out at the giant shining creatures who sat so distantly around the table. The huge seesaw sounds they made could not be folded into her tiny ears. She saw Andrew lean over to Jane and say something. She saw Dee Dee watch with adoring round-eyed humility as Andrew and Jane looked at each other and laughed. Far away next to her, Carl nodded pleasantly. Why didn't he help her?

"Carl, Carl!" Dee Dee called, and Márta could hear again. Dee Dee was pointing at a plate passing overhead, on which a squat glossy hummock lolled under a quivering sauce. "Can I have that for desert?"

"Of course," Carl said. "Whatever you like." He and Jane and Andrew gazed at Dee Dee with a tender, elegiac indulgence, as though she were an event that had taken place on earth many years earlier, before some great catastrophe.

"You know what?" Dee Dee said happily.

Recalled, the others looked at her with a false brightness. Evidently she had nothing to say.

"You know what?" she began again, and achieved traction. "Carl, do you know how Mother met Kevin? He works at an auction house, and she went to cruise an escritoire, but she came home with him."

Jane tipped a little bird bone in tribute. "Good for her."

"Yeah," Dee Dee said. "That's true, but—" She stopped, and turned the dark color that precedes tears. "But what if he doesn't . . . I mean, what if he only . . ."

"How well I know the type," Andrew said as Dee Dee fell into a despondent silence. "Jane, isn't that your friend Blaisdell over there?"

"Where?" Jane said. "My God."

In the far reaches of the room, a party of red-faced young men—rich simpletons, Márta calculated, barely out of public school—looked up as a woman announced herself with the aid of a toy trumpet. One of the men was wearing a paper hat. They all pounded on the table as the woman, singing "Happy Birthday," proceeded to take off her drum majorette's outfit.

It was all just barely audible. Carl appeared to be paying

no attention, though Dee Dee watched with interest, and Jane was regarding the spectacle with sparkling, narrowed eyes. "Excuse me," she said.

Jane reached the table just as the woman with the toy trumpet refastened a final button and hurried off. Jane sat down and draped an arm around the man in the paper hat. He, and the others too, stared at her with the joyful, wondering incomprehension of men who are about to pass out.

Andrew leaned across Dee Dee to Carl. "See the one in the hat? Guess who took Jane to Paris a couple of weeks ago when you and I were in the South of France."

"Really," Carl said.

"You were just in the South of France," Márta observed.

For an instant the room was a tableau. Every face, every object frozen, haloed with a warning brightness.

"Just for old times' sake, really," Andrew said. "We only stayed a few days, because Carl became incredibly shirty over something."

Carl pushed his plate away. "Not at all," he said.

"No?" Andrew said. "Well, good. I can't think why you would have done." He turned to Márta. "Has Carl told you about Cubby and Kaye?"

Márta looked at Andrew. The South of France. During the whole time Carl hadn't called, when she might reasonably have assumed he was working, he had been in the South of France.

"Well, but after all," Andrew said, "there's nothing to tell. Evidently they were friends of my father's—from Kenya, possibly, but no one really remembers. It's all lost in the mists of time and brain damage. They're English classics, Kaye and Cubby. Titled, demented—generations of primordial aristocratic inbreeding."

Dee Dee listed suddenly against Andrew's arm. He brushed

her hair away from her forehead. "We used to go to their place from time to time on holiday. Carl and I. Especially if my mother was off someplace. The idea was, we'd be getting looked after." He looked at Carl. "Which was indeed the case—we long ago came to the conclusion that the servants were wardens in disguise."

Carl raised his eyes to Andrew, then looked down with a faint, self-mocking smile.

"Dee Dee—" Márta said. Dee Dee's head was sliding along Andrew's arm. "Dee Dee, do you want to go?"

"No," Dee Dee said.

Andrew resettled her against his shoulder. "But Carl hadn't been for years and years," he said. "And Cubby was forever saying, 'Wasn't there some other little chap?' or 'Where's dear, dear Carl?' or however it all happened to come up in his mind at that particular moment. So he and Kaye were simply over the moon when I told them Carl had gotten in touch with me and was going to be staying at my place for the summer."

"Did I get in touch with you?" Carl said mildly.

"Oh," Andrew said. "That's right. You ran into me. By chance. And then you got in touch with me."

Into the sudden hollow of silence at the table, Dee Dee inserted a little hiccup.

"I think," Márta addressed Carl, "that it's time to take your sister home."

"Jane?" Dee Dee sat up. "Where's Jane?"

"It's all right, ducks," Andrew said. "Jane's found a friend."

Outside, it was still drizzling. "Will you come with us?" Carl said to Márta as he opened the taxi door for Dee Dee.

"No," Márta said. "*Thank* you."

By the time she reached her flat she had to fight the clamor pressing in on her just to get the key into the lock. Carl had looked at her as he said good night with a trace of surprise. Oh, that innocent face! In fact, he was so slippery that he had made her not be able to understand why she was angry herself. Which was worse behavior in its way than István's.

Judit sat at the kitchen table eating, directly from its deli wrapping, a cheese-and-pickle sandwich on limp English bread. "Up so late?" Márta spoke insouciantly in English.

Judit sighed. "I was just getting some work done. Have a nice evening?"

"Lovely," Márta said. "Carl took me to the most marvelous place. Do you ever wonder why London is such a quiet city? It is because everyone who lives here is inside this restaurant. On the street, it is all chauffeurs waiting."

"How pleasant," Judit said.

"Very," Márta said. "We had a great deal of champagne because Carl's baby sister has come to stay with him. And Carl's friend Andrew brought with him the most beautiful girl, Jane."

"So," Judit said. "Your life is glamour and more glamour." She wadded up the deli wrappings; they landed in the garbage with a deadly little plop.

In the morning when Márta awoke, anger lay next to her like a cover that had slipped off during the night. She felt around for it and readjusted it over herself.

What a hateful evening. How remote Carl had been, how abstracted. But how handsome! Oh, the world of difference between the banquet he seemed to offer and the crumbs that fell her way. Why, with all their talk of traveling that evening in the French restaurant had Carl not even mentioned that he was going to the South of France? What a shrew he made her feel.

Poor Dee Dee. That poor little pit pony! Alone, a foreigner—all she had was Carl! Márta imagined herself—in a little suit, perhaps—showing Dee Dee around London; really, Dee Dee was rather cute, if you managed to think about her in the right way. Márta eyed the phone. There were swans in a park somewhere, she understood—she could show them to Dee Dee. Take her shopping. Explain to her peculiar English customs, like tea . . . How well, she wondered, did Dee Dee actually know Carl?

Dee Dee was late, of course, and the restaurant Márta had designated—one whose name had echoed, potently English, all the way to Márta in Budapest—was crowded with Saturday shoppers. Their faces looked ashen and fatigued against the prettily colored walls and carpets, and the uniformed hostess eyed Márta with suspicion. Márta cleared her throat. "Yes, I'm waiting for my—" Her what?

"Excuse me?" the hostess said. "Of course. Well, there aren't any tables at the moment anyhow. You can see for yourself. More and more crowded all the time now. Where do they all come from? Days when you hardly hear a word of English spoken." She lifted one foot, then the other, as though she were accustomed to perpetual pain. "I don't know if you've noticed the change. Perhaps you don't remember. It's only in the last few years that London has become so"— she cocked her head conspiratorially to indicate the roomful of tea drinkers—"*cosmopolitan.*"

"Hi," Dee Dee said from near Márta's shoulder. In her yellow slicker she looked like a huge bathtub toy.

"You'll have to keep your coats," the hostess observed morosely. "The cloakroom's closed for renovations."

"That's okay," Dee Dee said. She rubbed at her nose with her wrist.

"Well, management doesn't care for it," the hostess said. "It lowers the tone."

Márta burned with self-consciousness as she poured out the tea. It was all so primitive and complicated. At the tables all around them women in tweeds or chadors and men in pinstripes dealt with the fussy pots and tongs and strainers with the ease of tycoons handling ticker tape. And what about this pot of plain hot water, Márta wondered. Was she supposed to be *doing* something with it? No matter. Dee Dee appeared not to notice her awkwardness. In fact, for all Dee Dee appeared to be noticing, Márta could have taken her to the filthy corner caf. There was no sign of life from Dee Dee at all. Not even self-pitying monologues, let alone meaningful discourse about Carl. No, Dee Dee was quietly absorbed in stacking up the expensive little cakes that tasted like Kleenex filled with toothpaste, and eating them mechanically, one after the other.

Dee Dee's eyes were fixed on Márta's plate, where a little cake sat inscrutably, bitten. She was trying to think of something to say. It was difficult, though—especially since Márta had been frowning since they'd sat down. Dee Dee felt cold and rubbery. What if Márta hated her? What would happen then?

After her mother had announced to her that she was to be sent to Carl for the summer, Dee Dee had been racked by rapid alterations between joy and misery, hope and panic. She had seen Carl only once. When she was a child, probably around four. Where had they been? She, Carl, their mother, of course . . . It was a big house. The floor shone, there were flowers in huge vases, several women—tall, broad-shouldered, with long, whooshing skirts; a fat man with dark hair. Someone said, would the baby like to see the pony? Carl took her hand. *She was the baby.* Carl led her outside, the house darkened behind them. In a grassy little enclosure a white creature pranced and curvetted. Dee Dee stared straight ahead. *Was she feeling her own hand holding Carl's, or was she feeling Carl's hand holding hers?*

Dee Dee carried the memory privately, a picture in a locket. She never asked her mother about it. At the worst times, she allowed herself to take it out and contemplate it. The angelically serious boy stayed older than she was; he was ahead of her, drawing her along as though she were secured to him by some unseverable attachment. As indeed she was.

When Dee Dee descended the stairs the morning of her departure for London, her mother had looked at her narrowly. "You've simply got to lose five pounds," she said. "Ten would be better. You can get away with things as a child that you can't at your age, you know."

All right. All right. If Carl was ashamed of her, if he didn't want her around, Dee Dee would take off on her own somehow. She had with her a reasonable amount of money—her mother and her father had been separately, guiltily open-handed, and at an early age she had cultivated the prudent habit of skimming small amounts from her mother's unguarded cash against unforeseeable eventualities. There were times, during the savage quarrels between her parents, between herself and her mother, when, her face stiff from the strain of shame or tears or fury, she imagined herself liberated— cast out, fugitive, all the trashy screen of words left behind; words and the trashy names of things and accusations and expectations. The rocking of the darkened carriage, the purifying monotony of hooves, of tracks. Looking out at the flowing night, clean, unknown, dignified, new. Dependent on no one, loved by no one . . .

But when Carl greeted her at Heathrow there was no sign of recoil. He kissed her on both cheeks and picked up her bag. She had recognized him immediately; he was just as he ought to have been.

Early in the evening Dee Dee had awoken in her new room.

The walls were covered with something green, like ribbon. Silver-framed photographs were scattered on a polished dressing table. Standing in the doorway was a woman with long, blondish hair. "Hello," Dee Dee said.

"Hello," the woman said.

Where was Carl? Where was Andrew? "I'm Carl's sister," Dee Dee said.

"Right." The woman shook out her hair. "Carl said." She sat down on the foot of Dee Dee's bed and yawned. "I'm Jane," she said. "Here for long?"

Jane was wearing a kimono and her feet were bare. "I don't know," Dee Dee said.

"Mm," Jane said. She reached for one of the silver-framed photographs. "I suppose not . . ."

Dee Dee crawled out from under the covers and peered over Jane's shoulder. The photographs were all of people from some other time. They looked not real at all—implausible, approximate, costumed. "Who are they?" Dee Dee said.

"Andrew's posh relations, I should think," Jane said. "This must be his mum—looks enough like him, doesn't it?"

She handed Dee Dee the photograph. It was true; as Dee Dee saw Andrew's face within the woman's, the opaque surface of dated style melted. The woman's skin warmed, her curls had just sprung back from a breeze. A starry, dangerous blur of excitement hung in front of her eyes like a little veil, and her beauty rose from the black-and-white paper like steam, so evanescent it suggested imminent fatality—a car, a boat, a wild animal . . . Dee Dee handed the photograph back to Jane.

"What?" Jane said, glancing at her.

"I don't know," Dee Dee said. *London.* Only a few days earlier she had been talking to her mother, and they had started to quarrel, and her mother had said, "All right, I've had it. I'm sending you to Carl." Dee Dee looked at Jane in amazement. "I was just there," she said, "and now I'm *here*. Mother and I were just *talking*, and now I'm here . . ."

Jane stood up. "Well," she said. "That's the way it works, isn't it. Anyway"—she smiled kindly from the doorway as Dee Dee pulled on her jeans—"Carl's pleased."

Dee Dee stared soberly into the silver-framed mirror and carefully combed her hair.

That's the way it works. She wandered out to the stairway. *Carl's pleased.*

It was pitch-dark when Dee Dee next woke up. What had awakened her? There was the familiar unevenness in the air of recent disturbance.

But where was she? She felt around for a light—oh, yes. Andrew's house. She felt a bit strange. From dinner maybe. She remembered: she'd drunk a lot of wine. It had been very noisy. Jane had been there, and Carl, and Carl's friend Márta, and Andrew. How nervous she'd been! She'd talked a lot. But what had she said? And how had she gotten upstairs?

She listened carefully into the lush undergrowth of silence. At first she could make no sense of it, but then she heard something from downstairs. She got up, as she had so often at home, and crept out to the landing. All the closed doors around her! More frightening than the faint light from below.

Dee Dee edged herself down the stairs, halfway to the next landing. Legs extended on the sofa into her view. Andrew's —those were his socks. "I'm sorry," someone said quietly. Carl. He sounded far away. "Really," he said. "I really am."

"Must we discuss it?" Andrew said.

Dee Dee strained into the silence.

"What?" Andrew said. "Did you say something?"

Dee Dee could feel Carl sigh. "No," he said.

"But *I* said, must we discuss it?" Andrew said.

Carl cleared his throat. "No," he said. "I'm sorry."

"What?" Andrew said. "You're what?"

"Don't," Carl said. "Please."

"Don't *what*," Andrew said. "Please *what*. Oh, God. Why are you *here*?"

"I don't know," Carl said. "I'm sorry."

"Don't be sorry," Andrew said. "Just tell me why you're here."

"I thought it would be—" Carl said. "I don't know."

"You don't know," Andrew said. "Of course you know."

"I wanted to be—I thought we'd be able—"

"You see," Andrew said. "Oh, how idiotic. You see, this is what you say now. This is what you always say. But then it's *you* who always—"

"I know," Carl said. "I'm sorry. But not anymore."

Darkness boiled up around Dee Dee. After a minute Andrew spoke again. "Then why are you here?" he said. His voice twisted like a wilting flower. "Why are you here?"

The next evening Dee Dee was waiting on the sofa when Carl returned.

"Where is everyone?" Carl said.

"Jane never came back," Dee Dee said. "I guess. And Andrew wanted me to tell you he was going somewhere with Timothy."

"Ah," Carl said. "Hm. Well, in that case." He looked around at the walls as though he were trying to remember something. "Takeaway all right?"

Dee Dee stretched out on the sofa, her empty plate balanced on her stomach. Carl sat in a high, straight-backed armchair; he appeared to be sitting in a bell jar of light. The boy who had hovered by her, always available in moments of extreme need, who had led her from one year to the next—had that boy become this man? "Carl—" Dee Dee said.

"I was thinking," he said. "You know, it's idiotic, your being here in Europe and just lying around the house."

"It's only Friday," Dee Dee said. Where was *Carl*? "I only just got here yesterday."

"I ought to take some time off," Carl said. "Or arrange with my firm to go someplace."

"Go someplace?" Dee Dee sat up. "I mean——"

"Someplace else," Carl said. "After all, why should you stay in London? It's so—well, and also it's . . ."

Dee Dee ran her hand over the velvety covering of the sofa. It was only last night that Andrew had lain in this very spot.

"And you know," Carl said. "It occurs to me. What did you think of Márta?"

Carefully, Dee Dee felt her way toward the answer. "I liked Márta," she said. She looked at Carl gravely. "I felt very comfortable with her."

"Because I was thinking," Carl said. "Maybe Márta should come with us."

The restaurant was emptying out. There were only a few remaining parties of ladies, and, at the next table, a hunted-looking man whose pinstriped shoulders carried a dusting of white. Márta's little frown intensified, and Dee Dee's heart began to beat rapidly; what had she done now? Oh, no—and what had happened to that bitten little cake on Márta's plate? She had some impression that she herself had . . .

"So you say Carl is planning some sort of trip," Márta said. She turned her teacup in her hands.

"Well," Dee Dee said. Had Carl expected *her* to ask Márta? "I mean . . ."

"He really ought to let us know, don't you think?" Márta said crossly. "That brother of yours really ought to let us know when he is sending us on trips."

"Didn't he call you today?" Dee Dee said timidly. "I'm sure he tried to call you today."

Márta looked at her blankly, she seemed to be concentrating, as though she were identifying some faint piece of music.

"Márta?" Dee Dee said.

"Shh," Márta said. She leaned toward Dee Dee, lowering her eyes. "Do you think that man is attractive?"

"What man?" Dee Dee said. The only man she could see was the one at the next table.

"Don't look," Márta said. "He is very aware of us." Márta gazed in unearthly majesty at her teacup, and a hush consumed the room as a marmorial glow lit her face, her arms, her throat. But then she burst out laughing, causing a renewed murmur of conversations and teacups. "Oh, what a ridiculous country this is!" she said. " 'The cloakroom is closed for renovations—' " She imitated the hostess's pruny expression. "The cloakroom! Closed for renovations!" She burst out laughing again and smiled over at Dee Dee with a merriment that seemed entirely unwarranted.

"I had a nice time today," Dee Dee said that night to Carl. They were in a room on the second floor that held a great number of books. "With Márta."

"Good," Carl said. He peered at a horse print on the wall in front of him.

"Have you had a chance to—I mean, I'm glad you're going to ask her to come on our trip," Dee Dee said.

"You know," Carl said, "I spent a lot of time in this room when I was your age."

"Excuse me—" A boy a few years younger than Carl leaned around the door. "I can't find a corkscrew."

"There's one in the drawer to the right of the sink," Carl said.

"Oh," the boy said. "Well, I couldn't find it."

Carl shrugged. "Sorry."

"The thing is," the boy said, "I can't find Andrew, either."

Carl sighed and pushed back his hair. "Andrew went out," he said.

"Oh," the boy said. "Well, when you see him, tell him Christopher and Angelica and I waited."

Carl nodded.

"Thanks," the boy said. He looked at Carl uncertainly and then withdrew. Carl put his head in his hands.

That miraculous hair of his—so like their mother's. "Carl?" Dee Dee said after a moment. "Could we take a train?"

"A train?" Carl lifted his head. "If you like." He sighed. "Well, I suppose I'd better call Márta, hadn't I, before it's too late."

"Carl?" Dee Dee said. "It isn't too late . . ."

"Yes," Carl said. "I mean, it's already after ten."

From high under the grimy glass, two pigeons swooped over Dee Dee as she hurried along. On their way—who could guess from where to where? The line where Carl and Márta stood arguing tensed and rippled as Dee Dee approached, like the tail of a nervous animal; the train would be boarding any minute.

"What is the matter?" Dee Dee heard Carl say. "Why are you angry?"

"Why ask me?" Márta said. "When you know very well."

"Know what?" Carl said. "I don't know. What have I done?"

"Done," Márta said. "You haven't 'done' anything."

"Then why—"

"It's what you *think*."

"I see," Carl said. "And now you know what I'm thinking."

"I happen to," Márta said.

"Very good," Carl said. "But you could be wrong."

"I happen to know," Márta said. "And I happen also to be right."

"Yes?" Carl said. "Good. So what is it that I'm thinking?"

"You know what you're thinking," Márta said. "Why should I tell you? You're thinking that you don't want to go."

"I'm thinking that I don't want to go!" Carl said. "On this trip? Of course I want to go. This trip was my idea—why wouldn't I want to go?"

"I don't *know*—" Márta said. "I don't know why not. You tell *me* why not."

For a moment the line paused in its progress, then continued around Carl and Márta into the open doors of the train. "Márta," Carl said. "We have to get on the train now. Where's Dee Dee? Oh, there you are."

"You get on the train," Márta said. "You get on the train since that's *what you want*. But what am I going to do?" Her eyes shone, furious and teary, and a freezing little laugh hung in the air. "Now I've taken time off from my job. I have no money. You don't care whether I live or die—"

"Oh, please," Carl said. "Márta—Márta, please. We have to go now."

"We?" Márta said. "Yes? Why should I go somewhere with you when you don't know the difference between me and a . . . *suitcase*. I will stay here, where at least there are certain people who do want to see me."

Carl looked at her. His face closed over. "Oh, what is the point?" he said. "Why should I say anything? No one ever believes me. I'm sorry, Dee Dee—" He put his hand on Dee Dee's shoulder. "We'll have to work this out before we—"

But Dee Dee slipped out from under his hand. Hugging her bag of magazines and candy bars against her chest, she mounted the steps of the train.

Carl's and Márta's shocked faces glowed as she fled along a corridor. The train breathed and shuddered. From the other side of its metal membrane Dee Dee could feel all the last sad leave-takings, torn away, fluttering idly upward in the station like slips of burning paper, floating as the dead words curled into the faint edge of flame, darkening into ash . . .

She opened the heavy door onto one of the compartments. She felt in her pocket for her ticket, and took a seat. She was alone. Would Carl and Márta be looking for her, pacing up and down beside the train? Or would they still be arguing, each trying to get the other to say what they needed to hear? But perhaps, in fact, Carl had already capitulated, and Márta, victorious, was already abandoned. In which case Carl—well, Carl could go on his way back to Andrew's house.

The door of Dee Dee's compartment opened; the train slid into motion. A stooped, elderly man appeared. He stood briefly, balancing, then took a seat across from her. In the gauzy dimness he looked to her impersonal, unformed—like a mound of clay on a sculptor's table. Yes, she thought; that's how she would look to him.

The carriage swayed, the train roared into a tunnel. How was she going to take care of herself, Dee Dee wondered. Still, how does anyone? *From far away Carl had accompanied her.* In darkness Dee Dee gazes out the dark window—faint lights bobbing in the silver frame. Any moment, she knows, day will pour in, extinguishing the lights, molding onto her face and the face of her traveling companion the masks of themselves: a man made ordinary by evasions and fears; a girl who won't engage our sympathy or hopes. But just for the moment, aren't they free? What rare, dear beings are hidden here now by these shadows?